A CORNISH MAID

Autumn 1909: Edith Trewin, the general maid in the Killivert household, and Miss Alicia, the young lady of the house, are social worlds apart, though they share a streak of independence and intelligence. The two young women become unlikely allies after a kitchen maid inexplicably disappears shortly after her arrival at the house. The two unite in the search for her as they experience love and loss as the Great War overtakes the world.

*Rosemary Aitken titles available from
Severn House Large Print*

From Penvarris With Love
The Silent Shore
Stormy Waters
The Tregenza Girls

A CORNISH MAID

Rosemary Aitken

Severn House Large Print
London & New York

This first large print edition published 2011
in Great Britain and the USA by
SEVERN HOUSE PUBLISHERS LTD of
9-15 High Street, Sutton, Surrey, SM1 1DF.
First world regular print edition published 2009 by
Severn House Publishers Ltd., London and New York.

British Library Cataloguing in Publication Data

Aitken, Rosemary, 1942-
    A Cornish maid.
    1. Social classes--England--Fiction. 2. Women household
    employees--Fiction. 3. Missing persons--Investigation--
    Fiction. 4. Great Britain--History--George V, 1910-1936--
    Fiction. 5. Love stories. 6. Large type books.
    I. Title
    823.9'14-dc22

    ISBN-13: 978-0-7278-7906-6

Severn House Publishers support The Forest Stewardship Council
[FSC], the leading international forest certification organisation. All
our titles that are printed on Greenpeace-approved FSC-certified paper
carry the FSC logo.

Printed and bound in Great Britain by the
MPG Books Group, Bodmin, Cornwall.

For Rob with love

Part One

Summer – Autumn 1909

One

'Edith!' Cook came out on to the kitchen step to shout, and her voice echoed down the yard and into the back garden like a clarion. 'Edith! Drat that girl, where has she got to now?'

Edie could see and hear her from the orchard at the back, where she had been out seeing to the hens, and dawdling contentedly under the apple trees. Mrs Pritchard looked like an outraged chicken in a pinafore herself, Edie thought – standing there with her stout hands on her stouter hips and turning her beaked nose from left to right: it was exactly what Biddie – the black hen – was doing this moment, looking for a worm. All the same, when Cook was calling you like that, it didn't do to dally and Edie picked up her basket and hurried to the house.

'I'm here, Mrs Pritchard,' she said breathlessly. 'I only went out to feed the hens and get the eggs.' She offered the basket like a trophy as she spoke.

Cook took it with a sniff. 'I don't know how it took you all that time, I'm sure. What you been up to?'

In fact, she had been staring at the trees trying to think of the right words to describe the misty green frilled lichen on the grey grooved bark,

9

spread out like the map of some enchanted fairy-land. But you couldn't say that kind of thing to Cook. 'Had to stop and do it all myself, today, for once. Sammy's helping Mr Gribbens do something with the hedge.'

Mrs Pritchard made a tutting noise. 'No other staff to do it for him, I suppose. One boy and a gardener to run a great place like this. I don't know what the old Colonel would have had to say, I'm sure. Time was when there were twenty indoor servants in this house – and that's not counting the occasionals.' She turned back into the kitchen as she spoke. 'And now look how it is. Since Violet left to marry that daft young man of hers, apart from Queenie coming in each day to scrub, there's only you and me to manage everything.'

Edie smiled. This was one of Mrs Pritchard's favourite themes – but as long as she was fretting about the lack of help she wasn't grumbling at indoor maids for loitering out of doors. Edie ducked past into the pantry and said cheerfully, 'Though of course there is that nurse now, for Mrs Killivant, and Miss Alicia has talked her brother into sense and got him to agree to send the laundry out.'

'Don't you answer back to me, my girl!' Cook aimed a slap in the vague direction of her ear – though it would not have stung much if it had connected. 'Pity your hands are not as busy as your tongue! There's the poor mistress waiting for her tray, and Miss Alicia will want her meal as well – though she'll come down and breakfast in the morning room, no doubt. You have laid

10

the table ready, I suppose?'

Edie flushed. 'Yes, Mrs Pritchard,' she answered patiently, though it would make you mad. Of course Cook knew perfectly well that she'd done that first thing – as soon as ever the bedroom fires were swept out and relaid and the water taken up for Miss Alicia and the nurse. It was one of the dozen tasks that fell to Edie's lot these days, before she came downstairs to give a hand to Cook. Just as well that there was Queenie to do the skivvying, or she might have found herself doing that as well – scrubbing the pots and mopping floors and polishing the stairs. Queenie was a tiny woman with half a dozen kids, thin as a broomstick and never known to smile. She came in each morning from the town and worked till half-past two, and then went home to do the same thing at her little cottage in the town. You could hear her this minute, clanking at the pump, fetching fresh water for the kitchen in a pail which was half as big as she was and must have weighed as much.

'The mistress has ordered scrambled eggs today.' Cook's voice startled Edie from her reverie. 'So you can crack half a dozen of those fresh ones into that basin there – make sure there aren't any of those nasty spots in them – and then you can take madam up her tray and come back for Miss Alicia's when you've finished doing that. Well, then,' she went on, 'what are you waiting for? Those eggs won't shell themselves. Thinking about something else as usual, I suppose?'

Edie said nothing but set to work at once, and

by the time that Queenie struggled in – puffing and blowing with the water-bucket – she had already half-finished with the eggs. They had to be cracked into a teacup – slowly, one by one – each inspected and sniffed carefully to make sure it was fresh, and then transferred into the mixing-bowl. She was secretly delighted to find a reject, too – one with the tell-tale 'nasty spot' in it – which Edith knew was only the beginnings of a chick – and she put that carefully into another cup. She and Queenie would have that for their own breakfast later on, if Cook did not decide to use it in a cake.

Queenie was only a casual of course, and not strictly entitled to anything at all, but a kindly heart beat under Cook's floury pinafore, despite her sharp rebukes. 'Only decent bit of food that woman sees all day,' she had said to Edie once, in a rare burst of confidence. 'The Colonel would never have begrudged her – and I'm sure the ladies won't.'

It was true. The Killivants had always been generous like that. If there was a bit of anything left over from upstairs, the staff were welcome to enjoy it for their tea – even in these days when the purse was tight. Mrs Pritchard could remember times, before the master died, when the house was full of visitors and there were guests to dine, and she'd given Edie mouthwatering accounts of what had been 'sent down' for the servants then.

'And it wasn't just the good plain meats we have on Sundays now – roast beef and lamb and that sort of thing. There were proper, rich folks'

12

things. Venison, I've tasted, and jugged hare once or twice. Potted partridge – though I didn't care for that, all bones and little bits of lead, it seemed to me. Or, if there was a dance, there might be sandwiches – potted chicken some-times, or egg in mayonnaise – all with the crusts cut off: so light and tasty that they're gone before you've hardly had the time to relish them. And as for the desserts! If you ever get a chance to taste a charlotte russe – you make sure you take it. Melts in your mouth it does...' And Cook had shut her eyes and pulled her lips in tight, as if the sensation might still be lingering, before she added, in a brisker tone, ''Course, we really never got a lot of anything – there were dozens of us then. No more than a mouthful or two, by the time we'd shared it out – but it was that delicious it's a wonder there was any leftovers at all.'

Must have been lovely, Edith thought, though it was years and years ago. There hadn't been a dance here since the master died. It would have been nice to see one – if it was only once. Miss Alicia in that pretty dress, perhaps, that Edie had noticed in the wardrobe once or twice...

'Edith!' The voice was so sudden that she almost dropped the bowl. It was lucky that she caught it just in time and saved the precious eggs. Cook had come up behind her to speak sharply in her ear. 'Tear yourself from dream-land and take madam up her tea.'

'Yes, Mrs Pritchard. I am on my way.'

And after that she did pay attention to her tasks.

Alicia was waiting by the window-seat. She forced herself to stand there, looking out on to the garden, instead of prowling restlessly around the breakfast room. Nor did she go to the table and sit down, although a place at the far end had been laid for her. She looked at the cheerful chequered tablecloth, the gleaming china, glass and cutlery and the crisp white napkin in its silver ring. Stupid really, all this fuss for one. She ought to do as Mama did and have a tray sent up. Edwin thought so, too; he had said so several times in the daily letters which he sent to her – pages of meticulous instructions and advice.

'Liss,' he had written in his latest note (he always called her Liss, as if she were a child), 'it is quite preposterous you sitting there alone, rattling around in that great room like that. Think of the servants, and the extra work you make...' – that was true, she thought, a little guiltily. But then he had added the words which hardened her resolve. 'If you were a fellow, it might be different – a chap needs a good breakfast before he goes to work and a chance to sit down with the mail – but in your situation you should think it through. Have you considered what it must cost in extra coals, simply to heat the breakfast room each day?'

Typical Edwin, she thought angrily. He did not have to live here, in this half-empty house – and when he did come he would never dream of breakfasting upstairs. Because he was a 'fellow' and that was different!

14

Things would have been otherwise if only Charles had lived. Charles had been her eldest brother, and the dashing one – following his father's footsteps into the regiment and thence to that terrible business in South Africa, serving with the same careless distinction which he showed in everything. He had won a medal and been mentioned in dispatches too, before a Boer sniper got him through the heart while he was accompanying a column of supplies.

The unlucky bullet had killed more than young Captain Killivant: Mother had gone at once into a terrible decline (she had rarely left her sickbed in the seven years since), and Father succumbed soon after to a careless wound. He took a painful bullet in the thigh – nasty but minor compared to wounds he'd had before – but this time he caught fever and within a week was dead. Perhaps he had simply lost the will to live – whereas a month or two earlier he would have fought back and survived.

The Colonel's death had proved a turning-point. He had left the house and contents to Edwin in his will – as might be expected for the second son – though Mother had the right to stay there while she lived. To Alicia herself he had left a tidy sum, but with a proviso which made things difficult. 'Learned my lesson dealing with my wife,' he had been heard to say, and it was true that poor Mama – a charming, nervous soul, who could paint and play the piano like an angel in her youth – had no head for figures and had once got into debt: so he had set aside five thousand pounds in trust, which would come to Alicia when she reached thirty years of age, or on her marriage – whichever happened first.

Alicia heaved a sigh. It was no good reminding herself that this was no deliberate slight to her, and that he had made similar provision for her older sister too. The other daughter – Mary, whom Alicia had adored – had the good sense to marry very young and so qualify for her inheritance at once, though she had died in childbirth several years ago. Alicia still missed her sister very much.

So now there was only herself and Edwin left, and since Mama accepted Father's view of things – in this as in all other aspects of their life – it was Edwin who had taken charge of family affairs. Edwin, who had been sickly as a child: a solemn boy with glasses who was scared of getting wet, and refused to join his siblings in their childish pranks. And he wasn't all that different now he was adult. Pompous, careful Edwin, who had become a clergyman and in due course had married a woman as boring as himself.

There was a letter from him on the tray, she saw. That cramped and careful hand was unmistakable. She picked up the letter-knife and slit the envelope. 'Our dear sister...' He always began his letters in that way, as though he were writing a sermon to be read aloud. He was just six years Liss's senior, but it might have been sixty from the way he wrote sometimes – like some aging uncle, giving good advice to a dear but wayward child who could not be expected to understand the world.

16

Her eyes flicked down the closely written page. It was much as usual. The necessity of keeping up the 'small economies' (Alicia smiled grimly. Edwin was very keen on urging them to thrift – though he never applied this to his own expenditure) and had Mama remembered that the land-rates were due? He supposed that the nurse and laundry bills were real necessities and he would arrange to have the money made available. Alicia smiled sourly. How very kind of him!

'Madam? Miss Alicia?' The maid's voice startled her.

'Ah, good morning, Edith.' She looked up from her mail.

'Breakfast, Miss Alicia.' The girl put down the tray. Toast, Alicia noticed, and a dish of scrambled eggs. You could think it quite inviting if you did not recall the way the sideboard at one time used to groan with food – porridge, fresh fruit, bacon, tomatoes, kidneys, the sausages that Father liked, and several kinds of tea.

She allowed the girl to serve her and then said with a smile, 'I shall want you after breakfast to take something to the post. A reply to Mr Edwin. I think we have a stamp?'

'Yes, Miss Alicia, and fresh blotting paper too. I put a new piece in that roller thing only yesterday. Funny sort of device. Never seen one till I came to work for you. Puts me in mind of a rocking-horse, a bit.'

'Very good, Edith, that will do for now.' Alicia made an effort not to grin. The girl had an inventive turn of phrase sometimes – Charles would have thought so. It would have made him laugh. The recollection of her brother took her by surprise, and instantly robbed her of all desire for mirth. She went back to her breakfast – the eggs were very good – and not until she'd finished did she speak again. 'Thank you, Edith, you can clear the table now. I'll go into the library and see about that note.'

She put her napkin down and rose slowly to her feet. She didn't want to write the letter, it was a tiresome chore, but Edwin had made it clear that he expected it – a daily account of everything that happened in the house and a proper accounting of all expenditure. If only she had access to that money of her own. She would mention it to Edwin – for the hundredth time – though there wasn't much that he could do, since it was in the will. 'You'll have to find someone to marry, Liss, that's all. Then you can have the money instantly.'

No chance of that, she thought indignantly. How was she ever to find anyone to wed, cooped up with Mother in the house like this? It wasn't even possible to go out visiting her friends, let alone attend a party or a ball: if there was an invitation, she couldn't really go, because there was no chance of entertaining anybody in return. Surely Edwin must be aware of that.

Though, to be fair to him, he had done his best. He'd attempted to find her a husband, more than once. He and his wife had invited her to stay and he had introduced her to a series of young men – earnest young curates, for the most part, prematurely bald. He invited them over to take a cup of tea, and shamelessly extolled her virtues as a prospective bride. He couldn't understand why, before the week was out, his sister was begging to be taken home again. 'Paraded like a prize cow at a market,' Edie had said, when Alicia had told her all about it, later on.

She sat down at the writing desk and took the paper out, fitted a new steel nib on to the pen and dipped it carefully into the inkwell on the stand. 'Dear Edwin...' She had got as far as that, when she was interrupted by a tapping at the door, and Edith stood there with her apron on.

'Miss Alicia, I am sorry to intrude, but there's a Mr Tulver come to ask for you. It seems that Mr Edwin told him he should call. Come from the bank, he tells me – should I show him up, or will you go downstairs? I've left him waiting in the blue sitting-room.'

Alicia put down the pen without regret. 'I'll come down and see him. From the bank, you say? And Edwin sent him? I wonder what he wants.'

Tim Tulver sat stiffly on the corner of the chair, pressing together his ankles and his knees and making a steeple with his fingertips. He wanted to look neat, and make a good impression when Miss Killivant arrived.

He glanced at the mirror above the mantelpiece. It was a large one but he could not see his reflection from where he was. He wondered about standing up and having a swift check – the set of his tie and trousers, and the condition of his hair – but thought better of it. It would never do to have her come into the room and catch him in the act. He coughed and went back to staring at his fingertips.

It was a good decision, because here she was striding imperiously across the room to him. Not very much like Edwin, on first appearances. He was small and mousy, she was tall and fair – and held her head extraordinarily upright on her neck. Not exactly pretty – she was too strong-featured for that – but attractive, damned attractive, with those flashing eyes, and she looked disturbingly directly at you, for a girl.

He felt himself flushing as he struggled to his feet – the more so because he knocked his brief-case over as he rose. 'Miss Alicia Killivant?' He held out his hand. 'Timothy Tulver, from your father's bank in town. Your brother Edwin suggested I might call...'

Her handshake was as brief and formal as a man's, and her voice was disappointing – brisk and businesslike. 'Mr Tulver. I've not heard him speak of you. What business brings you here? Something about the provisions of the trust?'

He retrieved his briefcase while she watched, unmoved. 'Your brother thought I should explain to you...' She made no answer or murmur of support. It was unnerving and he gestured to the chair. 'May I?'

'Of course,' she said, with the ghost of what might have been a smile. 'But I think I should tell you, Mr ... Tulver, did you say? ... that I am quite familiar with the terms, I think. The money comes to me when I am thirty years of age, but up to then I cannot call on it at all without the agreement of the two trustees – my brother and a person from the bank, who used to know my father very well, I understand.'

'Mr Symons, yes.' Tim Tulver cleared his throat. 'That used to be the case. Indeed, that's why your brother thought that I should call. Mr Symons is unfortunately not with us any more.'

'Indeed?' She was looking at him sharply.

He could see what Edwin meant. 'Wilful, you'll find her. Lovely girl of course, and very attractive if you like that kind of thing. But wilful with it. Headstrong as a horse. Don't say I didn't warn you. Though she's a handsome catch. Comes into five thousand on her wedding day.' But she was saying something. He tried to concentrate.

'Mr Symons has retired from the bank?'

For a moment he could make no sense of this. Then he gave a rueful little laugh. 'In a manner of speaking, you might say so, I suppose. Mr Symons passed away last week.'

She sat down suddenly. Her face was serious. 'So my brother Edwin is now the sole trustee?'

'Oh, no, Miss Killivant. It doesn't work like that. The bank is entitled to appoint another trustee in Mr Symons's place. In point of fact...' He ran a finger round his neck. His wretched stiff collar seemed to be too tight. 'In point of fact,' he said again, 'they have appointed me.'

For some strange reason this news made her laugh aloud. That was dispiriting. He felt he cut a dashing figure in his working clothes. 'You?' she repeated, in a tone of disbelief.

He was affronted. 'That's right, Miss Killivant.

21

Any request that you may make for funds will – in the meantime anyway – require my signature.' He rummaged in the briefcase. 'I have the papers here. I'll leave them with you, so you can read them through. They will explain all this. Perhaps you can return them to the office later on. 'He snapped the briefcase shut. 'And now, if you'll excuse me...'

She was blushing now. 'Mr Tulver, I'm so sorry. It was the shock, that's all. And Mr Symons was my father's age. I did not expect...' She trailed off and made an apologetic gesture with her hands. Then suddenly she stiffened, and said in icy tones, 'This arrangement was my brother's doing, I suppose?'

'I believe that Mr Edwin did suggest it, yes. I have had dealings with him once or twice before.' He gave her an ingratiating smile. Why did she make him feel that he must apologize?

'I see. So I must face the phalanx of the pair of you, if I so much as want a pair of shoes? I have always felt that Edwin would be unwilling to comply – unless it was a medical emergency, I suppose – but Mr Symons was an impartial voice. Not that I ever needed to appeal for funds. But now that the co-trustee is Edwin's friend...'

He interrupted her. 'I assure you, Miss Killivant, you have no need to fear. I have a professional reputation to sustain, and I promise I will consider any claim you make with all the impartiality that you could hope for.' Drat the girl, why was she smiling now? Had he sounded as if he'd back her every whim? He hastened to correct the impression she might have. 'Of

22

course, I cannot guarantee that funds would be released – that would require your brother's signature as well. Though I hope I might have some influence on him.' Why had he added that? Perhaps because she was crossing to his side and holding out her hands to him, quite unexpectedly. Did she hope that he would take them? Oh, the documents. He handed them to her. She took them with a smile.

'There you are, Miss Killivant.' Had she realized? He could feel that he was turning pink again. 'If there is anything that I can do to help...'

'Thank you, Mr Tulver. You have been very kind. Now, may I ring the bell and get the maid to bring some tea?'

He would have loved to linger, but he did not dare.

Two

'You should have seen him, standing at the door. "I'm Mr Tulver from the bank," he said.' Edie put on a comic voice to imitate his tone. It was her half-day Wednesday, and here she was at home, crushed up in the corner of the kitchen on the bench, with the younger ones clambering all over her, and begging for a story as they always did. She was obliging with an account of what had happened in the week. 'Well, I had to let him in. So full of self-importance you'd think that he would burst. Dressed up in black and white like that penguin in Donny's colour-picture book he won at Sunday school. Same shape as a penguin, Mr Tulver was, as well – little head and big round body – toddling along the passage with his briefcase and his hat. Perhaps he was a penguin. What do you think of that?'

Five-year-old Donny gave her arm a playful punch. He was at school now and learning how to read, which made him feel grown-up – and made him a proper stickler for the facts of things. 'They don't have penguins in the bank, you goose! They have things like ... I don't know.' He looked at Edie but she couldn't help. None of them had ever been inside a bank. He suddenly had an inspiration. 'Cash registers,

24

I suppose.'

Edie grinned. 'Well, he did look a bit like one of them, I suppose, when he was sitting on the chair – all black and upholstered and stiff as anything. Do you think that if I'd pushed the buttons on his coat his eyes would have gone spinning round inside his head and come up with numbers, like cash registers in shops?'

A general roar of laughter greeted this remark, and Edie gently disengaged herself. 'I'd better go and give Meg and Ma a bit of a hand. Can't stay here sitting like the Queen of what's-its-name, expecting to be waited on.'

She meant the Queen of Sheba, but Donny misinterpreted. 'She's called Alexandra,' he supplied. 'And the King's called Edward, just the same as Pa. We've got a picture of them on the wall at school.'

'Wonder if they call him Teddy when he's at home?' Edith said, and they laughed again though this time all of them looked shocked.

Edie smiled. She skirted through the narrow space between the kitchen table and the wall, and two more paces took her to the scullery. Ma and Meg were in there, and there wasn't room for more, so she stood at the doorway. 'What can I do to help?'

Ma turned, her worn face lighting with a smile. 'You can get the cups and saucers from the dresser if you like, and put the kettle on the range to boil. There's jam tarts in the oven waiting to come out, and there's pressed tongue ready outside in the safe. Meg and me are washing up the children's knives and plates and we can lay the table ready for our tea. But be sure and leave a decent plate of everything for Pa. He'll be good and ready for a bit of a meal – he might come early, knowing you are here.'

Edie went out into the yard, where the zinc safe was nailed to a shady wall. She opened the perforated door to get the meat. Pressed tongue sandwiches and jam tarts as well – a year or so ago, it would have been a choice between the two. And this safe was new.

She knew it was partly because she'd gone into service now. She brought home her wages and divided them each week – three and six for mother and sixpence for herself. It made a bit of difference, and the fact that she got her keep and uniform obviously meant that there was one less mouth to feed, and one less set of clothing to provide. Or to sew and wash and mend, she told herself, as she took down the bowl of tongue and took off the weighted saucer that Ma had put on to 'press' the meat.

She sniffed at it. Delicious. It did keep things cooler, now they had the safe – especially if you put a bowl of water to evaporate – and milk and butter kept much better than they used to do indoors. She took the pat of butter in her other hand – it would be wanted for buttering the bread – and set off back across the yard with it. Just at that moment, Meg came trotting out as fast as her fourteen-year-old legs would carry her.

'Want the milk and butter, we do. I forgot before.'

'Jug's still in there,' Edie said, nodding her

chin towards the butter-pat, in the dish which she was holding, though it was invisible under the muslin cover with the beads to weight it down. 'Didn't have a hand free, by the time that I'd got both these.' She said it with an apologetic smile.

Edie occasionally felt a twinge of guilt about her younger sister nowadays. Ma needed someone to help around the house, and that had been Edie until a few short months ago. But now Meg had got old enough to 'leave that school and lend a bit of a hand', Edie had been freed to find a paying job and the schoolteacher herself had been good enough to put in a word for her to go into service with Mrs Killivant. 'You've got the intelligence to make something of yourself, but you'll have to remember to speak properly and keep your mind on things. I don't have to tell you, it will be hard work.'

It was. Yet, remembering the scrubbing and the laundry and the mending that were required at home – let alone the sewing, shopping and preparing meals – Edie sometimes thought life wasn't half so hard these days, and what is more, she now got paid for what she did. There were Abel and Reuben, the two boys of course, almost old enough to go to work, but poor Meg had no sister who could take her place in turn – not until Suzanna, and she was number six. Only eight years old, with Jake and Adam in between, so it would be years before she would be any real use to Ma, and by that time even Rosa would be going to school – not underfoot and threatening to fall into the fire as soon as anyone took their eyes off her. No wonder Meg was looking tired and glum.

'I'll get the milk,' Edie told her now, 'you've got enough to do. And after tea I'll help you with that blouse you're altering. Lovely bit of muslin that it was made of, isn't it? Belonged to Miss Alicia, so you can tell it's good. Pity she spilt blackberry all down the front of it. But you take in those pleats the way I told you to, and it will fit you lovely and you'd never know. And you've still got the edging – it will look a treat.'

Meg cheered up enough to flash a smile. 'Well, if you're sure that you've got time enough? I'll never be as handy with a needle as you and Nana are. I take after Ma for that. Give me a pair of knitting needles and some sock-wool any time.'

Edie laughed. With five boys and Pa there were always socks to knit, and it was a job she'd hated since she was a little girl. 'Of course I'll help you, Meg. Though we'll have to look sharpish. I can't be late tonight. Mr Edwin's coming down from London tomorrow, on the train – and it's always bedlam while he's in the house. Mrs Pritchard will be tearing out her hair. She tries to make things nice for him, but it is never right. If the meal's delicious, we have spent too much – and if it's rather plain, it isn't good enough.'

Unconsciously she had been imitating him and Meg gave a little giggle.

Edie smiled. 'Tell you the truth, Meg, I'm glad I'm here tonight. Everyone will be as cross as sticks back there. And there's Pa come already, I can hear his step. Let's go and have a bit of tea with him, poor man – and then we can get the little ones to bed. I'll tell them a story if they're very good. And afterwards I'll help you with that blouse before I go.'

Teddy Trewin took his boots off and hung up his cap and scarf on the nail beside the door. Not that he was dirty, he had stopped off at the 'dry' to wash and change his clothes before he left the mine: never came home 'reeking' if he could help himself – poor Minnie had enough to do to keep things something like, without him trailing red dust everywhere.

He looked round. Edie and Meg were already on the step and Rosa was reaching up to fling her arms around his neck, and he bent down to scoop her in his arms. 'Well, here's your pa then, Edie. Got a kiss for him?' he teased, and of course she had, but somehow he didn't feel the usual flush of joy.

Truth to tell, he was simply grateful to be home. It was not just that he was weary and ached in every bone – he'd been a miner long enough to be quite used to that – but there was also something else that worried him. He'd been doing that coughing and spluttering again when he came 'up to ground'. 'Course, he tried to hide it as he always did, but Cap'n Maddox had noticed all the same.

'That's a nasty cough that you got there, old son.' He came over to where Teddy was sitting, panting, on the grass.

Teddy shook his head, too short of breath to speak. 'Shouldn't 'ave come up they ladders,' he muttered, when he could. 'Foolish thing at my age. I'm rising forty now – can't come racing up them the way I used to do. It's nigh on a mile. Should have waited for the cage with all the rest of them, and rode up on the winch.'

He tried to smile but Cap'n Maddox didn't look convinced. 'If you say so, Teddy, but I think it's more than that. I've heard you like this for a week or more –and you're greener than that grass you're sitting on. I've seen all this before when miners cough like that. You want to see that off before it gets a hold. Go home and go to bed. And don't go worrying about wages while you're there. The Fund would see you through it, if you lost a day or two.'

Teddy looked at him. This was likely to be more than a day or two, he thought, and Cap'n Maddox was aware of that. But the Miners' Benevolent was very good, of course – it not only paid out to people when they couldn't work, it helped with funeral expenses and that sort of thing. And there'd be a whip-round for the widow, very like, as well. But it hadn't come to funerals – for a little while at least.

'No need for that,' he said, dismissively. 'It's just a bit of cold.' He struggled to his feet. 'Though I think I must have got something in my throat. Haven't been quite right since that charge went off last week.'

He said it lightly, but even the memory almost made him gag. He'd been lucky really, he had not been hurt, but the incident still gave him nightmares every night. It was so unexpected, that had been the thing. The self-same 'pare', or team, as there had been for years. They had bored the rock as usual, and put the charges in: the powderman had set the fuse and they had all retired. But this time something hadn't been quite right. They'd hardly cleared the level when the boom rang out and the shock-wave had caught them sharply from behind. Teddy was thrown forward on his face, bruised and winded, and when he scrambled up it was to find that it was impossible to breathe. The air was impenetrable with smoke and granite-dust, making it equally impossible to see. He tried to find the others by stretching out his hands, but there was nothing but rockface. The candles had gone out and he'd had to grope blindly down the tunnels in the dark, holding his breath until he thought his lungs would burst, until he blundered into a ladder and half-slithered down, into a lower adit where the air was clear. There he'd rested, panting – thinking that he was as good as dead – until they came to look for him and a pair of strong hands hauled him back to safety and fresh air. His powderman and kiddlyboy had been less fortunate. The first had lost his fingers and the other died outright.

'Should have gone home then, boy,' Cap'n Maddox said. 'Only you wouldn't have it.'

Teddy shook his head. 'Minnie would only worry if she knew. Thank you for finding a new "pare" to put me in.' He meant it, they were nice lads, though it couldn't be the same – and they were wary of him in case the bad luck stuck to him. The kiddlyboy's death had been a shock to everyone. It was a faulty fuse, they reckoned, but you could not be sure – it might have been

31

the powderman who made a slight mistake, and Teddy knew he should have checked the fuse in any case.

'And this confounded cough has plagued you ever since?' Maddox shook his head. 'You want to take care, Teddy. You know what it can mean. Perhaps you ought to think of coming up to ground. There's a place going in the sheds directly, so I hear, supervising the shaking-tables where they sort the tin. Harry Pearson's leaving for America next week, and they'll be needing someone who can take his place. Might suit you very well. Needs a steady person, who can concentrate, but there's nothing to it, once you've got the knack.'

Teddy was staring at the man, appalled. 'Are you suggesting that I should go for that? Me, who has spent my whole life underground?' It was almost an insult. Working in the sheds wasn't a proper man's job, Teddy thought.

'I can see it doesn't appeal to you very much, old son. But you really ought to give it a little bit of thought. And don't take too long about it, or they'll have appointed someone else. It's a decent sort of job, and the pay is steady too – though it's a bit less than if your pare strikes a good seam, of course – and I'm sure they'd have you if I recommended you. I really think you ought to take the chance while it is there. Otherwise you might be underground – and not the way you mean.' He grinned. 'And this way you'd get to see your family now and then.'

Teddy sighed. He'd been working 'doublers' up till yesterday, meaning that he had been

32

working two shifts on the trot – sometimes as much as sixteen hours down the mine. It was not compulsory, he volunteered for it. But as he said, 'Got to do something, with all these mouths to feed.' He hardly saw daylight, sometimes, for a week on end – though he'd been hoping that since Abel would soon be old enough to join him down the mine, money would be a bit easier than it used to be.

And now this! It was enough to try the patience of a saint. He'd thought of nothing else the whole way home tonight.

He put his arm round Edie. 'Let's go in,' he said. 'Your mother promised there'd be pressed tongue for tea.'

Might as well take advantage of these things while he could.

Edwin's visit was a brief and tense affair. He came down, as usual, on the sleeper train, and – again as usual – didn't sleep a wink.

'People are so inconsiderate,' he complained to Liss as they trotted up Market Jew Street in an ancient hansom cab, after she had come to meet him from the train. 'Banging their suitcases and slamming doors all night.' He gazed disconsolately out into the street. It was so provincial – bicycles and carts, the small old-fashioned shops with piles of merchandise stacked round the entrance ways – he counted shoes and saucepans, carpets, eggs and fruit. So different from the elegant stores one found in London now. And hardly a single motor vehicle in sight.

'But, Edwin, you always say you're wakeful

on the train.' Alicia's answer cut across his thoughts. 'So you can hardly blame others for your predicament.'

She was right, of course, which didn't help his temper in the least. 'Oh, please don't concern yourself, Liss, on my account,' he said, adopting a tone of patient martyrdom. 'I am a little cramped and short of sleep, that's all. It does not signify. It is the price for coming down to visit you and dear Mama. I hope I know my duty where such matters are concerned.'

They had reached the house by this time, and the driver stopped the cab. Edwin swung out of it and saw his case brought down before he paid the man – which Alicia rather pointedly stood by and let him do. It was a reminder that she had no money of her own.

'If you are so wearied, Edwin, I should go and rest,' she said, as the housemaid seized his suitcase and led the way indoors. 'Fortunately, you should have no trouble here – it's the same bed that you slept in every night when you were a boy. Edith can take your case up straight away, and then bring some brandy to the library perhaps. Unless you'd rather have some vinegar and lavender water to bathe your aching brow? I'm sure Mrs Pritchard could find some, if we asked.'

She was looking at him in that mocking way she had. He glanced at her, nonplussed, but she simply smiled, as though the comment had been purely innocent.

He answered rather curtly, 'I know my wife has often made such a request, but she has not

34

come this time – in her condition I could hardly ask her to. In the meantime I will have that glass of brandy, please.'

The servant looked sheepish and took the case upstairs, and Edwin followed his sister into the fusty reading-room, which had not changed a whit since Father's day. He found it oppressive, and said tetchily, 'Even so, I cannot be too long. I must discuss with Mother about replacements and repairs, then I have an appointment with the manager at the bank – I believe you have some papers signed for me to take?'

'Of course I've signed them, Edwin – what else was there to do? And of course you will have to discuss things with Mama, but I don't know why you have to treat me like a child. I'm the one who sends you the accounts, and points out that the roof is leaking in the loft.'

'You should have the servants check it every week or two.' He spoke before he thought – and he knew what she would answer before she said a word. She was always complaining about the lack of staff and now he had given her an opportunity.

She took it, naturally. 'The servants? Edith and the poor old cook? Be reasonable, Edwin, they have far too much to see to as it is, what with Mother ill in bed. It's only fortunate that I went up when I did – to find an old blouse that I'd promised to the maid – otherwise the damage might have been a great deal worse. Or perhaps you'd like me to have the gardener in, or ask the scrubbing woman to inspect the roof? I presume that even you would not expect to ask the nurse.'

'Ah, yes, the nurse,' he said, anxious to draw attention to the fact that he had agreed to that – though of course the doctor had suggested it. 'That's working well, I trust? Nurse Morgan has proved to be satisfactory?'

'Nurse Morgan runs the sickroom like a barrack-room,' Alicia said. 'Everything in order and no disobedience brooked. I'm sure you will approve. I admit I find her difficult at times, but Mama adores her, which is fortunate. Rather reminds her of Father, I suspect.'

Edwin ignored the jibe. 'In what way difficult?' He had a right to know, he told himself, since after all he was the one who paid the bill. He felt a certain sympathy for the nurse, quite suddenly. Liss did not take easily to authority.

'Well, she does cause friction with the kitchen now and then. Cook takes her orders from Mama of course, and Mama will ask for something that she has a fancy for, so Mrs P will cook it and send it up to her – only to have Nurse Morgan send it back and order something bland instead, like poached fish or blancmange. Says it is better for an invalid. Other than that, she fits in very well, though of course doesn't mix much with the other staff – she takes her meals with Mama and sleeps in the ante-room next door in case she might be wanted in the night. But you'll find Mama's much better than the last time you were here. You can thank the nurse for that – bullying Mama into doing as she's told, perhaps, and making her take her medicines and do as the doctor says.' She gave him a triumphant smile. 'I'm sure you'll find your money is well spent in that regard.'

She was making little points at his expense again. He hastened to repress her. 'And what about that food that gets sent back again? I trust it isn't wasted?' He saw her stubborn face. 'Liss, I know you think that I fuss about such things, but believe me, if you saw the sights I sometimes see, you would be troubled about wastefulness, as well.'

'Well, I don't know,' she muttered snappishly. 'I suppose the servants eat it, if I've had my meal. Do you want me to give orders to Cook that it is to be saved and served to me next day?'

She meant to be sarcastic, but he gave that nod again. 'A good idea, Liss. I'll mention it to Mrs Pritchard when I speak to her. And speaking of the servants, where has that brandy gone? It must be minutes since I ordered it. I presume you still have a little in the house?'

'Brandy?' she said, pretending to reflect. 'I believe we do. We have not economized in that direction yet I account our brandy as medicinal supplies. The nurse gives some to Mother, when she cannot sleep.' She looked her brother directly in the eye, and suggested with apparent innocence, 'Perhaps you should try some, Edwin, before you catch your train back home.'

She was being disrespectful and it took his breath away. 'It seems that I may have to wait till then before I get it, too. What's happened to that maid? She needs a talking-to. It shouldn't take her all this time to bring a simple drink.'

'I dare say she's been called away to help with the beef tea. Mama always has it at this time of day – Nurse Morgan's orders – and I've heard Cook say before that it takes hours to make – pushing raw steak through a sieve. Now if we had another maid to help...'

It was the beginning of an argument which lasted half his stay, so he was more than usually happy to get home again. He hung his hat and coat up, gave his suitcase to his man, and went into the sitting-room at once to find his wife. He looked around with satisfaction at his modest home: the Morris wallpaper, the solid book-cases, the simple but comfortable chairs – so different from the old-fashioned dusty plush, ornate mahogany and overstuffed sofas of Hol-vean House.

'Home already, Edwin?' Claire looked up at him, proffering a scented cheek for him to kiss. Her voice was lilting, soft and high – as unlike Liss's as it was possible to be. It was true that in her 'interesting condition' it could sometimes turn into a whine, but nonetheless it was the sort of voice a man expected of a girl. 'You look exhausted, dearest.'

He sank into a chair. 'It proved to be a very difficult few days. It's always trying, all this rushing up and down, and I know you are always begging me to stop, but a fellow has to try to do his duty, after all. Father gave me the responsi-bility, and it's up to me to shoulder it as stoutly as I can. But it isn't easy when I have to keep an eye on Liss. She's so unlike the average sort of girl. It's hard to know what one can do with her.'

Claire made a face at him. 'I don't know why you say that, Edwin dear. She's nice enough to look at – in fact one or two young men you asked to tea thought she was very striking. Though I suppose they were always put off in the end.'

He groaned in agreement. 'It's her manner, Claire – the way she strides about and is apt to look a fellow in the eye – more of a boyish swagger than a modest gait. I remember once – when she was up here – you and she were out walking in the street. It struck me then how different you were.'

Claire took this as a compliment and coloured prettily. 'Well, I'm glad of that. But don't let her distress you. You're home now, Edwin. Let's talk of something else.'

But he couldn't let it rest. 'She's so headstrong sometimes,' he went on earnestly. 'I know I irk her with my carefulness, but she's far too ready to rush into things. Never willing to think things calmly through. I suppose she must feel a little restricted now and then, having to live with Mama and with no money of her own, but – as I've tried to tell her a number of times – compared to many, she is very fortunate.' He meant it. If his sister lived in London and had seen what he had seen – young women who had nothing and nobody to care, orphan-girls worried into early graves by responsibilities and debt, or hapless females who had been forced into degrading lives – she would be grateful for the blessings of a comfortable home, adequate money for her needs whenever she asked for it, and a loving brother to see to her affairs.

If only his sister were a little more like Claire.

He looked at his wife now, sitting by the fire, knitting some white garment with elaborate care, and drawing her pretty brows into a concentrated frown. She saw him looking and glanced up at him.

'What is it, Edwin? Are you still fatigued?'

He smiled indulgently. 'I was just thinking how glad I am to be back home again, with my pipe and books and fire – and my pretty little wife.'

She dimpled sweetly. 'I don't know why you go there, Edwin, if you dislike it so. Surely you can organize affairs and pay the bills from here? If you had a living, instead of working with the mission to the poor, you would not be able to go down there the way you do, you would have to stay here and minister to your parishioners. And I feel the want of your company, you know – the more so as the baby's time comes near.'

He rose and went over to stand beside her chair and put a hand on her shoulder. 'Of course, my dear. And I do not go so very often, after all. Only once a quarter, as a general rule. But I did think that with the change in the trustees...'

She shook his hand away. 'Oh, Edwin, don't bother my poor head with such affairs. I never did understand that business of the trust, but I am quite sure that whatever provisions you have made, it will be for the best. Your sister should be very pleased that you have taken such pains on her account.'

'They were hardly my provisions, Claire, my dear...' he began, but she reached up and placed a playful finger on his lips.

40

'You are too modest, dear. Did you not tell me that you'd proposed a friend as trustee and that you hoped he'd make Alicia a match? What a clever thought. Though you're right that finding her a husband will be hard. Far too fond of her own way, it seems to me.' She went back to her knitting, frowning as she said, 'You know, when she was up here I found that she'd gone out one day, deliberately to listen to a speech by one of those dreadful women who keep disrupting parliament? Next thing you know, she will be joining them. The sooner you get her married, Edwin, the more relieved I'll be.'

Edwin shook his head. 'I sometimes think my sister would have made a better man. She was clever at her lessons, you know, when she was at school.' Better than he was, though he didn't mention that.

Claire put down her needles with a little sigh. 'Well, I don't want to criticize your family, Edwin dear, and of course she's very charming and all that sort of thing, but I do find her rather tiring and exuberant. Speaking of which, I'm feeling rather tired myself just now. I think I'll go to bed. Would you be an angel and ring the bell for me, and get the girl to bring me up a little cup of tea? I'm sure they will have done the fires and warmed the beds by now.'

'Of course.' He dropped a fleeting kiss upon her head. 'That's another thing that worries at me, you know. Liss wants another maid. Yet Mother already has two servants living in and another woman who comes in to clean, and two men to do the garden, to say nothing of the

41

nurse. That's six staff to look after just the two of them. While we make do with five. She says we have a courtyard while they have lots of grounds. Won't let the matter rest. In fact we had some heated words about it in the end.'

Claire smiled vaguely. 'Did you, Edwin dear? No wonder you are vexed. Now you won't forget to ring down for my tea, will you, dear, and don't be too late coming up yourself.'

He did arrange to have the maid take her tea, and bring up a glass of brandy for himself, but he stayed for a long time staring at the fire and it was after midnight before he went upstairs.

Three

It was a dreadful day. Rain was lashing down 'like stair-rods' as Mother would have said, filling up the gutters till they overflowed, and turning the garden paths to muddy pools. Blowing half a gale as well, with a wind that cut straight through your skirt and blouse and shawl, so that even going out to get the eggs was soaking, chilly work – like one of those Polar expeditions you heard so much about.

Though she didn't get as wet as she had expected to. Sammy had already collected up the eggs today and was waiting with them ready in the basket when she came, which was a kind of mercy; though Edith was never quite certain where Sammy was concerned. There was something about the way he looked at her and eyed her up and down, grinning all over his cheeky freckled face, which made her not quite comfortable with his company.

But there he was, hiding from the rain, inside the poultry hut – a small low shed where the chickens had their roosts. The hens had obviously taken shelter too. They were sitting, looking damp and bedraggled on the straw and clucking with outrage at the indignity, while Sammy leaned, half-squatting, against the further wall – the hut was low and he was far too tall to stand upright. His battered hat was hanging on a hook and he was giving her that unnerving, impudent, slow smile as she came in.

She felt herself going pink, but there was no help for it. She had to go in there, it was so wet outside.

''Ello, Edie!' he said cheerfully. He straightened up to push the egg basket into her outstretched hand. 'I thought you'd be along. Some awful weather, innit? I picked these up for 'ee. And, don't worry, I've already checked around to see if there were any laid outside. Save you scrabbling about in all the wet.'

She found that she was blushing. 'That's very kind of you.' Now why had she said that? It was part of Sammy's duties to pick up the eggs, if he wasn't wanted for doing something else. And why didn't she just say 'thank you' like anybody else? She sounded like that Mr Tulver, all prim and la-di-da.

Sammy, however, did not seem to mind. 'Too wet today for doing much outside.' His grin grew even broader. 'Unless you have plans to cut down trees and make an ark, that is. Mr G is in the glasshouse, pricking seedlings out, and he sent me over to get some extra pots – and while I was about it, to pick up the eggs. Glad to get in here and be out the rain, I was.' He gestured to his shirt. 'Look at me, I'm soaking – and you'll be just as bad if you go straight out there in all this wet again. Why don't you stay here and shelter for a bit?'

He was right, there was a passing squall. The

44

rain was bouncing even harder off the roof and forming a kind of waterfall across the chicken hut door. Even Mrs Pritchard couldn't very well complain if Edie stayed a moment till the rain had eased.

'Perhaps I could do for a minute,' she conceded grudgingly, and found herself adding, 'just till this stops a bit, mind!' – as if she were staying on his account somehow or might have been tempted to linger anyway.

'Nice to have a minute to have a chat to you. Don't get to see you in the normal way.' He edged towards her.

The shed was a small one, but she edged away. Not that there was any harm in Sammy Hern, of course. He was a nice boy, so Queenie always said, and she should know because her cousin had been at school with him. But he made Edie feel uneasy. She wasn't used to boys, except as relatives or the lads in her class when she was young – and they never used to look at her like this, as if she were an iced cake and good enough to eat.

'Mind out!' he was saying. 'Don't lean against that wall. It's all over dust and cobwebs. You'll get yourself mucky on your uniform. There, you have done, look. Got it on your shoulder, where your shawl moved back. It's on your blouse. I can see the mark from here.'

'Where?' Edie craned around and tried to look. 'I can't see nothing. Is it very bad? Clean on this morning, this was – and my other's in the wash.' She scrubbed a hand vaguely at her shoulder blade.

He shook his head. 'It's lower down that that. More towards the middle. Here, hold still. I've got a handkerchief. Turn round and let me see. Bend down so I can reach it.'

She did as she was bidden and felt him rub her back, but it was not until his other arm came creeping round her waist that she jumped upright and turned to face him, scarlet-faced. 'Sammy Hern! You devil. There was no mark at all.'

He held up his hanky. 'There was a cobweb, honest. Just a little one. But of course I wanted to get close to you. I've wanted to for ages, you must know I 'ave. What fellow wouldn't, pretty girl like you? Besides, you rather like it – I can see you do.'

She realized that his left arm was still around her knees. He hadn't moved it when she jumped up. She twisted herself free. 'Well, Sam Hern, that's just where you are wrong. You had no right to go and put your arm round me like that. It was presumptuous and I didn't care for it at all.' She was doing her Mr Tulver act again, and her confusion made her speak more sharply than she meant.

The hurt on Sammy's face surprised and startled her. 'Of course, Miss Trewin. I had no right at all. I'm very sorry. Truly I am. I didn't mean no harm. I thought that you liked me, and it was just that you were shy, so I waited here on purpose so we could have a bit of chat. And now, I suppose, I've gone and frightened you and very likely you won't speak to me again. Wish I'd never come here for they dratted eggs today.' He picked up his battered hat and jammed it on his head, then shuffled, still stooping, over to the door. He looked like a despondent hunchback from the fair.

She couldn't let him go like that, she thought. She hadn't meant to wound him: she hadn't realized that he felt like that. Suddenly she rather wanted him to stay.

'Here, Sammy!' she said quickly. 'Don't go off like that. We're as bad as each other. I shouldn't speak so sharp.' He turned back towards her and she saw his smile. She went on hastily, 'But don't you get ideas. It wasn't proper, creeping up and getting hold of me like that. Don't you do that, ever, without I say you can.'

A slow, delighted smile lit the freckled face. 'You saying that you might tell me that I can, one day?'

She realized that she had said that, without quite meaning to. 'Possibly,' she said. Suddenly, it seemed, he was no threat at all. The world had turned about and instead of him teasing her, as usual, now she was teasing him. Her heart gave a strange and unexpected lurch. 'I aren't making any promises. I don't hardly know you – but given time, perhaps.'

'You saying that you're willing to walk out with me a bit?' he asked. 'Find out if you like me well enough for me to be your proper beau?'

She coloured. 'I suppose I am. But don't go saying so. Mrs Pritchard will have me out of here as quick as wink, if she thinks that I've got a follower.'

'Then we'd best be careful.' He gave a cheer-

47

ful wink. 'Starting this minute, if you've any sense. You'd better take those eggs in. The rain has nearly stopped.'

It had too. You could hardly hear it on the roof. 'Oh, Sam, you are a devil,' she muttered as he grinned. 'How didn't you say so earlier? Mrs Pritchard will be furious.' And she pushed past him and scurried down the muddy path.

Cook was grilling kidneys when Edie reached the kitchen door. 'Oh, there you are, Edith. What took you all that time? I'm waiting for those eggs. You've been so long, I thought you must have been laying them yourself. Now, mind you take that shawl off, you're dripping on my step. And scrape those muddy boots before you come inside.'

Edie did as she was told. 'I waited in the hen hut till that shower passed.' She handed Cook the basket.

Mrs Pritchard tutted. 'And in your own world, dreaming as usual, I suppose? Well, now you're back amongst us, make yourself of use. Give your hair a rub-down and get yourself upstairs. I can hear the doorbell. Go and answer it.'

'A caller, Edith?' Alicia was sitting at her looking-glass, putting her own hair up. She wasn't good at it, and it collapsed in a cascade of hairpins as she turned her head to look at the housemaid, who was standing at the door. 'At this time of day? We're not expecting anyone. Who is it, anyway? Not that dreadful Mr Tulver from the bank, by any chance?' She would not have put it past him to have called again.

48

The maid shook her head. 'It's a young woman, Miss Alicia.' She made a doubtful little face. 'Well, hardly even that. Just a girl, she looked to me – she might be sixteen.'

Alicia frowned. 'A girl?' She twisted her wayward tresses in a coil and pinned them up again. It wasn't any good. She'd have to ask Edith to help her by and by. You couldn't look fashionable doing it yourself. 'I can't think of anyone of that age it might be. Unless it's someone from Mrs Worthington's Academy for Girls. Someone whose sister I might have known at school.'

'Shouldn't think so, Miss Alicia.' Edith had come up behind her, and in two moments had the chignon neatly pinned in place. 'She didn't look the type. Not unless her family have fallen on hard times. There!' She handed the hand-mirror so Alicia could see the back.

Liss nodded her approval and put the mirror down. 'Fallen on hard times? What do you mean by that?'

'Well, poor thing, she's skinny as a rake and not very well turned out. Neat and clean and quite respectable, but not what you'd call smart. Only a coat and bonnet to keep off the rain, and all her hems is soaked. I'd have turned her off, except she asked for you by name. Said she had to talk to you. She sounded desperate. I've took her coat and hat and left her in the hall. I could not put her in the drawing-room. What should I say to her?'

Alicia leaned forward to select a brooch. She wanted to look elegant before she went downstairs, but there was no hurry by the sound of it.

Who was this visitor? A thin girl, not very well turned out, who asked for her by name? She racked her brains but could not think of anyone at all. 'Did she say what she wanted?' She looked up at Edith's reflection in the glass.

The figure in the mirror shook its head. 'I asked her what she wanted, but she wouldn't say. Just that it was urgent and she had to speak to you.'

'And she didn't give a name?'

'Wasn't going to, till I pressed a bit, and then she said that I could tell you it was Fanny come. Couldn't get her to say Fanny what. Said she'd explain it when she spoke to you – almost as if you'd know what it's about.'

'Well, I don't,' Alicia said firmly. 'I've never heard of her. No one of that name at all, as far as I recall. Though I confess that I am quite intrigued. I wonder who she is. Should I see her, do you think? I've half a mind to have you send her off again.'

But of course she did nothing of the kind. Visitors to the house were novelty enough and this little mystery was too curious to miss. Though when she came downstairs a little later on she wondered if she had made a mistake after all. The girl was standing stiffly by the chair near the door, as if she were too nervous to sit down on it, and was staring vaguely at the family portraits on the wall. Her fairish hair was cut in front into a ragged fringe – which had clearly never seen a proper hairdresser –while the rest was scraped back into a damp and skinny plait from which stray wisps were attempting to

50

escape. She was clean and neat enough, as Edith had said – apart from muddy hems – but the clothes were threadbare and the boots were worn and her pale face in profile was pitifully thin. The figure in general had a sort of humble, hang-dog air. More like a servant than a visitor.

Alicia sighed. She should have told Edith to send the girl away. It looked as if she was from some charity; one of Edwin's good causes, possibly, who knew the family name. Well, in that case he could deal with it himself. One couldn't make oneself available to any waif who happened to call by.

'Miss Killivant?' The girl had heard her come, and had turned to face her now. 'It's good of you to see me.'

Alicia did not smile. 'I am Alicia Killivant,' she said. 'And you are Fanny, I am led to understand. I don't think I know you. Fanny what?'

The pale face coloured. 'Yes, Miss Killivant.'

'Pardon?' Alicia was puzzled.

The girl looked up at her, and swallowed nervously. She was a good deal shorter than Alicia. Suddenly she gave an awkward little smile. 'I mean, yes, Miss Killivant, that's the answer – see. Fanny Watt. My name is Fanny Watt.'

She was so young and flustered that Alicia had to smile. 'I see. No doubt you are tired of people making jokes of it. Well, Miss Watt, should I have heard of you?'

She spoke more kindly and saw the girl relax. Some of the tension went from round the eyes. 'Not really, I'm down here seeking work. My parents died, see, a little while ago and I came

51

down here to try to find my aunt, but when I got here she had moved away. Gone to Australia to be with her son, and now I'm on my own.' The Cornish accent was suddenly broader – and not quite like Edith's, Alicia observed. 'And now I don't know what I'm going to do. I've come from Launceston way. I had a bit of money, but I spent it getting here...'

Alicia held up an interrupting hand. 'You were sent to look for my brother Edwin, I assume. In that case, Miss Watt, I fear you've come too late. My brother was here recently, but he's returned to London now and I am in no position to help you. If you are in want of charity, I suggest you write to him – or apply to one of the charitable bodies in the town.'

The girl was staring at her in dismay, and Alicia saw that there were tears in the grey eyes. 'I aren't after charity. That's how I came to you. I'm not afraid of working – and I was asking round. Somebody told me you might need a maid...'

Alicia was frowning. 'You came to seek a post? Then why did you not come to the tradesmen's entrance, may I ask?'

Fanny Watt dropped her gaze and stared down at her boots. 'I know I should have done, Miss Killivant – but what would happen then? They'd only shut the door on me – you know they would have done. They would just have told me there was no vacancy. That's what the coalman told me anyway. "Go and ask to speak to Miss Killivant herself," he said. "There's that great big house there with hardly any staff. Used to have no end of servants a few years ago, and they must be wanting an extra pair of hands – though her brother up London most likely won't agree. But she's a nice young lady, and she's got a lot of sense. Ask for her in person and I'm sure she'll hear you out." So I thought I'd try it. It's the workhouse for me else.'

Alicia said frostily, 'The coalman told you that? I must have words with him. I don't care to have this household the subject of idle gossip in that way.' Though secretly she was flattered that he thought her sensible.

The girl looked stricken. 'Oh, don't do that, Miss Killivant,' she cried, urgently. 'I hate for him to be in your bad books over it. He was trying to help me, and he meant it to be kind. And now I've brought trouble on him as well as me. I'm very sorry. I'll be on my way. I can see I shouldn't have come and bothered you like this.'

The tears of desperation were threatening again, and Alicia's conscience moved her to enquire, 'And where will you go to?'

Fanny shook her head. The eyes were brimming now. 'I don't know. I might try somewhere else. I'm sure I don't know where.'

'A factory or something?' Alicia suggested. 'I hear they're taking people at the laundry in the town.'

Fanny nodded. 'Girls, they're looking for. I did go down and ask. But it's not enough to live on, without you've got a home, not to pay rent and buy new boots and have enough to eat. I thought if I could find somewhere that would give me board and keep...' She tailed off.

53

Alicia nodded sagely. 'There may be something in the paper. I'll have a look for you. They do have advertisements for servants there, sometimes.' It made her feel important, offering advice and help, and she found that she was speaking in a patronizing tone – rather like Edwin, talking of the poor. She moved towards the drawing-room where there was a bell, and said in her more normal, forceful tone of voice, 'I'll ring for the maid and have her bring a copy up...'

'No!' the girl spoke with such passion that it stopped her in the act. 'No, not the paper. It would make it far too...' She had gone brick-red again. 'That is, they wouldn't want to have the likes of me. They would only take people with experience – or at least a written character...'

'And you don't have one?'

Fanny shook her head. 'Did have one, one time. A very nice one, too – I worked for a family for a month or two, and they wrote how they were sorry that I had to leave. But' – she sighed and gave a helpless shrug – 'I've gone and lost the envelope and that's the end of that.'

Alicia was frowning. 'Lost it? How lost it? You don't lose a thing like that.'

There was a silence and then Fanny blurted out, 'Got burnt, didn't it? While it was at our house. Nothing I could do.' Her voice was harsh with a kind of angry grief.

'There was a fire? At your home?' Alicia said, struck by a dreadful thought. 'Surely that wasn't how your parents died?'

She was answered only by a tearful sniff and a
54

reluctant nod.

'You poor young woman.' Suddenly Alicia felt a wave of sympathy. 'And that's why you can't go home again? You've got no home to go to?' Another tearful nod. 'I see now why you came down here to try to find your aunt. It must have been an awful shock when you found out she'd gone. But surely she must have told your parents that she planned to emigrate?'

The girl looked up at her. 'She was never on good terms with my father, I believe, and the households hadn't corresponded properly for years – though I think my mother used to write a note sometimes, and get a friend to send it when my father wasn't there.'

'But she never got an answer?'

Fanny shook her head. 'Not that I'm aware. She would have been afraid my father would find out. He would have knocked her head off, if he'd ever known.'

Alicia shuddered at this picture of the Watt family at home, and said quickly, 'But after ... what happened ... you still tried to find your aunt?'

Fanny said bleakly, 'What else was there to do?'

'You have no other family?'

'Not any more I don't.' The girl swayed slightly and seemed about to faint, as if the memory was more than she could bear, but putting a hand on the table appeared to steady her.

Alicia was uncomfortable at this evidence of grief. She said, rather fretfully, 'I don't know quite what I can do for you. As I told you, there is no vacancy.' Or rather, she thought bitterly, thanks to Edwin and his careful budgeting, I cannot afford to take on extra staff – and I wouldn't have authority to do so, if I could. She forced herself to smile. 'You said you found employment with a household once and they were sorry when you had to leave. Perhaps you could go back there, if I let you have the fare, and they might find you something if you applied to them? At least they might give you another testimonial.'

But Fanny simply closed her eyes and shook her head, as if the very thought of returning was horrible. 'It's kind of you, Miss Killivant – but don't ask me to do that. I couldn't bear to go back there after ... you-know-what. And the family that I worked for have moved on, anyway. I can't go traipsing round the country after them. No, I'll have to try my luck somewhere else down here today, and if I don't find something ... well, who knows what I shall do? Better I find the river and make a hole in it. Or it'll have to be the workhouse, I suppose. Starve most likely, else. I haven't eaten anything for two days as it is.'

Was that why she was faint? Alicia saw an opportunity. 'Perhaps I could give you a bite to eat, at least. I'll send you to the kitchen, and they can feed you there. And while you are about it, you could dry yourself a bit. I can see that you're wet through and shivering.' This time she did reach the bell and ring downstairs. 'I really don't know what more I can do for you.' If she had the running of this house, she thought, she could

56

take on this poor young woman and save her from despair. She could imagine it – a devoted Fanny, grateful all her days, serving her faithfully till she was old and grey.

It was a delightful image, and it was quite impossible. Edwin would never sanction the additional expense.

'Bless you, Miss Killivant,' the girl burst out. 'I'd be more grateful for a bite to eat than I can say. I'm that hungry my stomach thinks my throat's been cut. But I wish I could do something for you in return. I meant it when I said I wasn't wanting charity. Perhaps I could scrub the floor or clean the steps – they are going to need it after all this rain.' She brightened suddenly. 'Here, look, Miss Killivant, that gives me an idea. Why don't you take me for a trial – just for a month or two. I don't want paying, I'll work for just my keep – and if I suit, perhaps you'll take me on, or give me a character so I can find a post. I swear you won't regret it, but if you do for any reason, you can turn me out at once. It might be a help to you – from what the coalman said – and I can't tell you what it would mean to me.'

Alicia was about to shake her head. It would be most irregular – and what would Edwin say? She was very irritated with her brother, suddenly. Perhaps that is why Fanny's unexpected, bold suggestion had a strange appeal. Though, if there was any arrangement of that kind to be made, it was for her to suggest it, and not this wretched girl.

But the 'wretched girl' was speaking, in a

dejected tone. 'I'm sorry, Miss Killivant, I'm speaking out of turn. I can see from your face that it wouldn't do at all – I expect your brother wouldn't like it anyway.'

It was the mention of Edwin that made up her mind. 'I'll deal with him later,' Alicia replied. 'In the meantime...' she broke off as Edith came panting from downstairs. 'Edith, this is Fanny Watt, an orphan who has lost her parents in a fire. Take her downstairs and see she has some food. You can tell Mrs Pritchard that we shall need a bed – you can open one of the unused attics up again, and no doubt there's still bedding somewhere from before. Fanny's come to join us – just for a week or two. She can start this after-noon, when she is fed and dried. No doubt Cook can find her some useful jobs to do.'

The expressions on the faces of the two girls were comical. Fanny was beaming in obvious delight, and Edith was gaping in near-disbelief. 'Coming to join us? Just like that? Does Mr Edwin know? What is he going to say?'

Alicia's last doubts evaporated at these words, like the water still steaming from Fanny's drag-gled hems. 'I'll deal with Mr Edwin. You leave that to me. Mrs Pritchard is always saying she could do with extra help. So here is a solution. I hope she will be grateful. It's the best thing all round. Now, off you go, the both of you. What are you waiting for? And, Edith, you can bring me a cup of tea into the drawing-room in half an hour.'

Sammy was double-digging the bed for the

broad beans that afternoon. It was back-breakingly sticky, after all the rain – but that was most likely why old Gribbens had put him on to it.

'Teach you to take all morning over seeing to the 'ens,' the old man had muttered, grinning round his pipe. 'Make sure you do it proper, too – two spades deep, and see you fork in a bit of something from the heap, before you start backfilling – like I showed you how. And get and do it quickly while this rain holds off. I've put the beans to sprout and they'll be ruined if they wait.'

So here he was, knee-deep in mud and filth, running as much with sweat as with the rain, with a barrow beside him full of compost from the 'heap' – the stinking mix of household rubbish and seaweed from the shore which was kept rotting in a corner to improve the soil. The 'heap' was Mr Gribbens's pride and joy, but Sammy hated it. It had to be laboriously turned by hand from time to time, and woe betide Sammy if he didn't 'find the plank' – the piece of wood which Mr Gribbens always hid beneath the pile, and which had to be uncovered for inspection every time, to prove that the turning over had been thorough.

All this for a bucketful of miserable broad beans, he thought, standing upright for a moment to ease his aching back. But his resentment vanished as he saw a familiar figure in a cape. 'Edie?' He left the trench and padded to the path. 'What you doing here at this time of the day? Thought you and Cook were cleaning chandeliers this afternoon?'

She rolled her eyes to heaven with a despairing look. 'Some chance of that! I'm sent to find a mirror that was put out in the shed – wanted for the attic, if you ever heard the like. You'll never guess what's happened. A girl came off the street, and Miss Alicia's gone and took her on as extra help. Only on trial for a month or so, but it is all arranged.'

He pushed back his cap and whistled with astonishment. 'Just like that? She never did.'

' Yes, she did. Couldn't hardly believe my eyes and ears,' Edie replied.

'Whatever did Mrs Pritchard have to say to that?'

Edie grinned. 'I was sure she'd have my guts for garters when she heard – she always hoped that if there was a post here, they would give it to her niece. But there was nothing for it. I had to take this Fanny down and tell Cook that she'd come. Well, Cook was making pastry, and you should have seen the look. And when she said, "Whoever heard the like?"' (she did an imitation that made Sammy laugh aloud), 'I thought that she would burst. But if Miss Alicia said so, there wasn't much that she could do. Just said, "Come here, Fanny – is it? – and let's take a look at you." And then she wiped her hands and looked Fanny up and down, for all the world as if the poor girl was a fowl, or a bit of rabbit that the butcher's boy had brought.' Edie gave a giggle. 'I half-expected Cook to come and pinch her arm, just to make sure the meat was really fresh. Though it was so skinny there was nothing much to pinch.'

It was preposterous, but Sammy had to grin. You always did when Edie told a tale. 'Sounds pretty wretched from what you say of her. One of Mr Edwin's charity cases, is she?'

'Don't believe so.' Edith shook her head. 'Lost her family in a fire, it seems, and came from Launceston looking for an aunt who's gone away, and someone told her that we might be wanting help. So she came to ask. Us or the poorhouse, from the sound of it.' The words were kindly, but she looked a little bit put out.

'Still, it will be a bit of company for you.' He tried to sympathize.

She made a face. 'I'm not so sure of that. She doesn't say a lot. Managed to speak to Miss Killivant all right, but she was that white and silent when we went downstairs, that you'd have thought that I was talking to a ghost. I had to stop and block her way before she'd speak to me. "Cat got your tongue?" I said. "Or aren't I good enough to talk to, is that it?" And then I felt awful, 'cause I made her cry.'

Sammy scratched his forehead with a muddy hand. 'Probably the poor girl's terrified to death. And if she's lost her family – like you say she has – no wonder she doesn't feel like chattering. How would you feel yourself, if it was Donny and all the rest of them?'

He saw the look of horror dawning on her face, and wished he hadn't been so forthright, but she said, 'Of course, you're right, Sammy – I hadn't thought of it like that. I'll try and be a bit more friendly when I get back to her. One thing about it, she won't have time to brood. Mrs Pritchard will have her running round till her feet won't remember when they last hit the ground.'

'Opposite to me, then,' Sammy put in with a grin. 'My feet are that stuck up with earth, from being on the ground, it's a wonder I can find them if I wanted them.'

'Sam Hern, you are a caution!' She was pretty when she laughed. He would have liked to touch her, take her hand at least, but he was so muddy that he didn't dare.

She must have read his thoughts because she took a step away. 'But I can't stand here gossiping,' she said. 'I got to find this looking-glass – if it isn't broken into smithereens. Be covered in spiders, I shouldn't be surprised.'

'And you don't like them?'

'Hate the jolly things. And it will be worse when I get back inside. It's all very well for Miss Killivant to say "open up the attics", but it means a lot of work. It will be the smallest attic, where there isn't so much, but nobody's been in there since the last tweeny left – and that was years ago. We'll have to move the dust-sheets and air the mattress through – to say nothing of scrubbing down the floor and walls. Need a bit of bleach, I shouldn't be surprised – you don't want mouldy patches and a smell of damp. And Cook says to take a duster and dustpan when I go, because it must be knee-deep in cobwebs in that room by now.'

'Wish I could come and kill they spiders for you then!' he said, hoping he sounded a little like St George.

'Oh, Fanny's going to help. She's having a

drop of soup first, and drying out beside the fire. She has got a change of clothes at least, though they are wet as well. She left them in a bundle out beside the gate, because she didn't like to bring them in with her, she says. Not much when she's got it, but there's a skirt and blouse – seems they gave it her the last place that she worked – and that's a mercy, 'cause there's nothing here that would have done. My stuff wouldn't fit her – I'd make two of her. Makes me feel a proper fatty, by comparison.'

Sammy gave her a grimy, rain-soaked smile. 'Look pretty good to me.' And then there was no time for saying more because Cook was on the doorstep, shouting down the path. 'Edith! Drat the girl. Where has she got to now?'

Four

Edwin was furious when he got the news. Claire was reading a letter of her own and he startled her by thumping on the breakfast table with his fist.

She looked at him. 'Edwin, dear!' she said reprovingly. 'I wish you would not do that. You alarmed me, and in my condition that is not good for my health.'

He gave her a brief, apologetic smile. He should have been more thoughtful, he supposed. 'I'm sorry, Claire, my dear. But I am sorely tried. What do you suppose my foolish sister has done now? Listen to this...' He read the page aloud.

Claire listened, but – for once – she did not do what he expected and instantly support his point of view. 'Well, I can see that it is vexing, dear – her appointing someone without consulting you at all. But she has always said that they need another maid, and you have opposed it on the grounds of the expense. It seems she's found an answer which satisfies you both. And, as she says, it's a form of Christian charity to save a poor orphan from the workhouse – just the sort of thing that you support yourself. I should have thought that you would have been pleased, if anything.'

Edwin gave an exasperated sigh. 'Really, Claire, I am surprised at you. There's no comparison with what the mission does.'

She looked at him, surprised. 'Why not? You deal with unfortunates who walk in off the street and have an unhappy background, don't you, dear?'

'Not like this,' he said impatiently. 'We do things properly. We look into things and have a proper place for girls like this to sleep. We don't just take them in and let them live with us. Someone we've never heard of in our lives, without a recommendation or a written character. For all we know the girl may be a thief – or worse. I shouldn't be surprised to have another note from Liss, saying that all the family silver had disappeared one night.' He picked up his cup and drained it in a decisive gulp – and rather wished he hadn't, because he'd let the tea go cold.

Claire, infuriatingly, refused to be convinced. 'But Alicia writes that this Fanny has settled very well. A good hard worker and the cook is pleased. Is that not enough? It's not her fault if all her papers were destroyed by fire.'

'We've only got the girl's own word for that,' Edwin said darkly, and felt he'd made a point.

Claire reached across and gave his hand a 'calm down, darling' pat. It was the sort of thing he usually did to her, and somehow it didn't calm him down at all. 'Well, it seems your mother has accepted it,' she murmured peaceably.

He put the cup down in the saucer very hard.

'If you mean that she's somehow been prevailed on to agree to having this girl, then, yes. I can't imagine how Liss managed to talk her into it. Usually she takes no interest in the running of the house. Liss has no doubt enlisted the support of that nurse I told you of, and of course Mama would fall in with anything she said.'

Claire went back to her letter, not at all concerned. 'And it's officially your mother's house while she is alive, which makes it difficult for you to intervene from here.'

'Precisely.' Edwin frowned. He signalled to the housemaid to pour another cup of tea. 'Well, there's nothing for it. I'll have to go down there again and sort it out in person, I suppose.'

Claire put her letter down and made a pouting face. 'But Edwin, you promised! You can't leave me now. Not until after the baby has arrived.' She patted her fat stomach. 'It won't be very long. Only another six weeks or so to go.'

'By then, by all accounts, it may well be too late. According to the letter, this girl is only there on trial.' Edwin relieved his feelings by buttering toast with much more vigour than the task required. 'I've met her kind before. I think Alicia should have turned the creature firmly out of doors.'

Claire gave him one of her vague smiles. 'Well, you can't have it both ways, dear. You can't both wish her gone, and want to talk to her. If the girl is a thief, or untrustworthy as you seem to think, the facts will no doubt quickly come to light. The biggest problem may be if she's satisfactory, it seems to me – then Alicia

66

will want to make her permanent, and if your mother supports her you may have to agree. Though I suppose that you can always stipulate that she must pay the wages from her legacy and not go calling on you for the additional expense.'

He looked at his wife with appreciative surprise. 'Well, of course, I could do that, couldn't I, my dear? And of course I could ask Tulver to go down there again – after all, he is the co-trustee, and money from the trust demands his signature. At least he can make sure this Fanny isn't wanted by the police, and he can let me know if she seems generally suitable or not. I shall write to Liss and say so.'

'I am sure you're right, dear.' Claire folded her correspondence, in her tidy way, and put it safely in its envelope, seeming suddenly more like her old compliant self. She smiled vaguely at him. 'That would be very wise. And if you are not planning to rush off to Cornwall, after all, could you contrive to visit my dressmaker today and ask her to call here? I fear some of my dresses need letting out again.'

He frowned importantly. 'I'm not quite sure when I shall have the chance. This week is a very busy time for me indeed, what with that meeting with the bishop, and the committee of the poorhouse guardians, and the opening of that mission hall to sailors down in the East End.' He had made her pout but her request had pleased him, all the same, reminding him that he would be a father very soon. He pushed back his chair and rose sedately to his feet. After all, he thought

67

indulgently, she could hardly be seen in public in her current state and it was his place to protect her when he could. 'Still, I am sure I can find the time somehow to run a precious little errand for my precious little wife.'

He dropped a kiss on her head and went upstairs to write to Liss. Quite a stiff note, in the circumstances. What nonsense would his wayward sister be getting up to next? He wished for the hundredth time that she were more predictable, and – well – respectable. Like his dear wife, who had just demonstrated her delicacy and decorum with her last request. If Liss had been in the same situation, he thought, she would simply have ordered a cab and – interesting state of health or not – gone out and called on the dressmaker herself.

He dipped his pen into the ink again and dashed off a brief letter to Tim Tulver at the bank, outlining the situation and asking him to call.

Teddy Trewin was riding to the surface in the cage. He was making himself do it every time these days, instead of climbing up the ladders and coughing all the way. He didn't want Cap'n Maddox to see him doing that. But ever since that dreadful business with the detonating charge, riding up like this had been a purgatory. It wasn't so bad, perversely, when he was underground – if he could see the tunnel, and the adit over him, then he could concentrate on the job in hand. But here, hemmed in by men on every side, he got that awful breathless feeling in his chest, and he had to shut his eyes until they got to ground.

'Getting out then, Trewin?' someone muttered in his ear. 'Or are you fixing to stop here half the night?' He realized that the whim had shuddered to a stop.

'Don't like it that much, Jethro,' he quipped, and tried to laugh – but ended up coughing in any case, of course. And, equally of course, there was Maddox watching him, as he stepped unsteadily from the cage and let the others surge past him out towards the dry.

Teddy couldn't help it, he had to stop and gasp. And the Cap'n came over, exactly as he'd feared. 'Hello then, Teddy. Still got that cough, I see? Thought any more about what I said, have you?'

Teddy said nothing. He pretended that he was still too short of breath.

Cap'n Maddox wouldn't let it drop. 'Pearson goes on Friday and you'll miss your chance. Have to make your mind up, if you want the place.'

Teddy still said nothing, but he didn't shake his head.

'I took the liberty of saying that I'd mentioned it to you, and I think that Cap'n Pearce would take your part if you went up for it.'

Teddy found that he was nodding. He knew Dick Pearce by sight. A big gruff man with hands like shovels and a famously loud voice who was the Captain of the settling sheds – just as Maddox was the Captain of the engines and the winding-gear. Those two Cap'ns were un-

69

likely friends, but they had worked together at the mine since they were boys.

Maddox saw the nod. 'I'm glad that you see sense. I'll put your name forward then, old son. Best thing all round. They'll get a good man and you'll do better there. 'T'isn't free of dust, of course – whatever round here is? – but it will give that chest of yours a bit of a chance, at least. Now, you get down the dry, boy, and get your street clothes on. Isn't that your eldest out there by the gate?'

It was. It was another Wednesday, and he knew that Edie would be home, but she didn't generally come down the mine like this. He hurried to get decent and strode out to where she was.

'What's all this then? Nothing wrong at home?'

She shook her head. 'Thought I'd come and meet you. I got time tonight. Miss Alicia's gone and got another maid – so I don't have to be back quite so quick to warm and turn down the beds.' She told him all about it. She sounded glum, he thought.

He fell in beside her and said, as they walked down the path across the field, 'So, what's the matter? Don't you like her very much?' And when Edie didn't answer, 'Must be something. 'T'isn't like you to take against another girl. 'Specially one who's had a sorry loss, from what you say.'

Edie made a face. 'I haven't took against her. But she won't be friends. Every time I try to talk to her, it's like talking to a wall. She answers a question, if you ask it straight, and that's all there is. Even then she doesn't tell you much. And if you talk about yourself, or the house or anything, she just says "really" and looks the other way. I don't think she ever volunteers a single word. Might say "good morning" if you pass her on the stairs – even give you a smile if you're lucky, too – but that's the most that you get out of her.' They had reached a stone stile, and she sat down on it.

He perched beside her, aware of the cold granite on his legs. 'Maybe she simply doesn't want to talk. How would you feel if it was us had died?'

She buried her head in his shoulder suddenly. 'That's just what Sammy said. It makes me feel a worm. But I have tried, honest. And she shows me up so much. Down every morning at the crack of dawn – and I have a struggle to be up by six o'clock, let alone be sweeping the rooms and setting fires.'

'So she's being helpful with the chores at least?'

Edie looked up at him, her mouth pulled down into a semi-playful pout. 'Oh, she does that all right. Too much, it seems to me. She's been a little whirlwind of work the last few days – and you have to hand it to her, she is quick and neat and doesn't need telling twice about how things are done. Obvious that she's done a lot of it where she was before. So prompt and eager, she quite puts me to shame – and Cook is worse than ever about how I'm in a dream.'

He put his arm around her and gave her a quick squeeze. 'And are you?'

71

'P'raps,' she admitted, with a rueful smile. She got up suddenly and set off across the stile. 'It's very well for Fanny,' she said resentfully, 'I don't believe she goes to sleep at all. She doesn't seem to need to. I can hear her through the wall – tossing and turning and pacing up and down. Seems to go on half the night sometimes. Good thing the mistress didn't make us share a room – or neither of us would ever sleep a wink.'

He was panting to keep up with her. His breath was short again. He managed to control it well enough to say, 'Got bad dreams, I expect. It can't be easy, losing your family in a fire.'

She turned to stare at him. 'That's just what Sammy said.'

He grinned. 'And who's this Sammy I hear so much about?'

She blushed, but – as he'd rather hoped – she was much more cheerful talking about this lad. But it made a man feel old. His little girl, Edith, walking out with a young admirer of her own.

The twinge around his heart was not entirely caused by the dust, or even the worry about the change of job. He hadn't told anyone about that yet, of course. Not even Minnie – though he'd have to do it soon. Who was he to go giving anyone advice? But Edie was looking at him hopefully. He gave her arm a squeeze. 'Well, why don't you go to Fanny sometime soon, and tell her outright that you were wanting to be friends. Can't do any harm – you can hardly make it worse – and if she's shy and grieving, it might even help.'

'I believe I will. I'm glad we had this talk.' She
72

turned and hugged him, and he smiled at her. She was so young and lively – like her mother used to be. That Sammy Hern the gardener was a lucky chap. It was to be hoped that he was good enough for Edie, that was all. Perhaps – when all this business at the mine had settled down – he'd try to get his daughter to bring him home sometime, and let her family have a look at him and see.

Edith woke in a cheerful mood. She lay beneath the covers, listening to the rain. If it had set in wet again, she thought, that meant there was a chance that Sammy would be there when she went out in a little while to collect the eggs. She was glad that she'd told Father about Sammy, after all, and Father had seemed actually to quite approve of what he heard. She lingered for a moment, savouring the thought, then realized that her reverie had lasted far too long – again.

She climbed out of bed as quickly as she could, rinsed her face and hands in the cold water from the jug and rubbed her teeth with salt and soda till they gleamed. Then she pulled on her newly sponged white blouse, put on her gingham uniform and set off with the slops. Thank goodness that, these days, there was not so much to do first thing or she would never be ready to take the breakfast up. There were only the upstairs fires to sweep and lay. It was Fanny's job now to do the downstairs ones and brush the carpets.

As Edie hurried down the back steps with the pail – you never used the main stairs except

73

when working there – she paused by the baize door that led from the servants' staircase to the entrance hall. Yes, she could hear Fanny already hard at work: busy with the broom and dustpan by the sound of it. Edith scuttled to the kitchen as quickly as she could, but Cook was inclined to be rather sharp with her.

'And where you have been, miss? It's long past six o'clock. What time do you call this?'

Edith thought of saying that she called it seven minutes past, but instead she muttered something about sleeping rather late.

'Well, if that Fanny can get down on time, my girl, then you can do the same. She came down on the dot of six and she is hard at work by now.'

Edith flushed. She might have answered back, but remembered her promise to Father and said thoughtfully, 'She's looking a bit better, these days, isn't she? Filling out a bit and looking a bit less drawn and desperate.'

'I'll give you "desperate" if you don't make a start. Go and do those slops and then get yourself upstairs. Nobody would think that you had work to do. Oh, and there's bread and ham for you when you come down again at eight,' she added, not unkindly, and went back to scalding milk.

Edith emptied the contents of her washing bowl dutifully into the row of cabbages that Mr Gribbens had planted closest to the house – soap got rid of the bugs and things, so Sammy always said – then scuttled back upstairs again to do the fires. Then there were the upstairs carpets to scatter tea-leaves on – damp ones so that the

74

dust all stuck to it and you could sweep them easier – and after that there were the beds to make and all the rooms to air. When she had finished she paused at the baize door. She'd not been very nice to Fanny once or twice, she knew, and if she wanted to make a new start there was no better time than now.

Edie pushed the door open and peered into the hall. Fanny was standing by the window with the dustpan in her hand, staring out into the street.

'Fanny?' Edith called to her.

Fanny jumped, so startled that she dropped the pan, scattering the tea-leaves and dust across the floor. She turned, with a look of such desolation on her face that Edith cried aloud, 'My dear life, Fanny, whatever is to do? I only came to say I wanted to be friends. I know I've sometimes been a bit off-hand with you.'

'Well, a fine start you've made of it. See what you have made me do!' It was clear that Fanny was very close to tears.

'Here, I'm sorry. Let me sweep them up.' Edith came over and tried to lend a hand, but the other girl snatched the dustpan savagely away.

'I can do it.' She bent over and began to clear the mess away. 'Though I don't suppose it will do me any good. You've made it very clear that you don't want me here – and I'm sure you'll have your wish. In the end they'll throw me on the street again.'

It was almost the first time she'd volunteered a word – and Edith felt a proper worm for having been so cross. She tried to make up for it by being friendly now. 'Miss Alicia will keep you if she can, I think. It's only that her stuck-up brother might object.' She gave the younger girl a sympathetic smile. 'And she'd give you a good character if he does, I'm sure. You're a good little worker. Make me look foolish sometimes, the speed you get things done.'

The other girl gave her an uncertain smile. 'Don't worry about that. It's clear that Mrs Pritchard is very fond of you. And I'm not after your job, I want one of my own.'

The idea of Mrs Pritchard being fond of her was rather a surprise, and Edith tried to earn the accolade by thinking of something sensible to say. 'Isn't there anyone to whom you could apply? Our Mr Edwin runs a mission, come to think of it. Perhaps he could help you find some other post.'

Fanny's 'No!' was like a cry of pain.

Edith felt as if she had been slapped. She shrugged and turned away. 'Well, if you won't be helped...'

'It isn't that, Edith.' Fanny's face was crumpling. 'It's just ... well...' She broke off. 'I can't really tell you. I can't go to any mission for the poor, that's all. It's just what people would expect that I would do.'

Edith turned and stared at her again. 'People? What people?'

Fanny shook her head and wouldn't meet her eyes.

'You're afraid someone will find you? But you said your folks were dead. So who is it then? The police? You're in some kind of trouble, is that what it is?' The conversation had taken a

76

most peculiar turn.

Fanny shook her head again. 'I am not in trouble. Not the way you mean. And it's not the police.' She turned away and bent down to the floor again. 'Now mind your feet and let me clean these tea-leaves up.'

Edie stood her ground. 'But there must be someone after you! Or you would not have said...'

Fanny's face was stricken as she looked up at her. 'Well, I'm afraid there might be – though I can't be sure. Someone that I've been afraid of all my life. And I don't want them to catch me. That's all it is. And now that my mother and everyone are dead ... There, now! I knew I'd go and say too much one day.' She broke off with a little sob.

'But surely no one could have a claim on you? Unless it's some relation?'

Fanny simply nodded. Tears were streaming down her face. 'I suppose you could say so. A very distant one. I hate him, Edie. And he's so horrible to me. You can't imagine it.'

'So that's why you didn't want to answer an advertisement? You thought perhaps this person would manage to trace you, is that it?'

'He might work out that I would come down to my aunt.' Fanny's words were coming out in sobbing bursts. 'And if he started asking questions...'

'Well, why don't you talk to Miss Alicia or Cook? I'm sure they'd understand. Who is it you're afraid of?'

A sob. 'I can't tell you that. I've said too much

77

already. Don't ask me any more. And promise me you'll never, never breathe a word to anyone. If he ever came and found me, I believe I'd kill myself.'

'All right,' Edith said, 'I promise. I said I wouldn't tell.' Of course, she'd had her fingers crossed behind her back, which – as everybody knew – meant that the promise didn't count. But she would never betray a secret told her by a friend.

'Thank you, Edith. I knew you were a chum, otherwise I'd never have trusted you like this. If they caught up with me ... you can't imagine what they'd do.' She shuddered, then went on in a more normal voice, 'In the meantime, I suppose I'd better clean the floor. I think I can hear someone coming up the stairs.'

It was Queenie, puffing and panting with her pail. 'Whatever are you two doing? You're wanted down below. I'm sent to fetch you, and Cook is spitting tacks.'

'My lor'!' Edith said, and ran downstairs at once. She expected to be sent out to the hen shed for the eggs, but Mrs Pritchard was too quick for her. 'Edith, you can take the mistress up her tea. Fanny can go out and get the eggs for once. And don't look like that at me. Do you think that I don't know why you're so keen on going out to the shed? I wasn't quite born yesterday, though you might think I was. So you can take that tray instead. Your breakfast will have to wait till you come down again. Serves you right for dallying half the day upstairs.'

So there was nothing for it but to go up with

the tray, and Mrs Pritchard kept her on the run for hours. It wasn't till much later that she met Fanny on the stairs.

'Didn't see anyone in the chicken shed, I suppose?'

Fanny shook her head. 'I didn't run into anyone at all. But the eggs were waiting in the other basket by the door, and there was a bunch of wild flowers on the top of it. I thought perhaps that they were meant for you, so I hid them in my apron and smuggled them upstairs. They're in your room behind the washstand, on the floor.' She gave a shy and conspiratorial smile. 'And of course I didn't say anything to Cook.'

So that morning was a sort of turning-point. Father had been right. Telling Fanny outright that she wanted to be friends had broken the ice between them in a dramatic way. They had shared each other's secrets, and – though by a kind of mutual consent they avoided talking of those secrets, even between themselves – there was a bond between herself and Fanny ever afterwards.

The flowers were wilting when Edie got upstairs, and of course she had to get rid of them next day, but it gave her a little flush of pleasure all the same. She'd have to thank Sammy when she saw him next – supposing that Mrs Pritchard ever let her near the chicken shed again.

Five

Tim Tulver was delighted when Edwin's note arrived and gave him an excuse to visit Holvean House again. Delighted, though naturally a little flustered too. He wondered when would be the most appropriate time to call. Not in working hours this time, perhaps – it was not directly trustee business, after all – and if he went then he would be expected back at his post promptly, so there would be no opportunity to linger if he was invited to take tea. Next half-day closing when the bank was shut and he could reasonably call there in the afternoon – that seemed the first available possibility.

He prepared himself with extra special care – went home and changed his coat, put on his new stiff collar and his best cravat, and combed his hair meticulously into place with brilliantine. His mother looked appraisingly at him as he came in to say goodbye, interrupting her letter-writing to demand in an accusing tone of voice, 'Going somewhere special, Timothy?'

He shook his head though, dammit, he was sure that he had flushed. 'Going to see a client this afternoon, that's all. One of Mr Symons's that I've just taken on. One wants to make a good impression, doesn't one?'

80

His mother pursed her lips into a knowing smile. 'Of course.' She presented a wrinkled cheek for him to kiss. 'Are you expecting to be home for tea? Or does that depend on how impressed she is?'

'Yes. I mean ... no. That is, I can't be sure.' Mater had made him disconcerted, as she always did, but – for once – he wasn't going to tell her everything, and he would not commit himself to being home betimes. He said in a deliberately portentous way, 'There's a lot of business to discuss. It may take me some time.' He went out into the hall and picked up his hat and coat.

It was not until he'd got outside the door, and was priding himself on how well he'd handled her this time, that he realized that he had tacitly agreed that the client in question was indeed a female. Dammit, twice! Now there'd be an inquisition when he got home, no doubt. He was still feeling foolish when he got to Holvean House, but he squared his shoulders, walked boldly down the path and rapped the lion-knocker on the heavy door.

He was admitted this time by a different girl – presumably the one that Edwin was concerned about, and it had to be conceded that his co-trustee had cause. She seemed to be nervous of answering the door: peered through an adjacent window like a frightened mouse before she opened it, though when she did she was entirely polite.

'It's Mr Tulver from the bank. I've come to see Miss Alicia Killivant.' He gave her what he hoped was a discreet appraising glance. 'Whom were you expecting?'

She turned an embarrassed brick-red at once. 'Why, no one, sir,' she stammered. 'It's just ... them boys from up the street. I think they know that Edie's got a half-day off, and they plague me by ringing the doorbell now and then, that's all. And of course I wasn't told we were expecting anyone. I wouldn't for the world have been so impolite.'

She looked so contrite that he almost smiled. 'Never mind. I don't have an appointment, but I've been asked to call. I hope I find Miss Killivant at home?'

She coloured up again. Quite a pretty creature, if she were not so thin – if you could think about a servant in that way. 'Of course, sir. Let me take your coat and hat, and if you would care to wait in here...' She led the way into the drawing-room. 'Mr Tulver, I believe you said? Am I to tell Miss Alicia what it is about?'

He could hardly answer, in the circumstances. Perhaps the girl guessed that this concerned herself, because she had turned that ugly red again. 'Tell her that her brother requested me to call. That's all, thank you, Fanny. You are Fanny, I suppose?'

A look of nervous horror flashed across her face. 'How do you know that? Oh, Mr Edwin told you my name, I suppose?' Her colour faded and she heaved a sigh. 'I knew that Miss Alicia would write to him about me in the end. You've come on his behalf to see me turned away?' She gave a bitter smile. 'I'll save you the trouble, sir. I'll pack my things and go.'

'Nonsense, child!' He had held up a rebutting hand, he realized – for all the world as Edwin would have done himself. 'I have come to discuss arrangements with Miss Alicia, that's all. So if you would go and fetch her – as quickly as you can?'

'Yes, sir.' And Fanny disappeared at once, to come back ten minutes later with Alicia Killivant. 'Mr Tulver, Miss.'

'Very well, Fanny. You can bring us tea.' Alicia was as striking as he had remembered her. Even her dress was unconventional. Her hair was caught up in a sort of snood, and her dress was of some shiny green material which almost matched her eyes – though the expression in them was as fiery as the ruby at her throat. 'So, Mr Tulver, to what do we owe the unlooked-for honour of a second visit?' And then she added, before he had collected himself enough to answer this, 'I understand my brother has instructed you to call. I am to be required to dismiss poor Fanny Watt, I suppose?'

'On the contrary.' He was making that gesture with his hand again! He put it deliberately behind his back. 'I have by no means made up my mind that she should be dismissed. Your brother asked me to call in and have a look at her, and make sure that she was an appropriate type of girl, that's all.'

'Meaning that he does not trust my judgement on that point? Or that of my mother? This is still her house.' She was confronting him. She sounded roused and she had pointedly not asked him to sit down.

83

He ventured a small, conciliatory smile. 'Edwin is concerned for your safety, Miss Killivant, that's all.' He had almost addressed her as 'Alicia', as he had done in his daydreams once or twice. 'He says you have no information about this girl at all. She tells you some story about a fire and claims that she only came down here to find an aunt, but she has no written reference as to character and you have no proof that any of what she says is true.'

Alicia looked triumphant – and magnificent, he thought. 'Except that the information about her aunt is verified. I asked Edith to check up on that for me – we didn't tell Fanny, so she could not interfere. Edith found out where the aunt was supposed to live, and went and asked some questions of the neighbours round about. And there had been a woman of that description there, who had suddenly packed up and gone to join her son abroad. None of the neighbours had any forwarding address – beyond that it was somewhere in Australia.'

He frowned. 'That might be a mere coincidence, of course. A great many miners' widows have sons abroad these days – with the goldfields in America, and South Africa and the other colonies.'

Alicia shook her head. 'One of the neighbours remembered Fanny calling by, and being quite distraught to find the woman gone. So that part was true, at least. It makes one feel quite churlish to have questioned it.'

That was aimed at him. He hastened to atone. 'So it seems that Fanny may be what she claims

84

to be. That's a reassuring fact. And she's hard-working, do I understand?'

'Invaluably so. A great many jobs are being done which have been postponed for years because we didn't have the staff. And it's not only that. Who would have answered the door to you today, if she'd not been here? Mrs Pritchard probably, the housekeeper and cook. Or possibly Nurse Morgan, if she had heard the bell. Neither of which is very satisfactory, as I'm sure you will agree.'

Jove, she was a splendid woman when she held her ground like that. Her brother called her 'headstrong' and no doubt he was right, but there was something damnably attractive about a girl with fire. He moulded his face into a sympathetic smile. 'I agree it is not customary to have the housekeeper greeting your callers in the afternoon. I'm sure she has many other pressing duties to perform. And the nurse as well, no doubt.'

She looked at him with obvious surprise. 'Exactly, Mr Tulver. You take my point, I see.' She sat down on one of the two fireside wing chairs and indicated – at last – that he should take the other one, before she said, in a much friendlier tone, 'And this is a problem which happens every week, or did, until Fanny came along. I have told my brother, it's an embarrassment when visitors are greeted by a floury pinafore.'

He essayed a little joke. 'Or a nurse's uniform and a syringe?'

'I see you understand.' She actually smiled.

'And Edith is entitled to her free half-day. She asked if she could have Thursday this week – it is her mother's birthday or something, I believe – and now that we have Fanny, I was able to agree. Just the sort of kindness you'd think my brother would approve.' She leaned towards him and added in a conspiratorial tone, 'Mr Tulver, you will explain all this to him when you write?'

He nodded solemnly. 'You can rely on me.' It gave him a thrill of pleasure to be able to say that – like a knight in shining armour. But she was looking at him sharply. He must not seem too easily impressed. He made another steeple with his finger ends. 'I can see that there is a need for someone else. But is this girl the proper candidate? She had a furtive manner, answering the door – as if she were too nervous to do the job at all.'

She was on her feet again, indignant and upset. 'And how do you imagine you would feel in her place? Knowing that my brother is anxious to have her sent away, and so lose – not only her position, though that is bad enough – but also the only place the poor girl has to live. No wonder she is nervous when she hears the door. She must have seen you through the window-glass and guessed that Edwin had requested you to call. We have so few callers in the normal way.'

'Miss Killivant...' He was about to point out that she was arguing against herself. If there weren't many callers, then they didn't need an extra maid for answering the door. But Alicia looked him in the eyes, and he was lost.

'Yes, Mr Tulver?'

86

'I think we might call Fanny in and tell her she may stay, on the conditions which you previously agreed. The fact that you have checked her story out – at least in part – puts a different complexion on the case. Even if you don't engage her when she's worked out her trial, I will help you to assist her afterwards by giving her a character so she can find a post. I'm sure that Edwin could not object to that.'

Alicia looked at him with laughter in her eyes. 'Then, Mr Tulver, I fear that you don't know my brother very well.' She reached over and took his hand in both of hers. 'But I am very grateful to you for your support. I hope you'll write and tell him what your conclusions are? And here is Fanny with the tea, so we can tell her the good news.'

'Well, did you ever?' Edie exclaimed next day, turning the corner by the gate and finding Sammy there. She was going to collect a pair of Miss Alicia's boots, which were being mended by the shoemaker, and he was up a ladder trimming back the hedge. 'Imagine seeing you.'

He grinned his freckled grin. 'No good waiting by the hen-house any more. Only get that Fanny coming for the eggs.' He put down his shears and looked up and down the street. There was no one coming, and he came down the steps. 'She tells me that fellow from the bank called yesterday, and is telling Mr Edwin that she's got to stay. Make your life a bit easier with an extra pair of hands, but I can't say I'm delighted. Never get to see you in the morning now.'

'You're seeing me this minute,' she said playfully.

'Only 'cause Fanny told me you were being sent to town.' Which meant that Sammy had lain in wait for her, and timed the task to meet her walking by.

She giggled. 'She didn't, did she? That was good of her.' She looked into his eyes. 'And thank you for the flowers. She told me about those.'

'All the same, I'd rather you'd found them for yourself.' He looked both pleased and pink. 'Still, I'm glad she told you. Funny sort of girl. Doesn't seem to want to talk. If you ask her questions she's like a startled goose. And then she'll blurt out something like your coming here today – and anyone would think she really wants to be a friend.'

Edie grinned. 'It's like I told you when she came here first. She's hard to get to know. But she's quite nice really, when she thaws out a bit. Like as if she didn't trust you, when she first arrived – look how she hid her package of clothes out here in the rain.' She squeezed his fingers hard. 'Good thing you hadn't cut the hedges when she came. She couldn't have hid anything in them now.'

She'd meant it as a tease but he was frowning suddenly. 'But hang on a minute – how did she come to have anything at all? If the house was burnt down like you said it was? How weren't her things all lost in the fire? And you might say the same for her. How is she the only one that got away?'

88

She looked at him, astonished. She hadn't thought of that. 'What are you saying, Sammy Hern?' she cried. 'You think there's something fishy about her story, then?' She shook her head. 'I don't believe there is. Fanny's a good sort. I was a bit put out at first when Madam took her on, but I've got to like her in a funny way. And I'm sure she's honest. Cook put all the traps out – left money on the floor, even put a half a crown behind the hall-stand by the door – and Fanny picked it up and brought it back to her. And the part about her aunt is true. Miss Alicia sent me out to find the place.'

He had let her go. 'So Miss Alicia had her doubts as well?'

Edie was impatient. 'Well, there wasn't cause to have. I found the house at once. Funny sort of place. Miles from the village, like a sort of tiny barn with a stone staircase outside to the upper floors. Belonged to the mine-owners, so the neighbours said, and they let the woman keep it when her husband died. I looked in through the window, but I couldn't really see. Somebody else there now by the look of it. But there really was an aunt and she really moved away. A Mrs Polcurnooth, or some strange name like that. Something that I'd never heard of in my life.'

'But I thought that Fanny's name was Watt?' He still looked unconvinced.

'This was her mother's married sister – what do you expect?'

He grunted. 'I suppose so. Yes, of course, you're right. But it's still funny about that bundle though. Unless she wasn't there. Not in the house when it caught fire, I mean. But in that case why would she have taken a change of clothes with her?'

There was an explanation, Edie thought. She slipped her hand in his again. 'I shouldn't tell you this. But there was someone up there – where she used to live – who she was afraid of. I don't know who it is, but she is obviously really terrified. You don't suppose this person ... I think it is a man ... might have set fire to the house, do you? Done it on purpose – but she got away? Knew he was coming, and escaped, perhaps – never expecting he would set the place on fire?'

Sammy was frowning down at her again. 'Seems a little bit far-fetched to me. You really think it might be something of the kind?'

She squeezed his fingers. 'I tell you, Sammy, she's frightened for her life. But you have to swear that you won't say a word. I promised faithfully I'd keep it to myself.'

He shook his head at her. 'Well, I hope you keep your promises to me a little better, then. You promised faithfully that you'd walk out with me and I've not seen you since. No' – he flashed his cheeky grin at her – 'I'm only fooling, Edie, don't look at me like that. 'Course I know you'd meet me, if you had the chance. And of course I won't say anything if you don't want me to. None of our business in any case, I suppose. So why are we standing, wasting time like this? Someone will be along directly, sure as eggs are eggs, and I shan't have a chance to put my arms round you at all.'

'Who said I'd let you?' she demanded with a laugh, but of course she did – and for two magic moments she stood there clasped to him, before they heard the butcher's boy approaching on his bike. They only just managed to leap apart in time, and Edith had to scurry into town and get the boots.

Edwin's next letter was cool in the extreme, but somehow it didn't irritate Alicia very much this time. In fact it was rather inclined to make her smile, such was the tone of affronted injury.

I understand that Mr Tulver has approved your choice. I cannot say that I am over-joyed, but since I requested him to act in this for me, I suppose I am obliged to abide by his advice. You may keep this Fanny, on trial or otherwise, until such time as I can come down for myself – although I fear that with Claire in her current state of health, that may not be for weeks. I need hardly say that if you persist in this and want to give the girl a permanent position in the house, you will have to finance the expenditure yourself. I wash my hands of it, apart from signing the necessary consent. No doubt you can per-suade Mr Tulver to agree, since you seem able to persuade him of almost anything.
Your affectionate brother

She put the letter down. 'Affectionate broth-er'! She almost laughed aloud. You could tell he was incensed. And yet – like the time that

91

Charles had helped her cheat at Snap – she was guiltily aware that somehow she had won. It was not a sensation that she was accustomed to. It filled her with a kind of proud, defiant glee, as if she had found a mental strength she didn't know she had.

She had actually won the argument. And Edwin knew it. That was very clear. He had written as he might have written a grudging letter to a man. Not once in the letter had he called her 'Liss'. She was still smiling when the senior maid came in.

'Are you wanting me to clear the table, Miss?'

Alicia leaned back slowly in her chair, in the same posture she'd seen Edwin use. 'Do you know, Edith, I think I'll have another round of toast. Two new rounds, freshly buttered, can you see to that? And perhaps another pot of tea?'

'Of course, Miss Alicia, I'll fetch it up at once.' The girl looked so astonished that it almost made you laugh. Of course, it was an unusual request – the sort of thing that only Edwin ever did these days.

'Oh, and while you're down there, Edith, you can bring some marmalade. That special lime and ginger that Mr Edwin likes. I think you'll find there is some in the pantry still.'

Edith was still looking as if she couldn't trust her ears. 'Mr Edwin's marmalade?'

'The marmalade I buy for Mr Edwin, yes. I have a fancy to try a little for myself. I don't believe there's any rule that says I can't.'

The servant had turned very pink about the ears. 'Of course not, Miss Alicia. I wasn't meaning that. I'll go and fetch it up for you at once.'

It was delicious, too – though if it had tasted of aloes, Alicia would have relished it today.

Part Two

Christmas 1909 – Spring 1910

One

They closed the mine for Christmas – the only day they did, without there was an accident or something in the year. Only a few people were kept working Christmas Day: engineers like Cap'n Maddox to keep the pumps alive, and one or two people to check on safety underground – mostly bachelors, or older people who had lost their wives, and who didn't have much Christmas to go home to anyway. Pearce and two others were staying on in the dressing-sheds to clean the buddles out and check over the separating tables where the 'slimes' were streamed to extract the last particles of tin – but otherwise the dressing-workers were not required at all. So Teddy had the luxury of spending time at home.

For it had come to it. He had taken Maddox's advice and moved into the sheds, though the humiliation had been hard to bear. Had to go up cap in hand and ask the masters for the job – as though he were a fourteen-year-old coming straight from school. And they kept him waiting – said they'd let him know, and made him come back again next day to hear that they'd agreed – though Cap'n Maddox said later that they'd meant to have him all along.

In the end it had worked out all right, though

the other men were guarded with him, on the whole – turned out he'd been preferred over an old hand in the sheds – and Teddy sorely missed his friends from underground. The work was nothing like as interesting, besides – none of the excitement of finding a good seam. But at least the job was 'up to ground', and there was none of that choking panic that had come on him of late. Despite the dust – and there was lots of that – he was sure he wasn't coughing half so much these days.

Minnie's reaction had been a big surprise.

He'd been expecting trouble, when she learned about the change, and when he grasped the nettle finally and told her what he planned she put down her floor-cloth and sat down on the step, sobbing and burying her head in both her hands.

That alarmed him, because she wasn't one for tears, and he got down gently and squatted by her side. 'Now look 'ere, Minnie, it isn't settled yet. Of course I'll stay on underground, if that is what you want. I only thought of moving, on account of this here cough. If it wasn't for what Cap'n Maddox said the other day...'

He broke off. She was staring at him, tears still on her cheeks. 'Oh, be quiet, you daft lummox. I'm crying with relief. Don't you think I worry about you every day – you with that awful hacking, like my father had? Look what happen- ed – he never made old bones. And your lungs haven't fared much better, from what I hear of it. Miner's lungs, my father had, that's what the trouble was. I know that you were always proud of working underground, but I'd much sooner you were safely in the dressing-sheds.'

He shook his head. He'd never guessed that Minnie felt like that.

She seemed to think the gesture meant that he was not so safe after all, because she went on hastily, 'Of course, I know that there are sometimes accidents – there always is where there's machinery – but at least I won't be worried that you're blown to kingdom come, or buried under a load of rock somewhere. And it will be same with Abel, when he follows you. Get him a position topside, if you get the chance. Never mind the pay.'

Teddy nodded slowly. 'Might see if they need someone in the workshops, p'raps. Either the blacksmith or the carpenter. They're always short of boys. Of course, I can't afford a proper apprenticeship for him. He'll have to start by sweeping up, or fetching and carrying tools to be repaired, but make a good impression and you never know. The mine-owners sometimes let a youngster have an hour or two, to go down to the Workers' Institute and do an evening class, if the shift-cap'n thinks he shows something that they call 'huptitude.'

A nod. 'That would be something. Give the lad a trade.'

'He'd have to pay for classes, but we might just run to that, specially if he's bringing in a few bob himself by then. And Abel has always been handy with his hands.'

That made her laugh. 'Well, he isn't likely to be handy with his feet! And don't you go worrying about how we'll make ends meet. Better a smaller wage-packet than the "hurt" fund, any day. I'll make a nice Christmas for us, you see if I don't.'

And she had done, too. Wove a 'hoop' of greenery and hung it overhead, with apples and oranges dangling temptingly, less a decoration than a work of art. Mistletoe and holly were draped on every shelf, and come the day itself there was a pair of knitted socks or gloves for everyone in turn, as well as a penny whistle or some other treat all wrapped and set out invitingly beside the kitchen fire.

And the table was a triumph. They didn't have a goose, but there was cold roast and cold boiled and a piece of ham, and plenty of carrots and potatoes from the pile (he always dug them early and covered them in straw, and they came out delicious – just as these had done). And for afterwards she'd contrived plum pudding too, cooked in the copper in the outhouse in a cloth, and big enough for all of them to have a steaming slice, and a bit left over for when Edie came.

And Edie did come, shortly after lunch, laden with little parcels. She must have saved her precious sixpences for weeks, and for the first time ever had managed 'boughten' gifts, and the squeaks and squeals which greeted each of them was 'better'n a circus', Nana said. (Nana was Minnie's mother who had come in for the day.) There were penny dolls and spinning-tops and hair ribbons and drums, and then it was the adults' turn: a scented soap for Meg, a mouse-trap for Nana (very useful, that) and even a plug of best tobacco for himself. But the violet scent 'for Mother' was the best surprise. It must have cost Edie a whole sixpence, but it was worth it for the smile.

Then it was Edie's turn to open things. She was delighted with her pair of knitted gloves. And there were presents from the others, too. A cheerful peg-rug made of strips of rag, which had cost her sisters hours of patient work, some well-named 'rock buns' which the younger boys had made, in a useful tin which Abel had painted with enamel paint. Nana had looked out a lovely underskirt, made of red flannel and cosy as could be, and only a little bit worn around the seams.

'What a lovely Christmas,' Edie sighed at last, as they sat down to sandwiches of left-over ham. 'They can't have such a good one, even up at Holvean House. And, here, did I tell you what Miss Alicia gave us girls? Two pairs of lisle stockings and a length of gingham each, to make ourselves a brand-new morning uniform. And she told Fanny that she'd worked out her trial, and that after Christmas she'd be working for a wage. Only three and sixpence, and all found, but Fanny's thrilled to bits. Best present that she could have had, she said. Wasn't that handsome of Miss Alicia?'

He looked at his daughter. 'I suppose that was the only Christmas present your poor Fanny had – seeing as she doesn't have a family of her own.'

Edie blushed. 'Well, it wasn't quite the only thing she got. She had a linen hanky too – from

101

me. I had a bit left over when I made one for Sam, and I hemmed it up for her and put an "F" on it. She was that delighted, I thought that she would cry.'

Teddy cocked an eye at her. 'And Sammy too?' he said. 'Though, if you made it, I expect he'd like it anyhow.'

Minnie stopped pouring, the teapot in her hand. 'What's this about a "Sammy"? Something I should know?'

Edie coloured up again, and stared into her cup. 'It's only Pa's fooling. Don't you take no heed.' She turned to the littlest ones and went on, in a very different tone of voice, 'Now, did I tell you about the Christmas tree? Great big fir-tree bigger than that door. Mr Gribbens brought it in and stood it in the hall, and me and Fanny helped Miss Alicia dress it up last night. It looked a proper picture, when we'd done with it. Little wooden ornaments that we fetched down from the loft, and dozens of little candles set on tiny spikes. Like something from a picture in a story-book.' And she held them enthralled with stories from the house. She'd make a lovely mother sometime, Teddy thought – though not a patch on Minnie. Who could equal her? Who else could have made such a Christmas out of nothing much?

It was so cold and frosty when it was time to go that Edie was even more reluctant than usual to leave. She should have gone sooner, that was the truth of it, knowing that she faced that long walk in the dark. But there was no alternative; there were no horse-buses today, and no passing friendly farmer in a cart to offer her a lift – as sometimes happened – even a little way towards Penzance. She pulled the hood of her cloak round her ears and stamped her booted feet – already the icy damp was creeping in to nip her toes. At least her hands were warm – thank heavens for the gloves.

She sighed, and was about to set off on the path, when a voice behind her made her whirl around. It was her father, with a lantern in his hand.

'Can't have you walking all that way alone – not in this weather, and in all this dark. Here, let's have your basket, and I'll keep you company. Glad of a breath of air, in any case.' He was already through the gate and walking off along the road.

She hurried to catch him, grateful but concerned. 'You sure you're up to it? You don't want to catch a chill. I'm sure you've got something on your chest in any case.'

He grinned at her, the lantern throwing shadows on his face so that his cheekbones looked unnaturally high. 'If there's anyone got something to get off their chest, it's you. This Sammy, for example. I didn't mean to tease and make you all embarrassed in front of the younger ones, but it's time we heard a little more about him, seems to me. No, don't turn away, I aren't scolding you at all – but it's clear you're fair besotted with this young gardener-chap and – if that's the case – I think me and your mother have a right to know.'

She was glad of the dark to hide her blushes now. 'I'm not besotted. He's just nice, that's all. A good hard worker, Mr Gribbens says. Of course I know it can't be serious – not for a year or two at least – but if he can manage to get a gardener's job at some big house one day, there might be a cottage or anything, he says. And my skills would come in handy – they often take a couple, in a place like that.'

There was a long silence before her father said, 'So you've talked about it, have you?'

'Well, not in so many words. How could we, at the moment? But he asked me to walk out with him, and all that sort of thing.'

'Made it clear he'd like to think of marriage by and by?'

The flush behind her ears was making her feel warm, despite the wind. 'Well, not exactly that. But I'm sure that he's sincere. You should've seen the Christmas present that he made for me ... A pretty handmade wooden spoon with flowers and doves on it. Did it in the evenings. It must have taken hours.'

'Perhaps I should have seen it, like you say.' He helped her through the field-gate and fastened it again, then slipped an arm through hers and hugged it to his side, though he still held the basket in his hand. 'I'd like to have seen it, if you'd only brought it home. And, for that matter, this famous Sammy too. Don't you think your Ma and I would like to meet this man? Even if the little ones do rag you both a bit?'

'You want me to bring him?' Her heart was thumping now. Suppose they didn't like him?

But of course they would. Sammy was so easy, and comical and ... nice. So why was she feeling that he did not quite belong in that cosy, crowded cottage that she'd just left behind? Even as she asked herself, she realized what it was. 'His family aren't mining folk, of course, you know. Always worked in gardens, and that sort of thing.'

'Miners and gardeners – they both use picks and spades. I dare say we can find enough to talk about.' He was laughing at her.

She gave his ribs a nudge. 'Well, I'll try and bring him sometime, if that's what you want – though it's not as simple as you make it sound. He gets a half-day, same as me, of course, but it's very rarely that we're both off at once. And don't go saying that we could ask for it – if Miss Alicia knew I had a follower, she'd very likely dismiss the pair of us. Though Mrs Pritchard seems to be aware. She's told me off already for loitering with the hens, and she must have seen us after lunch today.'

'And what were you doing?' Her father's voice was sharp.

She pressed his arm against her. 'Nothing very much. Just exchanging presents. The outside staff were eating with us in the kitchen too, with it being Christmas, instead of having theirs in Mr Gribbens's quarters like they usually do. Well, when we had all finished, Cook went and got a tray and had Fanny clear the table, and asked Mr Gribbens to get some leeks for her. While they were busy they had their backs to us, so Sam slipped me his present and I gave him his

– and just as we were doing it, I saw Cook turn around.'

'Seems to me, she set it up for you.' They had reached the lane by now, and the going was easier. He held the lantern higher and grinned into her face. 'So she caught you in the act, eh? And what did the dreaded Mrs Pritchard say to that?'

It made her giggle. 'Just asked me for my saucer. Pretended she'd gone blind. But she'll have eyes like awls tomorrow – boring through the wall to watch you breathing if you don't look out.'

Father started laughing and it made him cough. Edie took the lantern while he doubled up and choked. She was frightened for a moment, but the coughs started to subside. 'Something in my throat,' he muttered, when he had recovered. 'I'm right as rain again. Or will be if you bring that Sammy when you have a chance. Now let's look lively. There's still a way to go. Can I hear carols? I believe I can.'

He took back the lantern and slipped her arm through his again, hugging it to him till they reached the house. And ever afterwards, when she looked back on it, it always seemed a magic evening between the two of them, walking through the darkness and listening to the evening bells, the 'curl' singers in the distance, and the sighing of the sea.

You couldn't envy Fanny, upstairs all alone. Or Miss Alicia either, if it came to that.

'Alicia has decided to give that girl a permanent

position,' Edwin said crossly, as he put the letter down. 'I was still hoping that she'd show a bit of sense and let her go.'

Claire didn't answer and he looked across at her. She was sitting, big and cumbersome, in her breakfast chair poking a desultory fork around her scrambled egg. She was grimacing too, the way she did these days. She'd done nothing but grumble in the last few weeks that she was uncomfortable and had an aching back. Christmas had seemed to make it worse, if anything, and she did not seem to welcome his attempts to help.

'Did you hear me, dearest?' he essayed, again. He had tried to make her take an interest in the papers and the mail – even talked to her about the latest fashions once or twice – but she scarcely answered him and (though she had chosen the menus for herself) she had fallen into the habit of picking at her food, as she was doing now.

She only shook her head as if she didn't care.

He took a careful spoonful of strawberry preserve and spread it on his toast. 'If you are as uncomfortable as you appear, my dear, perhaps you should consider retiring back to bed. Or perhaps we should take a little turn around the back garden before I go today. You know the doctor told you that you should move about – to help your circulation – since he says there are still two weeks or so to go.'

'Two more weeks,' she muttered. 'I think I'd rather die.'

'Oh, come now,' he said sharply. As a clergyman he couldn't let that pass without reproof. 'That's not a very Christian sentiment. You're in a delicate condition, that is all it is. It will be over shortly, and this will all have been worthwhile.'

She raised resentful eyes and looked him in the face. 'It's very well for you, Edwin. You don't have to endure it. Looking and feeling like a hippopotamus. Swollen feet and ankles, and an aching back, to say nothing of being kicked in the stomach now and then and getting fearful cramps. Nothing very delicate about it, would you say?'

The anger surprised him. Claire was rarely roused. He finished the last morsel of the toast and jam and dabbed his lips briefly with his napkin before he said, 'Now, now, dearest. Do not upset yourself. Perhaps a breath of air would be good for both of us. I'll stroll around the garden with you, when I've answered this – if I hurry I will still have time. But first I must write to Liss and tell her what I think.' He folded the letter back in its envelope.

She gave him that rebellious, hostile stare again. 'Why must you? I thought you said you'd signed the documents and washed your hands of it? It was your sister's problem now – that's what you said to me.'

'Dearest!' He intended the reproach. Claire was actually challenging his stated point of view! She was almost beginning to sound a bit like Liss. 'This is a matter of some significance.'

He rose and went to put his hand upon her arm, but she flinched away and after a moment said,

108

through gritted teeth, in a voice that was so strangled that it sounded like a hiss, 'For goodness' sake, Edwin, don't bother me just now. And go and write that confounded letter if you must. Though why you should care a whit about that dratted maid I cannot see. Can't you let it rest? You and your precious sister – it's all you think about. Liss, Liss, Liss, from morn till night. Can't you pay attention to your wife, for once?'

'But, Claire!' He was quite wounded. 'Of course I pay attention. Haven't I just said that I would take a stroll with you?' He tried to be magnanimous. 'Of course you're feeling a little under par just now. I try to raise your spirits. What more can I do?'

She didn't answer, and he saw that she had closed her eyes again and was grasping the table edge in both her hands. After a moment she let go of it, and said in a peculiar, urgent tone of voice, 'You can go and get the nurse you promised – that's what you can do – instead of standing wittering like the idiot you are! Can't you see that things are happening?'

He almost protested, but she let out such a groan that he set off at once, only pausing to ring down for the maid. He rushed downstairs, picked up his hat and coat and hurried out to take a cab and find the midwife's house. It was something he had meant to look into before. Fortunately the cabbie knew exactly where to go.

And of course when he reached the house, the woman wasn't there. Out dealing with another client, it appeared, since she'd not been expected to be called upon for weeks – though he was promised that she would come as soon as she got back.

He sent a message to the mission to say he would be late and went back to the house, but Claire had already taken to her bed. The room was obviously no place for a man, so he was reduced to hovering in the sitting-room, while maids went racing up and down with dampened cloths and ever louder groaning issued from above. It made him feel useless and incompetent, and that was not a sensation he was accustomed to.

Two

It was a full four hours before the woman came, and another twenty-four before they called him in. The doctor – he had sent out for a doctor in the end – came out on the landing and peered down into the hall, where Edwin was fidgeting on an upholstered chair.

'Congratulations, young Killivant. A daughter. Doing well. And your wife is pulling through. She's had a hard time but she should make progress from here on. You may come and see her – though not for very long. You must not tire her, she is very weak.'

He felt like a stranger in his own house as he went up the stairs. It was unsettling, having other people in control, and refusing you access to your own domain. But the doctor was standing by to show him into the darkened room.

He was quite prepared for bedlam as he walked through the door. The shrieks and groans had been quite terrible, and once or twice he'd had to leave the house. He had actually gone into church and fallen on his knees to pray that Claire might be delivered from all this – though in his heart of hearts he'd known that this was wrong. This was God's creation, and this was His decree. 'In sorrow shall you bring forth children.'

All the same, he'd prayed.

Then when he'd got back there'd been that dreadful hush, and then a burst of strange activity, servants clattering upstairs with bowls and steaming kettles and clattering down again with bloodstained towels and sheets. But he need not have worried now. The room was calm and orderly; only a strange, sweet, cloying smell hung in the air, while the doctor packed strange instruments into his Gladstone bag.

'Would Father like to hold her?' the nursing woman said, in the sort of voice one might use to a child. Without waiting for an answer, she thrust something in his arms, a little tight-wrapped bundle in a knitted shawl. He looked down at the child. It had a small, red, wrinkled face – rather like a monkey he'd once seen at the zoo, except that it was hairless and the eyes were tightly shut. He tried to feel a surge of proud, paternal joy, but nothing happened. The infant squirmed. It startled him. He gave it back again, fearful of dropping it.

The midwife cooed at it and placed it in the cot. His own cot, brought up from Holvean House by cart at great expense. Had he himself been small and wizened once? He supposed he must have been.

'...to spend a minute with your wife.' He realized that the doctor had been addressing him. 'The birth's been difficult, but she was very brave.'

Brave. He muttered a prayer of gratitude as he approached the bed. His wife and child had both survived the birth. Claire was lying on the pillow, not looking like herself. Her face was pale, her eyes and nose were red, and her pretty hair lay round her in damp, unbecoming hanks. They had put her in a nightdress and laid her in clean sheets, but he was uncomfortably reminded of those other sheets he'd glimpsed. It was so visceral, somehow, it filled him with unease.

Claire had opened weary eyes by now, and was murmuring his name. 'Edwin, is that you?'

'Yes, my dear.'

'Have you seen the baby?'

How did one answer? 'Very nice,' he said. And because that seemed inadequate somehow, he added, 'You did very well.'

'She didn't do it all alone. You had a part in it,' the midwife said in that arch tone again. She was collecting up strips of linen as she spoke. The doctor, he noticed, had packed his bag by now. 'Though it's just as well it was a girl this time. A bigger baby might have been too much for her – although she tells me you were hoping for a boy.'

'Next time, perhaps,' he muttered. It was a stupid thing to say.

Claire turned her face. 'There won't be a next time, Edwin. I can't go through that again.'

The midwife gave him a sidelong, knowing smile. 'They all say that to start with. She'll come around in time, just you wait and see. And the girl is healthy. Just give thanks for that. Have you decided on a name for her?'

The question quite surprised him. He had thought of names, of course, if it had been a boy. Charles, for his brother – or William possibly,

113

which was their father's name. But for a daughter he hadn't really made a choice. An idea struck him. 'We might call her Alicia Mary, I suppose.'

'Your family, Edwin? Can't we call her after mine? Didn't we say so, if it was a girl?'

He saw the look that crossed his wife's wan face. 'Dearest, we can hardly call her after you. We can't have two Claires living in the house. And Theodocia, for your mother, is not a name I like.'

'You could call her Holly, since it's this time of the year,' the midwife intervened. 'Or Ivy, that's a nice name – or what about Christine? Or even Caroline.'

'Caroline,' his wife said, faintly from the bed. 'Caroline Killivant. I like the sound of that.'

Edwin stared at her. Surely she must know that 'Carolus' was the Latin form of Charles. If they close that name the child would be called after his brother after all. But she seemed quite serious. He said, quite tenderly, before she changed her mind, 'Caroline it shall be, dear, if you wish it so.'

He paid the doctor and the nurse and went to register the birth. 'Caroline,' he told the man behind the desk. 'Caroline Edwina Alice Killivant.'

Claire would 'come around to it in time', as the midwife would have said.

There'd been no reply from Edwin for several days by now, although Alicia had braced herself for strictures, at the very least, when she'd

114

written to say that Fanny had been told that she could have a proper post.

Edwin had made it very clear that he did not approve: and though he'd given her the signed consent to access the money to pay Fanny's wage, he'd set the sum at three and six a week, in addition to the keep – considerably less than was usually paid. Even in a place as far from London as Penzance the average was at least a shilling more than that, and Edwin kept servants, so he must have known. He'd made it valid from the first of January, too, obviously intending to delay things if he could – but Alicia had calculated that she could still contrive to pay Fanny in arrears for the week which followed Christmas – as she'd pointed out to him in her last letter, rather gloatingly. Perhaps he'd taken umbrage, and was in a sulk.

Well, he deserved it, Alicia told herself. It had been quite embarrassing on Christmas Day, to summon Fanny to her and offer her the place at such a paltry wage. She would not have been surprised if the girl had asked to leave – though she would have given her a character, with pleasure, in that case. But Fanny had seemed genuinely delighted by the sum: of course, unlike Edith, she could keep it all herself, since she was not supporting anyone at home.

And now the time had come when she must first be paid, and there was no word from Edwin as to how this was to be done. Liss had received her usual allowance from the bank, but there was nothing extra to cover Fanny's wage. Well, she would go to town and see the bank herself. It was not a thing that she usually did, but this was money owed, and she would not allow Edwin's inactivity to prevent her from behaving properly as far as Fanny was concerned.

She rang down for Edith, who came up at a trot. 'Yes, Miss Alicia?' The girl had made a skirt and blouse out of the gingham length that she had given her at Christmas – it looked very well. The other one had recently begun to strain around the seams.

Alicia nodded her approval. 'Get your coat and take your apron off. I want you to accompany me. I am going to walk to town.'

The girl stood gaping. 'Walk, Miss Alicia?'

Alicia nodded. 'That is what I said.' She had privately decided not to take a hansom cab – Edwin would doubtless have queried the expense. Walking cost nothing, and it was not above a mile. Though she was not entirely confident of going without the maid – she had never had to find her way before. 'I have some business to see to at the bank.'

The girl was still hovering, looking unconvinced. 'You want me to fetch you an umbrella, Miss? It's not bad now but it might come on to rain.'

Alicia bit her lip. She hadn't thought of that. She had not walked, except for pleasure, since she had been at school. In fact, apart from going to church and the occasional visit to a dressmaker or friend – or going down to put Edwin on and off the train – these days she rarely left the house at all. The thought was sobering. She raised her head defiantly. 'An umbrella would be helpful, thank you very much. And you can look out my green bonnet, and the coat to match.'

'Now, Miss Alicia? Only Cook's expecting me – I'm supposed to be sieving that raw steak again to make some more beef tea for Mrs Killivant.'

Alicia made a dismissive gesture with her hand. 'Tell Mrs Pritchard that I am wanting you. Fanny will have to help her with the beef tea for a change. One advantage of having an extra pair of hands. Straight away, please, Edith.'

Of course it did take a little time to change for going to town, even though Edith came up and helped her with her hair, but half an hour later they had left the house. It was pleasant to be walking, even in the cold, and it made Alicia feel quite adventurous – except that her best white boots were new and inclined to pinch her toes. Besides, there were lots of other people in the streets – everyone from baker-boys and men on bicycles to stately ladies in impressive hats – so their presence excited no remark, though they were the only women to turn into the bank. Of course, she left Edith waiting in the entrance-way. One didn't do business with the servants looking on.

It was the first time Alicia had ever come alone, but the manager clearly recognized her face because he came out from his private cubicle at once. 'Miss Killivant, permit me...' He ushered her inside. She'd been in here before, when she'd come with Edwin once, and this time she was not so overawed by the impressive desk, all mahogany and brass, the rows and rows of files ranged on shelves around the wall, and the heavy door with 'Branch manager' etched in curly writing on the glass. The man himself had greying side-whiskers, and was as round and oily as an egg.

'To what do we owe the honour?' He indicated a battered leather chair where she should sit. 'Your mother's well, I trust?' He obviously feared she was the bearer of bad news.

She forced herself to smile. 'She's much as usual, thank you. But I'm not here on her account. I have called today about my own affairs. A matter of the trust. I understand that Mr Tulver is dealing with that now?'

'Of course, my dear young lady. I will see if he is free.' And he waddled off, although he looked a bit nonplussed. Alicia could see him in the main part of the bank, whispering to someone at the counter there, and a few minutes later Mr Tulver came – all pink confusion and eagerness to help. The business was concluded much more swiftly than she'd feared.

'Would you care for me to have it sent to you in future?' Mr Tulver was saying, as he counted out the cash. 'Save you coming down to get it every week?'

She realized that if she accepted this, he would be likely to come and deliver it himself, so she said hastily, 'There's no need for that. I'll come by once a month, and you can give me fourteen shillings then. The walk would do me good. Besides I shall doubtless have other things to see to in the town from time to time.' She said it confidently, though in truth there was nothing that generally required her to come, apart from an occasional visit to the dressmaker: most of the tradesmen delivered to the house.

Tim Tulver had turned scarlet and was saying earnestly, 'I shall look forward to your visits then. And if there is anything at all that I can do...'

'Thank you, Mr Tulver, you have been most kind.'

She proffered him her hand and he lingered over it, just long enough for the manager – who had been hovering at the door – to say, 'If you've finished, Mr Tulver, you may show the lady out', which made the poor fellow colour even more.

Edith had been shifting her weight from foot to foot, and wishing she was anywhere but standing at the bank, with everybody staring at her as they went in and out. She felt like one of they statues that they had in parks sometimes, 'neither use nor ornament', as Mother would have said.

It seemed simply ages before Miss Alicia came back, though it was only ten minutes by the big clock opposite, and the moment that she did so it came on to rain. Edith put the umbrella up, of course, and attempted at once to hold it over her mistress, but Miss Alicia was fearful for her hat.

'It's my very best one. I don't want it getting wet. And my best boots will spoil if we go out in this. It's only a shower. We'll shelter in the shops.'

'Yes, Miss Alicia. Shall we go in here?' Edith

did her best to sound merely dutiful, but secretly she was gleeful at the plan. Wouldn't Sam and Fanny be jealous when they heard? Half an hour to idle, with nothing else to do but look at the pretty merchandise in White's Emporium? Better than forcing horrid meat through strainers any day.

They had reached the shelter of the shopfront now, and Edith paused to shake the rain from the umbrella and close it up again, but as she turned to go into the shop she collided with a young woman who'd come in the other way, scattering the pile of papers which the girl was carrying.

'Oh, my dear life, what have I gone and done?' Edie was already scrabbling about, trying to retrieve the printed news-sheets from the ground, but the rain had been heavy and the pavement was all wet, so one or two copies had got very damp indeed.

Miss Alicia had obviously realized that something was amiss and had turned back from the inner doorway of the shop. 'What is it, Edith? What have you got there?'

'I'm some sorry, madam. I knocked her papers down.' Edith held up a sorry copy by one bedraggled edge, and almost succeeded in tearing it in half. The whole page had gone a funny colour with the wet and was already beginning to disintegrate.

'My dear young lady,' Miss Alicia exclaimed, turning to the owner of the papers with a smile, 'I must apologize. I fear my servant has cost you some expense. If you care to call at Holvean House a little later on, I will see that you are

120

compensated for any loss.'

Meaning it would come out of her wages, Edie thought.

The paper-bearer flushed. 'That is kind of you. It was as much my fault as hers. And some of the papers were already damp. I had them in an open leather bag around my neck, but when the policeman moved me on he broke the strap of it.'

Edie was astonished. 'The policeman did?' she said, so astounded that she forgot her place and joined in the conversation as a lady might.

The young woman nodded. She was nicely dressed – not fashionable, like Miss Alicia, but it was lovely cloth – and she spoke in an educated sort of way, besides. Not at all the sort of person to be arguing with the law. 'He pointed out that there's a law against what he called "hawking things on pavements". So I got in the gutter, though it was pretty wet – and he tried to move me on again. I refused to go at first, so he gave me a push. The bag got caught round a railing and the strap came off – and all the papers fell down in the street. So they were pretty wet before this incident. Please don't concern yourself on my account.' She gave a sudden grin – she had big teeth, but her smile still lit up her face. 'Anyway, it's my first time out with these. They won't expect me to have sold them all in any case.'

Miss Alicia looked at the sodden mass in Edith's hands. 'It says "Votes for Women". Are you one of them? I went to a meeting of the Movement once. But that was in London. I

121

didn't know they were down here.'

The young woman nodded. 'Oh, indeed we are. We don't enjoy huge numbers, but it's quite a lively group. Why don't you come and join us, if you are interested? There is a meeting every Wednesday night, and a guest speaker the first week of the month.'

Alicia took the paper out of Edith's hand. 'Well, I might do, if I find I have the time.' That was a wonder – what did Miss Alicia have to do, except sit and crochet or read a book or two? But perhaps it was simply that she didn't want to seem too keen, because she was asking in the same tone of voice, 'In the meantime, here is a penny for that newspaper. Where is this meeting?'

The other girl took the money and murmured an address. 'Seven for seven thirty. I'll look out for you. My name is Richie, by the way. Elizabeth Richie. People in the Movement tend to call me Beth.'

'Alicia Killivant.' The tone of voice was cool. 'People call me Miss Killivant as a rule.'

It was a definite rebuke, but Miss Alicia did hold out her hand, and the Richie person shook it, saying with a smile, 'Then welcome to the Movement for Women's Suffrage, Miss Killivant.'

Three

'Though what I can't for the life of me understand,' Edie said to her father the next time she went home, 'is why they call this meeting "Women Suffering". You'd think it would put people off from coming, wouldn't you? I s'pose it's 'cause the government's been putting them in jail. Miss Alicia was telling me about that – sounds simply terrible.' She glanced at her father. 'What you grinning for?'

They were out in the wash-house with the lamp alight, and Edie was helping him to make his inspection of the shoes – checking if the toes and heels were worn, and scraping the mud off with a knife so he could rub them clean and then apply the polish and brush it off again. It was a tedious business, with all those pairs of feet, but he'd taken to doing it the evening she was home – just for the pleasure of her company, she guessed. But he'd put the boot down and was laughing at her now. 'It isn't "suffering", Edie: it's some word like "suffrage" – they used to talk about the same for men. Fancy name for the right to vote for parliament, I think.'

Edie made a face at him. 'Oh, I see. But why would women want to do that anyway? What would the likes of Miss Alicia know about taxes and that sort of thing? It's a bit like asking you to go and choose a dress to cut a pattern from. You wouldn't know the first thing about where to start. Well, it's the same for her – choosing which man she wants to go to parliament.' He was still grinning, and it made her cross. 'And throwing stones at the Lord Mayor's banquet, up London, like those women did! How's that supposed to help?' She handed him one of Donny's little boots. 'This one's got a plate loose.'

'Make people take a bit of notice of them, I suppose,' he murmured peaceably, carefully selecting a couple of small tacks.

'I'd like to see what you would have to say if I started throwing stones to make you notice me! But with wealthy folk like Miss Alicia, it's different, I suppose.'

'As if I didn't notice you, young woman, as it is.' He turned over the 'cobbler's last' that he was working with – a strange-looking device with several iron tongues that looked a bit like feet, set so that you could stand it up any way you chose and have the size you wanted lying uppermost. It was very heavy and had cost no end, but Pa swore it had paid for itself a hundred times by now in what it had saved the family in cobbler's bills. He fitted the boot on to the smallest 'foot'. 'But all this suffrage business isn't just for the likes of Miss Alicia, you know. If these people have their way it will be Ma to vote as well – and you and Meg and Rosa and Suzanna one day, I suppose.'

'Have the Trewins running half the country,

shan't we?' Edie laughed. 'I wonder if Miss Alicia's thought of that?'

'Couldn't do much worse than the men do, seems to me. See what's happened now. Asquith and his Liberals are in a proper fix – got exactly the same number of seats as the Tories did, in that last election a month or two ago, and he's having to make pacts with the Labour men to form a government at all.'

Edie gave a doubtful laugh. 'Maybe Miss Alicia's women could get Labour on their side?'

Pa didn't answer. He had slipped the spare tacks between his lips, and was nailing on a plate – a little shaped piece of iron with a row of holes in it. This one was a toe-plate but there were 'heelers' too, tapped round the sole to save the shoe-leather – except that Pa's shoe-nails were apt to work right through and then he'd have to 'flat them over' at the end, though not before the wearer had time to notice it. No wonder Miss Alicia sent hers to the shoemaker, Edie thought.

Pa put down the hammer and picked up the polish-brush. 'Miss Killivant is going to this here meeting then?'

Edie giggled. 'She's gone to it, more like. Supposed to be this evening. Glad I wasn't there. She'll have taken Fanny with her, I expect. Mr Edwin doesn't like her going out at night without a maid. Though Fanny won't have welcomed that, I don't suppose. Left to herself, I believe she'd never go outside the house.'

She saw the brushing pause, and realized that her father was about to ask her why – and although she knew the answer, she couldn't

125

really tell. She'd already broken her promise to Fanny, when she talked to Sam. So she added quickly, before Pa had time to ask, 'Well, she's welcome to her outing – listening to some woman jawing on for hours. Worse than that Union fellow with his meetings down the mine. Though Ma says you've decided to join them, after all.'

He gave her a slow grin. 'She talked me into it. Said I should do something, now I'm working up to ground. Says if there was trouble like there was before, it might go hard with us.'

She nodded thoughtfully. She had been quite little when the miners last downed tools, refusing to buy their candles from the mine's own tally-shop – or something of the kind – when they could get them for half the price in town. There'd been a lot of whispering and worry in the night, but she had a fair idea of what had happened then: the owners had dismissed the lot of them and simply shut the mine, so there'd been weeks when nobody was paid. The miners won, of course, but at a dreadful price – there'd been a lot of hardship before the men went back again. She could still remember Mother arguing tearfully in shops, and going out to pick dandelion leaves for tea. 'That was bad enough,' she said.

Pa blew on Donny's shoe and rubbed it to a shine. 'Might be worse another time, as well. There isn't that bit extra to put aside to see us through, like there might have been when I was underground and found a decent seam – and the dressing-shed workers won't be the first ones taken back again. So your mother's right. I might need the Union, if there was trouble at the mine – though they might make it happen themselves, it seems to me, with all this talk about demanding better pay.'

He sounded so glum that Edie wished she hadn't raised the subject after all. She was trying to think of something sensible to say, when he added, 'End up like Jimmy Demster, if we don't look out,' and made her laugh.

Though it was not a laughing matter, when you came to think about it. Edie passed the Demsters' house a little later on, on her way to catch the last horse-bus back into Penzance, and she could not resist a glance.

There was a single candle burning in a downstairs room, and – since there was not a stitch of curtain at the windows anywhere – you could just see Jimmy Demster and his family in the room beyond, sitting on packing-cases round the glimmer of a fire. They had to sit on packing-cases, so the gossips said, because they'd bought a lot of fancy furniture from the tallyman for a bob or two a week, never allowing for how much extra it would cost in interest. Then when times were bad there was no money left for food, and they'd had to chop up all the chairs for firewood. That was the local rumour, anyway; though Ma insisted that a man had come and taken it all back, and she was kind to Jenny Demster when she came sidling down the path, begging to borrow a 'scart of butter' or a 'twist of tay'.

Surely the Trewins would never be reduced to

doing that?

It gave Edie so much to think about she almost missed the bus.

Alicia woke next morning with a gratifying sense that there was important business to be attended to. It gave the day a purpose, and she was suddenly impatient to be out of bed, so by the time that Edith came up with the tea she was already standing at the window with the curtains opened wide.

It was not at all her custom and it so surprised the maid that the little creature almost dropped the tray. 'Lawks, Miss Alicia. You gave me a fright. What are you doing standing there like that?'

Instead of rebuking her, Alicia merely laughed. She was feeling quite indulgent, for some reason, suddenly. 'Doing deep breathing, as we were taught to do at school. I've a lot to do today, and it's supposed to clear the brain. Like this...' She inhaled deeply, spreading out her arms, then hugged her chest as she expelled the air. The method seemed to work. She couldn't remember feeling so alive for years.

The maid glanced at her doubtfully as she put down the tea. 'Well, Miss Alicia, I'm sure that you know best, but mind you don't go catching your death of cold, standing in your nightgown in a draught of wind. Better to do your breathing when you've got something on. I'll go and fetch your hot water up so you can wash and dress. Will you be wanting your green figured silk and the embroidered blouse again today?'

Alicia was doing her breathing out again, and was ready to agree – but then she thought about it and changed her mind. 'You know, Edith, I don't believe I will. I think I'll wear that smart new navy blue instead. The one with the long jacket and the narrow skirt. And the white blouse with the jabot to wear underneath, just for a little softness at the neck perhaps. You can look it out for me. I've got someone coming to visit me today, and I want to make the right impression if I can. Oh, and tell Mrs Pritchard that we shall want elevenses – nothing fancy, just a biscuit and some tea, and perhaps some cheese and toasted muffin if we can run to that.'

'Yes, Miss Alicia.' Edith's eyes were round. You could see that she was bursting with curiosity. 'That Mr Tulver from the bank again?'

It was so outrageous that Alicia almost laughed. 'Not at all. One of the young ladies from the meeting yesterday. The one we met in town. She has asked me to assist her, and I've agreed to help.'

Edith was at the wardrobe, but she whirled around at that, her arms already laden with the clothes. 'You're never going out selling those papers in the street? Whatever would the mistress and Mr Edwin say?'

'Edith!' Alicia bridled. 'How dare you speak like that to me?'

'I'm sorry, Miss Alicia.' The maid had turned a gratifying pink and was looking appropriately abashed. 'None of my business. I should hold my tongue. It was only – I was worried on your account, that's all.'

'Very well. Then get on with your work. Lay the outfit on the bed and fetch that water up. And be quick about it.' She crossed to the dressing-table and sat down at it, to demonstrate that she was already waiting for the bowl.

Edith said, 'Yes, Miss,' and scuttled off at once.

Alicia smiled at her own reflection in the glass. She was getting soft. Edwin would say that the girl was impudent, and that she herself encouraged it by being far too tolerant. Which perhaps she was. She should have scolded Edith for her earlier remark about whether it was Mr Tulver who was coming here. But really, sometimes, it was tempting to confide. There wasn't anyone else that one could talk to, as a rule. Alicia had lost touch with all her chums from school. Perhaps this Miss Richie from the suffragists would turn out to be a friend. She seemed to want to be. She had made a point of hurrying over to speak to them last night as soon as they had arrived at the meeting.

'Oh, good evening, Miss Killivant. You did decide to come. And I see you have brought your maid – though not the one I saw you with the other day. Well, you are both welcome. We are all sisters here. And I'm so very glad to see you. I wasn't sure we would. So many people promise and then change their minds – and we did so want a decent turnout for tonight. The speaker has come all the way from London, specially.'

Alicia muttered something about looking forward to hearing the address – though, glancing round the draughty hall with its uncomfortable chairs, half of which were empty, she feared the evening did not seem to augur very well.

'Oh, I'm sure she will be thrilling,' Miss Elizabeth Richie said breathlessly. 'I was speaking to her earlier when she came off the train. The mood in London is quite remarkable – the Movement is simply going from strength to strength. However, no doubt she'll tell you all that for herself. Let's find you a nice seat where you can see and hear.' And she bustled over and found a couple of free ones by the wall, which were well placed but also thoughtfully discreet. 'I'm afraid I can't sit with you, I'm introducing this – and here comes the speaker and our local leader now. Amazing woman – she deals with all the mail. I'll try to introduce you to her later on.'

She gestured to the door, where a handsome lady in an enormous feathered hat was being ushered in by an eccentric-looking younger woman with wild auburn hair and a general air of having been picked up by a gale and blown haphazardly into her clothes. She was small and thin and energetic, in a jerky way, looking a little like a scarecrow come to life. If this was the 'local leader', Alicia thought, as the duo made their way towards the stage – the auburn-haired woman scattering hairpins and papers as she went – perhaps an introduction was not entirely a treat.

But once the speaker started, Alicia changed her mind. The Richie girl was right. It was a stirring speech. The stories of what Mrs Pankhurst and her followers had done – and which Alicia

131

had only heard of vaguely through the press – were much more thrilling than the papers said: and as for the way the police had treated some of those involved...! But perhaps it was the final words which really touched her heart: 'Why should men suppose that they have a divine right to make all the decisions in the world?' Alicia found herself on her feet applauding with the rest.

So when Beth Richie introduced her to the others later on, Alicia had murmured, 'What a splendid speech. I echoed the sentiment in every word.'

The wild-haired woman turned to her with a smile, and said – with an energy that belied her size – 'Then I hope you mean to join our Movement, Miss Killivant. We are in need of help from educated women such as you.'

Alicia stepped backwards – on to Fanny's foot. She had almost forgotten that the maid was there. 'I'm sorry,' she said hastily, in an apology which was somehow meant for everyone at once. 'I have an ailing mother – I am needed at home. I couldn't possibly agree to distribute literature.' Or take part in public marches in the street, she meant.

The scarecrow woman looked at her with contempt, but Miss Elizabeth Richie unexpectedly offered a way out. 'But you could assist in other ways, Miss Killivant, I'm sure. Our local group is drafting a letter to the government this week – you could help with that perhaps. A person of your obvious education...'

It was flattery, of course, but Alicia had been

happy to agree. Quite exciting, really, and – if truth were told – she was pleased to be able to invite Miss Richie to the house, 'To discuss the matter further, over a pot of tea perhaps?'

And it did prove a pleasant morning. Quite the most interesting she had spent for months. But – somehow – when she wrote to Edwin, she didn't mention it.

'Well,' Sammy said, when he saw Edie later on that day. He'd been digging over that dratted compost pile again, working in a pile of seaweed brought up from the beach, and he was glad to push his cap back on his sweating brow and rest his aching back a moment while he talked to her. 'Here's an unexpected treat. Imagine seeing you. Thought you'd be busy as a flea all day, with all that excitement in the house. What was it about? Some kind of visitor?'

Edie made a face at him. 'Sent out to fetch some more of they onions that are hung up in the shed. And we did have a caller. But how do you know that? Been working round the front and see them come, did you?'

He shook his head. 'Your friend Fanny came down the garden like a railway train first thing. I was carting in this load of seaweed then, a barrow at a time, but nothing would do but I should stop that straight away and cut a bunch of best camellias for the house. "Miss Killivant's orders", that is what she said. Never known her ask for that before, not even when Mr Edwin and his missus come to stay, so I figured out there must be something special happening.'

133

Edie kicked an idle foot against a turf of grass. 'Not all that special, you wouldn't have supposed. Just some woman from that meeting she went to yesterday, about some letter that they were going to write – but you'd think it was the King himself the way that Miss Alicia went on.'

He tried to look judicious. 'I suppose the poor soul doesn't have so many people come to call.'

Sammy turned another spadeful of the pile. 'Without you count that Mr Tulver, from the bank. And he's not very interesting, from what you say of him.'

'Well, this wasn't either,' Edie said, with vim. 'Enough to bore the socks off you, from what I heard of it – but Miss Alicia was simply thrilled to bits. She's agreed to go to all those meetings now – that Miss Richie will come and call for her, she says. That is a mercy anyway. At least me and Fanny won't be forced to go. I hate listening to speeches, they go on and on, and I'm not persuaded about this voting thing.'

Sam ran a grimy sleeve across his face. She made him feel protective – as she always did. He would have liked to reach out and take her hand in his, but he was mired in earth and the smelly contents of the pile. He contented himself with giving her a wink. 'Well, Edith Trewin, I don't know how you aren't. Sooner have your opinion about how to run the world than some that I could mention.'

'You mean Mr. Edwin?'

'I was thinking of old Gribbens, but either one would do. Or that Mr Tulver, come to that. I'm sure you've got more sense than he has...'

She shook her head at him. 'Well, you go to these 'ere meetings, if you're so keen on it. I'd sooner spend the evening in the house, myself, than sitting on a hard chair in that draughty hall – specially at this time of year when it's inclined to rain. And they're changing them from Wednesday, Fanny says – they've had to change the hall – so I'd have had to go, I suppose, if this Miss Richie hadn't offered to take Miss Alicia. Though Fanny might get dragged along in any case, if she doesn't look out – Miss Alicia thinks she's interested.'

It was so unexpected that it made him laugh. 'And you don't think she is?'

She kicked the turf again. 'Oh, I don't know. You can't tell what Fanny thinks. She was all fired up about it when she first came home – came into my room and kept me talking half the night, about how men had no God-given right to run the world – but when Miss Alicia was talking about going there again, Fanny didn't want to, that was clear as day.'

'Afraid of someone seeing her, perhaps?'

She looked at him sharply. 'I hadn't thought of that. I suppose that's what it is. Well, she'd better stop saying how the Movement's right, or Miss Alicia will take her there again. And me, most likely, if I don't look out – if the meeting isn't Wednesday, I'll have no excuse. But, talking about Wednesdays, have you talked to Gribbens yet?'

'Course I 'ave!' He felt the warm blood coursing up his neck, and turned a shovelful of pile to hide the blush. Quite a thing, it was, for her to

135

ask him home to tea. Made him feel quite nervous – though proud, of course, as well. 'Asked him for a Wednesday off, not next week but the next. There's some nurseryman he wants to go and see that day, so he won't be here in any case to be breathing down my neck. Didn't tell him why I wanted it, of course – and, thanks be, he didn't ask.'

'So?' she said impatiently. 'Did he agree, or what?'

He grinned. 'Grumbled a bit and made out it was very difficult – but said "yes" in the end. I thought he would. He'd rather have me here the weekend, helping him to plant – supposing that he gets the seeds and things he's looking for.'

Edie was grinning at him. She had turned pink as well. 'I'm some glad, Sammy. The family have been wanting me to bring you home for weeks. But we'd best be careful. We can't just leave from here. Do you think...?'

She broke off as a voice came ringing down the path. 'Edith! E ... dith! Where have you got to with those onions? I'm waiting to make stew.'

'Sorry,' she said breathlessly, 'I'm going to have to go, or I shall end up in the stew myself. I'll try and come tomorrow to pick up the eggs. We can make arrangements then.' And she darted off to fetch her onions, her trim little bottom bouncing as she ran.

Sammy watched her with pleasure till she was out of sight and then, reluctantly, turned back to the pile.

Four

'And did you have a good day today, my dearest?' Edwin said to his wife, with conscious heartiness. Too much heartiness. He had meant to sound cheerful but even to himself the effect was forced and rather unnecessarily loud.

Claire looked at him dully. The demands of motherhood seemed to make her very tired. Quite to be expected, until the child was weaned – although he'd engaged a nursery-maid, of course – but even now his wife was anxiously obsessed about the infant's health and seemed to spend a quite unconscionable amount of time visiting the nursery and cooing at the crib.

'It was too cold for Caroline to go out today,' she murmured now, as though that were sufficient answer to the question he had asked. 'It's already getting hard to find the coals to keep the rooms warm here, and of course it's quite impossible to find a hansom cab. I know you have some sympathy with these miners, Edwin dear, but it is hard when a baby has to suffer for their strikes.' Then she added, in a more animated tone, 'But she is blowing bubbles and when I picked her up today, I'm almost sure she smiled – although the nurse assures me that it's only wind.'

'That's nice, dear.' He flicked through the envelopes waiting on the tray. 'Nothing from Alicia again today?' He frowned. 'I know the mails have been delayed of late, but this is the third time in a fortnight her letter has not come – and they are getting shorter and vaguer every time she writes.'

'Really?' Claire's face was expressionless again, which showed that she was hurt. He hastened to exonerate his sister, if he could.

'Asks after you and Caroline, of course, and encloses the usual bills and expenditure accounts – then simply says that everyone is well, Mother is much brighter and there's nothing to report. None of the usual detailed complaints. Not like Liss at all. I'm sure there is something which she isn't telling me. Really, Claire, I'm getting quite concerned.'

'I don't know why you should be,' Claire said, rather snappishly. 'What is she to write? Life for her is very much the same from day to day – not like us, dearest, with a child to think about. She used to write and grumble that she needed extra help, but now that she has it, perhaps there isn't much to say. If there is any problem, no doubt she'll let you know. I'm almost glad that there is all this dreadful trouble at the collieries – at least you aren't talking about going down there again.'

His frown deepened. This was another change. Claire was taking issue with him much more often than she used. It was the result of restless nights, perhaps. But she was right, of course. It was not sensible to go down to Penzance while

138

the coal-miners were on strike, and threatening to deprive the railways of their fuel. He might find himself stranded at Holvean House for days.

He said, conscious of being admirably patient with his wife, 'All the same, my dear, I'm made uneasy when she won't communicate. It reminds me of the way she was when we were young: she and Charles would have a secret that they didn't want to share, and I could always tell because Liss would get evasive and wouldn't talk to me. And this is just the same. I'm sure there's something that she's trying to conceal. Something about that maid of hers, I shouldn't be surprised.'

Claire was not mollified. 'Dearest, you've got a positive obsession about that girl. And there is nothing you can do. I thought that Mr Tulver was taking care of it?'

He nodded. 'I've asked him to keep an eye on things,' he said, and went on sifting through the post.

She said, with such feeling that he looked up, surprised, 'Then I wish you'd let him do it, Edwin, that's all I can say. I sometimes think that you are more concerned with what goes on at Holvean House than you are about what happens in your own household here.' She struggled to her feet.

He watched her, wordlessly. She had got a little slow and clumsy since the birth, and she'd not regained her figure – much to his surprise. Not that he would ever mention that to her, of course. Though he had been hoping that as things went along she would return to normal and permit him to resume what he thought of as the privileges of a married man, but so far there had been no sign of that at all, and his attempts to woo her had simply earned rebuke. 'Edwin, have you no delicacy at all? It is only recently that I bore your child!' He had been obliged to retreat into the other room, with a vague sense that he'd behaved like an unfeeling boor.

She was looking at him with that same expression now. 'Won't you come up to the nursery with me presently, and take an interest in your little girl? Isn't that more fascinating than what your sister does or doesn't do?'

'Of course, my dear,' he murmured, though inwardly he sighed. When he was shown a baby every night, what was a man to do? The child wasn't very different from one day to the next, and there was a limit to the things that one could say. But something was expected, and it meant a lot to Claire, so he resigned himself to being lured upstairs. There he was given the sleeping infant to admire, under the nursemaid's disapproving gaze. The child was getting bigger, there was no doubt of it, and he seized on that to venture a remark.

'Looking very healthy,' he volunteered aloud. Much too loud, in fact. He had disturbed the child. It wriggled and turned red. Now it was about to cry, he thought, and he made to hand it back.

And then it looked at him. His daughter looked at him. Her eyes were unexpectedly wide and deepest blue and for a moment they seemed to fix on his. A frown of sudden concentration crossed her face and then the corners of the mouth turned up in what might have been a smile.

Edwin felt a strange emotion somewhere in his gut. Odd, he thought – according to the poets it should have been his heart. For the first time in his life he was possessed by love, overwhelming and wholly unforeseen. This was his child, the product of his loins. The baby screwed her face up and let out a mighty howl. But this time it was with a sort of tender pride that he relinquished her and gave her to the maid.

'She is quite perfect, isn't she?' he murmured to his wife as they went downstairs again. 'Did you see her smile? And you are right, of course. I'm absolutely certain that it wasn't merely wind.'

His reward was another surprised and fleeting smile.

The day for Sammy's visit had come round at last. Edie was so impatient that she'd been counting off the days. They hadn't dared to meet at Holvean House, of course, but here he was now, hurrying down Causewayhead, coming to meet her underneath the clock as they'd arranged.

'Left it till last moment, didn't you?' she said. 'I was getting worried that we were going to miss the bus.'

He looked uncomfortably up and down the street. 'Well, we didn't want anyone seeing us together and telling tales, did we? Anyway, here

141

comes the horse-bus now. Look all right, do I?'
he added, as it drew up to let them on.

She punched his arm. ''Course you do, you
daft thing. You look as smart as paint.' A fat
woman with a basket had reluctantly made
room, and Edie and Sammy sat down in the
narrow space, so crammed together that their
sides were forced to touch – not that Edie
minded. Neither did Sammy, by the look of him.

He bent towards her and said in a low voice,
'Put on my Sunday best, although I wasn't sure.
Don't want to look like parson, but on the other
hand, I want your Pa to think that I've got
prospects, if...' He didn't finish the sentence, but
it was clear as daylight what he meant by that,
and she could feel herself coming over all pink
and flustered at the thought. It was the first time
that marriage had been openly hinted at.

'Sammy!' She dug him sharply in the ribs, and
he lapsed into silence for a mile or two, until
they reached Sancreed and it was time for the fat
woman to get off. Edie didn't know her, but the
woman winked. 'Good luck to you, my lover.
And your young man, too.' And she got off with
her basket, leaving an embarrassed Edie staring
after her.

'Now see what you've done!' she hissed to
Sammy as the horse-bus moved away, knowing
she was scarlet as the flowers on runner-beans.
'Everybody's looking! Move away a bit!' Sammy did so, by an inch or two, and they said
nothing more – staring in opposite directions
until Penvarris came in sight.

'Come on then,' Edie prompted, and they got

down from the bus. It was hard to realize that he didn't know the way, and had to wait for her to lead him down the Terrace to the house. Even then he seemed amazingly reluctant to go in.

'Well, go on. They won't eat you. It's only my family that you're coming out to meet – you're not being hauled up before the justices, or being tested by some stuffy old inspector like we used to be at school.'

He cleared his throat and ran an anxious finger round the collar of his Sunday shirt as if it had suddenly got too tight for him. 'Suppose your Pa decides that I'm not good enough for you? Or I make a bad impression? It could work out that way. I get so nervous sometimes that I can't think what to say and I look as if I'm simple – what will happen then?'

He looked so earnest, standing there, all stiff and starchy in his going-to-chapel best, that it almost made her laugh. But she could see that he was worried, and she said with a smile, 'You, looking simple, Sammy Hern? You wouldn't know how to, if you wanted to. Just be yourself, and you'll charm the boots off them. I have told them all about you in any case, of course. Come on, there's Donny at the window now – bursting to meet you. You can see he is.'

Donny proved her right by opening the door and running out to greet them. 'Is this your Sammy, then? Isn't as tall as you made out he was. And can he really tell you every kind of tree?' He looked at Sammy gravely. 'I grew one from an acorn. I'll show you if you like.'

'Later,' Ma said, firmly from the door. 'Let the

poor lad come in and have some tea. He'll think it's some madhouse he's come to, otherwise.'

Of course, they all liked him – what else would they do? He was used to children – he knew Queenie's brood – and it wasn't long before his best trousers were at risk because he had the younger children climbing on his knees while he gave them 'rides' by bouncing them up and down. The rest of the family tried to make him welcome in their way – Meg and Suzanna giggled and darted looks at him and the older boys made manly conversation about trains, while Ma plied him with home-made splits and tarts and jam. Then, after tea, Pa took him down the back garden to see the cabbages he'd grown.

Edie would have liked to go with them – not to see the cabbages but to listen in – but when she went to follow, Ma shook her head at her.

'Edie, lover, go and fill the bucket from the water-butt and come and give a hand with washing up the cloam!' And then she added, in a whisper which Sammy must have heard, 'Can't you see that your pa wants a chance to have a word alone?'

It had not occurred to Edie, but it was obviously true – and an alarming thought. She tried to sneak a look at them while she filled up the pail, but they were simply standing by the cabbage patch, deep in conversation, with their backs to her. And back in the scullery, it was worse of course. What were they saying? What would Father think? It made her so nervous, she almost dropped a cup – and her mother packed her off to put the little ones to bed.

When she came downstairs again, Sammy and her father had come inside and were sitting in the kitchen at the table by the fire with the boys, while Ma and the older girls were busy darning socks. Sammy turned scarlet when Edie first appeared, and seemed to be busy staring at his feet, but Pa looked up at Edie and gave his gentle smile.

'Knows his cabbages, your Sammy – I'll say that for him. Given me a hint or two on what to dowse them with – keep they damty white butterflies away. Says he'll show me next time, when you bring him home.'

And that was all – but Edie knew exactly what it meant. Sammy was accepted and could court her if he liked. And judging by the shy grin on his crimson face, Sammy knew it too.

The next time that Tim Tulver called at Holvean House his courage almost failed. He had thought of nothing else for days, and had spent a great deal of time in front of his mirror, rehearsing what to say. All the same it took an effort of will to ring the bell, and when there was a little pause before the housemaid answered it, he very nearly turned tail and hurried down the path.

But here was the maid now, opening the door – neat as ever in her gingham uniform and blouse. 'Why, Mr Tulver! Let me take your coat and hat, and I'll run up and let Miss Alicia know that you are here.' And then, of course, it was too late for retreat. He had to allow her to show him in to wait.

It seemed an eternity before Alicia came; an

eternity in which the tension in him grew and grew, as if every tick of the ormolu clock on the mantelpiece were the sound of a ratchet winding up a spring inside his head. He gazed at the drapes and heavy furniture without really seeing them, and traced the pattern on the carpet with his foot, mentally repeating the words he'd settled on.

'Miss Alicia, it is presumptuous, I know, but I have managed to obtain a pair of tickets for the concert at the Town Hall next week. They are difficult to come by, as I am sure you know, because the violinist is...' Drat it! He should have noted down the name! Something foreign. It had slipped his mind again. He amended his lines. 'The violinist is a person of international repute – but I would be honoured if you would consent to accompany me. And you need not be concerned. I have written to your brother and he does not object.'

Or should it be 'agrees that I might ask'? He was still pondering the question when Alicia appeared, and – though he had been waiting for her – her presence, as usual, disconcerted him. She was dressed more severely than was usual with her, in a simple dark-blue gown with white around the neck. It contrasted with her glowing hair and made her look superb. He swallowed hard.

'Mr Tulver!' (Was he imagining it, or was there a touch of irony in her tone?) 'To what do we owe the pleasure? What has my brother found to worry him this time? Or is it some question relating to the trust?'

146

He blurted out, confused, 'Oh, no, Miss Alicia. It is not that at all. It is not a question of your brother or the bank, I assure you. I am entirely here on my own account this time.'

'Indeed?' There was no doubt about it now. The voice and the expression were frankly quizzical. 'I am glad to learn that you are entirely here. And what can I do "on your account", as you so delicately put it?'

He hesitated. This was not at all the way he had envisaged this little interview. He ran a finger round his collar, which had got too tight again, and murmured, 'Miss Alicia, I do not wish to be preposterous...' Good lord, what was the matter with his tongue? That was not what he had meant! He tailed off in dismay.

His discomfiture made her laugh aloud. 'I am sure that is the last thing that any of us would *wish* to be.' She seemed to recollect herself, and said more soberly, 'I'm sorry, Mr Tulver. That was impolite. What were you hoping to communicate?'

'Presumptuous. I meant to say "presumptuous",' he said, wishing that the carpet would open up and swallow him.

She did not help him in his embarrassment. 'And why should I think you were?'

He took a deep breath and the words came tumbling out. 'The thing is, I've got some tickets for the recital at the Town Hall on Friday night. It would be quite proper, my cousins will be there.' In fact it was a cousin who had offered him the seats – with the evident assumption that he would take Mama. He glimpsed Alicia's face.

'But I can see that it was foolish. I should not have asked. I beg your pardon. It was wrong of me.'

She looked at him 'But you have *not* asked, Mr Tulver.' Was she teasing him? Or should he take this as encouragement?

He said, knowing that he sounded like an anxious child, 'Well, would you do me the honour, Miss Alicia? Would you attend the concert in my company?' She seemed to be considering, and he added hastily, 'I have written to your brother and he does not object.'

The smile left her face. 'Friday night, you say? I'm afraid that makes it quite impossible, Mr Tulver. I have already engaged to attend a special women's meeting at the Workers' Educational Hall that night.'

She had been baiting him. He felt his ears go red. 'Of course! I should have realized that you would not care to go. Forgive me for having intruded on your time.' He turned to go, aware that there was hurt and humiliation in his voice.

She seemed to feel it, too. 'On the contrary, Mr Tulver. You mistake me there. I don't wish to be unkind. I have a genuine engagement, and therefore cannot come. I appreciate the compliment you pay by asking me.'

He turned back to look at her. God, she was magnificent. And lovely when she blushed. His heart was thumping till he thought it must drown out the clock. 'So in other circumstances...?'

She smiled, not unkindly. 'I might have thought of it. I do not wish to give you false expectations, Mr Tulver, but I might have thought of it. My life is not so exciting that I lightly turn down invitations that are kindly made.'

'Unfortunately, the recital is for a single night,' he murmured glumly. 'But perhaps another time?'

'Perhaps. I make no promises. Provided that you do not write and ask my brother first. And I have to warn you, Mr Tulver, I am much engaged these days with these women's meetings,' she replied. 'Unless, of course, you'd care to come and join us there? We are in want of supporters, and you would be welcomed, I am sure.'

She was still smiling and he could not detect whether she was mocking him or not. But to his agitated mind it seemed there might have been a kind of invitation in her words.

He said, with as much dignity as he could summon up, 'I have seen the announcements posted in the street, and have considered attending before this – if only to discover for myself what the truth might be behind the public gossip and the newspaper reports.'

It was not a very accurate account – he had seen the posters in his cousin's company, and John had jested that they should both attend, dressed in female attire: 'If they want to act like men, then we'll pretend we're girls. Why should they have the prerogative of changing roles? Besides, I'm sure you would look ravishing in a bonnet, Timothy. Though we shouldn't wish to chain ourselves to buildings, I suppose – or start throwing stones, and get taken off to jail.' Tim had thought it very funny at the time.

He didn't tell Alicia about all that, of course – and just as well. She was looking at him with a different expression on her face.

'Really, Mr Tulver? You have an open mind? Then you are more intelligent than I had supposed. I presume that you have not consulted my brother about this? I doubt that he would much approve of your attending our little gatherings. Or even of my attending them myself. Of course, he cannot disapprove of what he doesn't know. Or shall you feel obliged to tell him when you write?'

There now! She had wrong-footed him again. He mumbled indistinctly, 'I am not answerable to your brother for everything I do.'

'So I observe. Well, I shall look forward to greeting you if you do attend sometime.' She was looking at him kindly – which rather gave him hope – and her manner was more gracious as she added with a smile, 'In the meantime, Mr Tulver, would you care for tea?'

Five

Alicia stood at the window and watched Mr Tulver leave. What a strangely awkward little man he was. She had thought him pompous, when she met him first, but she was coming to suspect that his careful wordiness was not the result of natural arrogance, but – perversely – covered up an inner lack of confidence. She was quite ashamed that she had made him squirm.

And his invitation had been flattering. Not that she could think of him as any kind of beau – it was 'preposterous', as he himself had said, that he should suppose she might be interested in him, and even more preposterous to write to Edwin for consent – but it was gratifying to find oneself so openly admired. She smiled again, remembering how tongue-tied he had been. Quite endearing, really, in a peculiar kind of way.

'Excuse me, Miss Alicia, shall I come in and clear the tea?' That was Edith, returning from having shown their caller out.

She nodded, briskly. 'Thank you, Edith. And when you have done that, you may come upstairs and help me get ready to go out. Miss Richie is coming to collect me later on. I am to help the Movement with some further work.'

151

'Yes, Miss Alicia.' The maid sounded doubtful and Alicia was irked. Of course, the newspapers were full of sensational reports – women throwing stones and marching in the street – and the stories of arrest and force-feeding were simply frightening. But no one would expect her to be involved in anything like that. Nothing of the sort was going to happen in Penzance. Locally it was simply meetings and a leaflet here and there, and she was rather proud of having been asked to help again. And, if truth were told, she was pleased to have Elizabeth Richie seek her company.

They had been together often, mostly here of course, though twice she'd visited Elizabeth at home – a charming little cottage on the edge of town, where the widowed Mrs Richie held a kind of cheerful court amidst a riot of flowers, paintings, grown-up sons and dogs. Beth had apologized, but Liss longed to go again.

But they were going to the local 'headquarters' this afternoon, and that pleased her rather less. Alicia had been there only once before, and had been a little shocked. It was a ramshackle terraced house along a narrow alleyway, with a neglected garden at the side of it – a horrid straggly wilderness of weeds and mangy cats – not at all the sort of place one wanted to be seen. The doors and windows were much in want of paint, and it was not a great deal better when one got inside.

The whole of the ground floor appeared to be given over to the Movement's office work. There was a large table where volunteers could sit – there had been two of them addressing envelopes the last time she was there – in the midst of chaotic piles of paperwork. Assorted circulars, leaflets and the like were stacked randomly on chairs, haphazard heaps of outgoing mail teetered on window-sills and the tops of furniture, while stacks of 'Votes for Women' circulars overflowed on to the floor. Yet the wild-haired leader – who came out to welcome them – seemed to live there, from what Elizabeth had said. It was hard to know quite where. There seemed to be no servants, and though the place was clean, nothing had been tidied in living memory. And when a drink of tea was offered it was brought out in a cup with a non-matching saucer and a tarnished spoon, and accompanied by bought biscuits still inside the tin.

It was a long way from the orderly arrangements Liss was accustomed to at home, and she was a little apprehensive about visiting again. Yet it was oddly thrilling too – a glimpse of what Edwin would have called a 'Bohemian' way of life. Perhaps, she thought wryly, it was the thought that he would disapprove that had made her agree to go with Beth today.

She looked up to find Edith hovering. 'Well, girl, what are you waiting for?'

The maid grinned back at her. 'Waiting to hear what clothes I should put out, Miss Alicia, that's all. I've taken down the tray and was going to go upstairs, only you hadn't said what dress, and you were in that much of a reverie when I came back, I didn't like to ask.'

153

Alicia sighed. She would have liked to wear the navy blue – she thought of it as her 'going-to-Movement-meeting' dress – it seemed appropriately neat and businesslike. But it was very cold this afternoon, and she did not expect that 'headquarters' would boast any heat at all. She said, 'My pink and puce, I think. Or...' she hesitated, remembering that there might be dust, 'perhaps my dark grey woollen with the black embroidery.'

'You mean your half-mourning, Miss Alicia? You sure? It's awful drab. Miss Richie will think that a neighbour's gone and died – or you've been attending someone's funeral.'

'I'll be attending yours, young woman, if you speak to me like that. My dark grey woollen will do very well.'

And it did, she thought, a little later – as Edith did up the tiny buttons at the back. Sober and businesslike, a bit like a man's outfit. That was the ticket. She looked in the mirror and smiled at what she saw. 'Get Fanny to polish my new black boots for me. And look quick about it. Oh, there's the doorbell now. That will be Miss Richie. Go and let her in.'

But it wasn't Miss Richie. It was a man. A strange man that Edith had never seen before. A man with a tight high collar and a brown buttoned coat that looked as if it had been made for someone else, the way it stretched around him and strained at all the seams. He had a florid bearded face and a mop of greying hair, and he pulled off his bowler hat and held it to his chest.

154

''Ave I the honour of finding Miss Killivant's abode?'

Edie looked him up and down. He had thick boots, she saw, and his trousers were the sort of thing that Father sometimes wore. And his fingernails weren't clean. Not at all the sort of caller you would expect at Holvean House.

'The tradesmen's entrance is around the back,' she said, and made to close the door.

He put his foot in it, so that it wouldn't shut. 'This isn't tradesmen's business. I'd like to have a word with this Miss Killivant,' he said. He was smiling quite politely, and his voice was a surprise – rough and determined and with a Cornish burr, but at the same time oddly teasing, as if they shared a roguish joke.

'I'm afraid Miss Killivant is not available.' Edith made to shut the door again, but his boot still wedged it.

He winked. 'Oh, come now, missie. We both know she is in. It is only half an hour since she had a visitor.'

Edith gasped. 'You've watched the house?' she cried.

'Only long enough to make sure I'd come to the right place,' he said. 'Now, are you going to fetch Miss Killivant, or not?' His thick lips were still smiling but the smile did not reach his eyes.

She felt a little prickle of fear run down her back. Should she leave him and run down and call for Cook? Mrs Pritchard would know how to deal with men like this. But if she left the doorstep she was sure he would come in, and who knew what he would do? Steal the china, or

155

the mantel clock, or something of the kind. He made her uneasy, even where he was.

'Miss Killivant is getting ready to go out. A carriage will be calling for her any moment now. I have told you, it is not convenient. If you have a message, I will pass it on. And kindly move your foot from my employer's hall. If we wished to use a doorstop, sir, we would have purchased one.'

She was being impertinent, she knew, but for the first time the man looked a little bit nonplussed. All the same he did not move his foot. 'I've got a right to be here,' he mumbled angrily. 'I want to talk to your mistress. I have reason to think she has my daughter Nellie – Nellie Rouse – on the premises.'

Edith shook her head. 'Well, I can save you the trouble. There's no Nellie here. There's me and Cook and Fanny – and Queenie now and then. And except for Nurse Morgan, that is all there is. But she isn't Nellie, either. I think her name is Ruth. So if you would be good enough to go away and let me shut the door...'

To her alarm he thrust his face into her own. 'I want to see your mistress. You think I am a fool? Well, look here, missie, you just hark to me...'

'No, mister.' It was Sammy, bounding up the steps, carrying a billhook in his hand. He must have been cutting back the weeds around the hedge. 'Seems to me, it's you that should be harkening! I 'stinctly heard the young lady telling you, you've got the wrong address. So take your foot away or you'll have me to answer to.' He was smaller than the stranger but he was

156

young and strong – and he'd stood up for her. The man stepped backwards – good old Sam, she thought!

She should have shut the door, but she was quite transfixed. The man had turned on Sammy. 'And who might you be, when you're 'ome? Some kind of under-gardener? Well, you don't frighten me.' His voice was threatening, and when he raised his arm, for an awful moment she thought there'd be a fight.

Sammy squared up to him – with that billhook too. Edie would not have believed that he could look so menacing. There would be murder any minute. She let out a scream. 'Don't you hit him, Sammy, there'll be hell to pay...'

Sam said, 'Don't you worry. He's leaving – aren't you, sir?'

The stranger simply stood there, breathing heavily. Edith never knew what might have happened next, because a voice rang out behind her.

'Oi!' It was Mrs Pritchard, coming panting up the stairs, and out into the hallway in her apron. 'What's all this commotion? I could hear you from the yard. Who is this person, Edith? What on earth's going on?'

Edith did not move her eyes from the caller as she spoke. 'It's a Mr Rouse – least I assume that's what his name is. Looking for his daughter by the name of Nellie Rouse. He thought she might be here, and he won't believe me when I say she's not. And he keeps putting his foot inside the door. Sammy had to come and make him take it out. I thought the man was going to

157

hit him, that's why I cried out.'

Cook could look terribly imposing when she tried. She looked imposing now. Even the stranger seemed to wilt a bit. 'Very well, Sammy, you get back to work.' She folded her arms across her ample chest and confronted the caller with a steely glare. 'And as for you, if you try and put your foot inside the door again, I'll send Edie out to get the police.'

The man was doing that friendly smile of his again. 'Only looking for my own daughter, missus – that is all. Can't blame a man for that. Come all the way from Trewendron – that's up Launceston way – looking for my Nell. And I was told you'd taken on a maid not long ago.'

'Indeed we did. A charity case – an orphan. This family is noted for its charitable concerns. Miss Killivant's brother is in the church, and runs a mission in London for the poor.'

He didn't seem to hear her. 'Thing is, the girl has run away and she is needed home. I am a widower, and I've a brood of children to bring up. Can't do it on my own. I need my Nellie to lend a hand with them – 'tisn't too much to ask of your own flesh and blood, you'd think.'

'Haven't you got ears, then?' Cook said frostily. 'There's no Nellie here. The girl has told you once. And now I'm telling you the same.'

He was wheedling now. 'And you don't know where she is? You'd let her father know? I don't know what she's telling people, but she's tried this trick before – doesn't like to have to work for nothing when there's others getting paid. I don't blame your Miss Killivant. I just want her back.'

'Mr Rouse – you've had your answer. If you don't leave this doorstep, I shall send for the police.'

And, to Edith's infinite relief, the man did turn and walk away at last – just as Miss Richie's carriage drew up at the gate. He pushed past the coachman who'd got down to help her out, and went off, muttering.

'What an ill-mannered fellow,' Miss Richie said, as she came up the steps. 'Whatever did he want? Is your mistress ready, Edith? I am sorry we are late. We had trouble with the horses. We'll have to leave at once.'

'Go and get her, Edie, and then send Fanny down to me,' Cook said, not unkindly, and Edith scampered off. The first part of her errand was easily achieved: Miss Alicia had been ready and waiting for some time – and seemed oblivious of the commotion on the step. There was no sign of Fanny, but Edie took her mistress down, and watched as she and Miss Richie drove away.

Edith didn't only shut the door, she barred and bolted it, and leaned against it for a minute, flushed and out of breath. Then she set off to hunt for Fanny, not only to say that Mrs Pritchard wanted her, but to warn her too. Because she was as certain as it was possible to be that this caller was the person that her friend was so frightened of.

Sammy had gone back to slashing weeds again. He would get a jawing for his antics later on, if not something worse. Half-threatening a visitor, and with a billhook too, he could get himself dismissed. It was a wonder that he hadn't been hauled up before Miss Alicia there and then. But what else was he to do? Edie had been frightened – he couldn't just stand by.

He took out his feelings on a clump of thorns, and he was sucking his finger when he heard a shout. 'Sammy!'

It was Edie, running from the house. If she had looked upset before she now looked ten times worse. 'Sammy, have you seen Fanny? I can't find her anywhere.'

'She hasn't come this way. I'd have seen her if she had. She must be in the house.'

Edie shook her head. 'I've searched all over. And Mrs Pritchard too.'

He put down the billhook and looked into her eyes. 'Have you looked in the cupboards and underneath the beds? I think she might be hiding. And do you know why?'

She nodded. 'I think so. You're thinking what I'm thinking, aren't you, Sammy Hern? It was Fanny he was looking for. Not Nellie Rouse at all. This is the person she was trying to escape.'

He said, very gently, 'It might be worse than that. You realize that Fanny might not be Fanny after all? Nellie might be what she's really called? She might have lied to us.'

Her eyes were full of tears. 'If you can call it that. What could be more natural, when you run away, than to change your name? It's the sort of thing I might have done myself – if I had been trying to escape that awful man. She said he was dreadful, and now I can see why. He gave me the heebie-jeebies, just by standing there. No wonder she wanted to run away from him. And he's the one that's lying, if anybody is. He can't be her father, because her father's dead.'

'We have only got her word for that, you know.'

He saw it dawn on her that this might well be true. She let out a little sob and came stumbling to him, and then – watching street or no street – she fell into his arms. After a minute she looked up at him, as if another dreadful thought had just occurred to her. 'Sammy! You don't think...? She wouldn't have done anything desperate?'

'I don't know,' he said. 'I'll help you look for her. Come on. Just tell Mrs Pritchard what we're a-doing of.'

Mrs Pritchard joined them, but they couldn't find the girl. Mr Gribbens, in the rose-beds, hadn't seen her pass, and nor had Queenie, who was scrubbing the back step. She wasn't in the kitchen, nor in the scullery, nor in the garden or any of the sheds. The boxroom was empty, and there was no one in the press. There was nothing missing, as far as anyone could see – in the little attic the bed was neatly made, and even Fanny's own few possessions were still ranged round the room, but of the girl herself there was no sign at all.

They did find a pair of Miss Alicia's boots, on the back staircase, as though they had been dropped, and one of the side windows was unaccountably ajar.

'Might have slipped out the orchard gate without me seeing 'er, I s'pose.' Mr Gribbens pushed

161

back his battered hat and scratched his head. 'But don't 'ee fret, young Sammy. These girls are flighty things. She'll be back before dark you mark my words, wanting to come in and have her tea.'

But of course she wasn't – not that day, or the next, or any day that followed.

Fanny Watts – or Nellie Rouse – had simply disappeared.

Part Three

Spring 1910

One

There was something up with Edith. Teddy Trewin could see that as soon as he glimpsed his daughter by the stile, where she was waiting to accompany him on the walk back home. She sometimes did that, on her half-day off – and usually it meant that she was keen to talk. But today, it seemed, was quite the opposite. Her normally pink and cheerful face was looking white and drawn, and though she summoned up a smile as he approached, there was none of her usual bouncy chattiness.

She just said, 'Hello, Pa,' and that was all.

He was tempted to slip his arm around her and hug her to his chest – the way he would have done when she was small – but she'd grown to be a real young woman now and it wouldn't be 'fitty' to do things like that. Besides, he knew he was all over dust – now that he was working 'up to ground' he didn't have to change his clothes before he left the mine – but you couldn't help a bit of dust, it got in everywhere, and he didn't want to dirt up Edie's walking clothes.

So he thrust his hands into the pockets of his coat (he found there was a little hole in one of them) and asked, with a pretence at unconcern, 'Hello, my 'andsome. How are 'ee getting on?'

If she wanted to confide in him, she would, he told himself.

She looked away. 'Oh, I'm all right.'

They had fallen into step together on the 'miner's path' back home, but he stopped. Dust or no dust, he took her arm and swung her round so she was facing him. 'Now, don't give me that, my handsome. You look worried half to death. Something happened, 'as it?'

She pulled away, and stared at one of the white-stones by the path – painted so that miners could find their way home in the dark. She wouldn't look at him.

He tried again. 'Look here, Edie, you can tell your Pa. What is it, my lover? You in trouble with the Killivants?'

She shook her head and said, with what sounded like actual relief, 'No. I'm not in trouble – or no more'n usual, for being a bit of a lie-abed sometimes. Don't you worry about that.'

'You've never fallen out with that young man of yours?' That would be a pity, Teddy thought. Not really good enough for Edie, he had thought at first – but then who would be? Sammy was all right – a nice, hard-working lad – and fond of Edie, anyone could see. Been looking forward to meeting him again. He'd even thought of asking if the lad might know how a man could go about finding a position gardening somewhere: a fellow could do worse than be in the open air if he was having trouble with his chest – and even working in the sheds, this cough had not cleared up. Though there probably wasn't enough money in Sammy's line of work, to keep a

166

family on. Not a family the size of Teddy Trewin's, any case.

He was so busy with his thoughts that Edie startled him. 'Fallen out with Sammy? No, of course I aren't.' She took his arm – as if the dust did not exist – and urged him gently down the path again. After a minute she added, in a strained, peculiar tone, 'This isn't about me. Not my business really, if you come to think. But you know that Fanny that Miss Alicia took on? Well, you won't believe it, but she's upped and run away.'

'She never!' It was so shocking that he caught his breath, and that made him stop and wheeze.

Almost before he'd finished Edie spoke again. 'She has, though! Disappeared without a word. Jumped out the side window by the look of it and no one's seen her since. Wonder she didn't break a leg – that ledge is three foot up. Happened when a man came knocking at the door.' He listened as she poured the story out to him. 'Couldn't really have been her father, could it, Pa? Though Sammy seems to think so. I don't know what to do.'

'What d'you mean, my lover? What else could you have done? This Rouse man asked for somebody you'd never heard of, and you wouldn't let him in. Doesn't sound like the sort of person that Miss Alicia would want inside her house. And, from what you tell me, Mrs Pritchard was the one that saw him off.'

Edith shook a mournful head. ''Course, we didn't know then that Fanny'd disappeared. That's what's upset Miss Alicia something

167

terrible. She's sure that Fanny is this runaway, Nellie Rouse, and that was her father coming after her. Says, "Why else would Fanny run away?", and blames herself for hiring her without a written character. And I'm sure that Mr Edwin will take on something cruel.'

'I suppose she's wrote and told him?'

She nodded. 'I believe she has – but of course she haven't said so to the likes of us. It must be hard for her. He was always against the whole idea of taking Fanny on. Miss Alicia will never hear the end of it, poor soul. She's had us counting the silver, and all sorts, ever since. But of course Fanny wasn't the kind of girl to steal.' She looked up at him. 'Thing is, I think I might know why she ran away. And it's not because she's afraid of a bit of hard work, like that man made it sound.'

She lapsed into silence and he had to urge her. 'Well?'

Even then he wondered if she was going to tell him after all, but finally she took a gulping breath and said, 'She told me there was someone chasing after her. Some distant relative, she said, who'd try to claim her back. And she was terrified of him – you could see that by her face. So I don't believe for a moment that man was her pa, or that he just wanted her to come back home and work. I'm sure he must have beaten her, or something of the kind. I think she'd tried to run away before, that's why she wasn't home when the family house burnt down.' She paused and looked at him. 'Problem is, should I tell the mistress, do you think? I promised Fan I wouldn't – but with things the way they are...'

He used his free hand to push his cap back from his brow, as though fresh air would help his brain to think. 'Well,' he said slowly, 'I know we always brought you up to keep your word on things, but I can't see how as it would do Fanny any harm now, if you did. No, my lover, I aren't going to tell you what to do, but I should tell Miss Killivant if I was you. Might make her feel better on her own account as well – if there was a proper reason for the girl running away.'

'I think perhaps I will, then. Sammy thinks I should.' Edie looked as if a burden had been lifted off her back. 'By the way, he says he's got some new mixture for killing cabbage whites, and he'll give you the recipe the next time he sees you.'

He squeezed her fingers in his own roughened ones. 'Well, then, you'd better see he comes and does it quick, before it gets too warm and we have the blighters eating all the leaves. If you think you could bear to invite him here a second time?'

Was it her delighted laughter that gave his heart a twinge? Or was it the result of that confounded cough again?

'What do you mean, you want to have a proper talk with me?' Alicia demanded, staring at Edith in the looking-glass, and breathing in while the maid did up the laces of her stays. 'Aren't we talking now?'

Edith's reflection wouldn't meet her eyes. 'This is something serious. It isn't just a chat.'

Not something to be talked about when her mistress was half-undressed, she meant. Alicia felt her heart sink. This did not bode well. She remembered two servants asking for an audience like this, when Father was alive: one to hand his notice in and the other asking politely for a rise. Which of these alternatives, she wondered, did Edith have in mind? She felt a lump of helpless dismay rising in her throat. Either way, it would be difficult, with that treacherous Fanny having run away: she simply could not manage without a maid at all, and Edwin would never agree to any more expenditure – he was already scornful and superior over the last débâcle. His response had been so scathing that it still made her blush – though no one else would read the letter, she had put it in the fire – and yesterday's letter had been even worse: a pained assurance that he'd spent a night of prayer and was ready to forgive her 'arrant foolishness', and promising that he would come down soon and 'take control of things'.

And – she had to face it – he had reason, too. He had been dispiritingly right, and she had been utterly and embarrassingly wrong. But she would not give way to the tears that stung her eyes, not in front of the servants. What would Edwin say to that?

Edith was still looking at her in that nervous way, with her mouth half-open, rather like a fish. Alicia mastered her voice enough to murmur, 'Very well, I'll see you in the drawing-room downstairs. Give me a moment to finish getting dressed. I can manage on my own. In the mean-

170

time, take the breakfast tray downstairs.'

'Yes, Miss Alicia.' And Edith trotted off.

It would have been easy to give way to weeping then, but one couldn't take the interview if one had reddened eyes. Alicia looked at her reflection in the glass. She appeared strained and dishevelled. She sat severely upright and pulled her shoulders back – breathing hard until she felt more like her normal self.

For she had not been her normal self these last few days. She'd been reluctant to get out of bed, and had resorted to having breakfast brought up to her room. She'd cancelled all appointments with the Women's Movement, too – written to Miss Richie to say she wasn't well – though of course she hadn't told her what the trouble was. Well, now she'd have to make an effort. She stood up and carefully pulled on her grey half-mourning dress – it seemed appropriate to her mood today – pinned her hair into a twist, and went down to the drawing-room to face the interview.

Edith was waiting for her, looking anxious and upset. Alicia raised her chin and took the upper hand at once. 'Now, Edith, what's this all about? Are you not satisfied with your conditions here? Or have you come to tell me that you wish to leave?'

The girl was clearly startled. 'Thinking to leave you, Miss Alicia? Well, of course I aren't. Whatever put such an idea like that into your head?' She turned a brilliant red. ''Course, I aren't saying that I mightn't give my notice, by and by, if I was planning to get married, or anything like that.'

'And are you?' Liss gave an inward sigh. Another of Edwin's warnings which she had ignored. He'd been quite firm about it, the last time he was down, telling her that she was far too lax with staff – allowing the girl to loiter in the chicken shed with that young whipper-snapper of a gardener's boy. He'd seen them through the study window, he declared. And it seemed that he was right. Heaven knew what the pair of them would live on, if that was the case.

Edith's face was a rather guilty red. 'I dunno where you heard that, Miss Alicia.' Obviously true then! But she hurried on. 'Maybe one day – but this isn't about me. This is about Fanny. Something you should know.'

Alicia closed her eyes. She had just allowed herself to feel relieved, and suddenly there were new revelations to be faced. 'What is it now? You've discovered something else? She's made off with something which we haven't missed?' The thought of Edwin's anger made her feel positively ill.

'No, 'course she hasn't!' The girl was so roused that she was quite impertinent. At any other time she would have risked a stern rebuke. But she was already adding, 'She hasn't taken anything at all that I can see. Not even her own belongings, most of them. Though she must have took her half-crowns with her when she went. She kept them separate in a little tin box underneath her bed – she was saving up for something, and she showed it to me once – but I went just now and looked, and it wasn't there no

172

more. But see what I found up there, in among her things.' She reached into the pocket of her apron and brought out an old sock which she emptied out on to the table with a clink: a shower of coppers and silver sixpences. 'Nine and sixpence, near enough ten bob. Almost three weeks' wages – you see what that must mean?'

Alicia frowned. 'You mean she saw that fellow coming – through the front window perhaps – so she ran up and only had time to seize the tin and flee? Well, of course, she panicked when she saw him, that's why she ran away. There's nothing new in that.' Alicia sank listlessly into a fireside chair, though the fire was not alight. In fact, she noticed, it had not been set – indeed, although it was almost ten o'clock, the hearth had not been swept. Another example of the fix that Fanny had left them in. 'Who would imagine that a girl would tell such lies,' she muttered bitterly, 'or flout her own father in that brazen way?' She was aware of a tell-tale tremor in her voice. 'She seemed a pleasant girl. How could I have so misjudged her character?'

'That's just it, Miss Alicia. I don't know that you did.' Edith knelt down on the floor in front of her mistress and looked into her face. For two pins, Alicia thought, the girl would pat her hand – and for once it might have been quite comforting. 'Fanny was very happy here,' the maid went on. 'She didn't want to leave. And leaving nine and sixpence! She wouldn't have done that. Must have been something terrible that made her run away.'

'Going back to help her family. We know what

it was.'

'Doesn't sound very likely, does it, when you come to think? Fanny was a worker, that wouldn't worry her. No, it was more than that. I think she's in danger. She was proper terrified of being found, you know. She told me that she had a relative who was a threat to her – and she was always frightened that he'd come after her. Remember how alarmed she got when she first turned up here, and you offered to look in the newspaper for a job for her? Perhaps she was afeared that if a post was advertised, it would be too easy to track down her address.'

Alicia nodded slowly. She did remember that. And one did hear sometimes of dreadful cruelty, people beating their children and that sort of thing. She said, reluctantly, 'But if he is her father he has a right to know. It isn't even as if the girl were twenty-one.'

Edith was looking up into her face. 'But supposing that it was not her father after all? If it was, why did he wait so long? Fanny'd already been here months and months.'

'Perhaps he'd only just discovered where she was,' Alicia said. She stood up sharply and walked around the room. What the girl was saying did make a kind of sense.

'Then why didn't he get the police to look for her before?' Edith had followed her to the window as she spoke. 'If he found her so easy, you'd think the police force might.'

Alicia turned to face her. 'Perhaps it was the police that she was trying to escape. We don't know that she's not a criminal.'

'Can't be that, Miss Alicia. We know that when she first came to Penzance, she went to find her aunt – we know that for certain, because I went to check. She only came here when she found the woman gone. That would be the first place that the police would look – so she wouldn't have gone there if she was on the run. Besides, I told the neighbours who I was and where I worked – I thought they'd talk to me more readily if they recognized your name – so they knew where she'd gone, and they'd have told the police. But there's been no one asking questions on the doorstep here, like they would have done for certain if the law was after her.'

Alicia nodded. She hadn't thought of all this, but it was obviously true. Edith was cleverer than you might have thought. It made one view her with a new respect. 'And then suddenly Mr Rouse came down all this way himself?'

'And there's another thing. Where are all these children that the Rouse man claims to have – he didn't bring them with him. So what's become of them? Yet he says he needs her to look after them.'

'You know,' Alicia said slowly, 'it is possible you're right. It is all a bit peculiar when you think of it that way. But why would he claim to be her father if he's not?'

'To get his hands on her. I dunno why exactly – but that's what she seemed to think.'

'But how could he expect to get away with it?'

'His word against hers, it would be, wouldn't it?' Edith replied. 'No one knows the pair of them down 'ere, except that aunt, and even she

175

has gone. And if it was Fanny and her so-called father, who would folk believe? It's like they say in those Suff'ring magazines – the woman's voice don't count. But of the two, I'm more inclined to trust what Fanny said. And we know he's after her, so if she was in danger then, I suppose she will be now. Though as to where she's got to, that's a mystery.'

'Yes,' Alicia said slowly. 'Clearly there is something very wrong in all of this. Fanny may be under threat, as you so rightly say. And we can't help her if we don't know where she is.' She was suddenly filled with interest and resolve. She would set out to find Fanny – before that fellow did. If there really was a legitimate reason for the girl to run away, it would give her some ammunition against Edwin, too. Though of course he wouldn't approve of her investigating this. She smiled. That was quite a reason for doing it, in fact. Suddenly the world seemed purposeful again.

She turned back to the maid. 'You know, Edith, this talk has done me good. You can lay and light this fire while I go and see Mama, and then you can bring me a pot of tea in here. I'm going to write a letter, so fetch your hat and coat because I'll want you to deliver it to Miss Richie when I've finished it.'

Beth was a person of action and ideas. Who else, after all, could she have asked for help?

Tim Tulver walked past the gate of Holvean House three times. He would not call. He wouldn't. Miss Killivant had humiliated him

176

quite enough. After all, he'd made his feelings clear, invited her to that recital at considerable expense, and she had snubbed him quite deliberately.

What a fool he'd been to turn up at that hall – lots of dreadful women in even more dreadful hats, listening to impassioned speeches about crackpot ideas – only to find that Alicia hadn't come. Just as well he'd given Mother and her friend the seats in the Town Hall, pleading a headache on his own account, so she didn't have the least idea that he'd been out at all. He had not even been able to beat a fast retreat, because while he was looking for Alicia in the crowd, a frightful, earnest young female had come and seized his arm.

'Looking for someone?'

And when he had been foolish enough to confess that he'd been invited by Alicia Killivant, she'd said briskly, 'Oh, then you must be Mr Tulver. This way then,' and borne him off in triumph to a seat in front. The two of them had obviously conspired to make a fool of him. He sat through the meeting. Alicia didn't come and there was no escape. He slunk off afterwards, feeling bitter and betrayed and swearing he would never seek Miss Killivant's company again. He went straight home and lay down in a darkened room, and when Mother came home a little later on, he was glad of the headache – a real one by now – so he didn't have to listen to her enthusiastic praise of the violinist and the concert he had missed.

What's more, since then he'd had to endure

constant well-meant enquiries about his health, and daily doses of iron tonic – which he loathed. A lot of people had a cold, his mother said.

Perhaps it was that which had made him wonder about Alicia, when she did not come as usual to collect the money from the trust. Had he been too hasty? Suppose she was unwell? Perhaps she had not intended to snub him, after all. Could he decently go up and ring the bell? He could enquire after her, perhaps, explaining that he had found himself in the area, and was concerned that she had not called in at the bank.

But suppose she was simply anxious to avoid his company? He might be snubbed again. She might send down to say that she was not at home. Or she might send a message that she was indisposed – and he wouldn't know if that was true or not. He was still havering in the gateway when a hansom cab drew up, and a young woman in a feathered hat came clambering out of it.

She had to walk past him to get into the house, and she glanced towards him with curiosity. She was plump and pleasant-looking, though she had enormous teeth, which she was baring at him in a cheerful grin.

'Looking for someone?' she enquired.

Surely he'd heard that voice before – speaking those very words? He looked at her more closely. Yes, surely it was the female from the meeting hall the other day?

She, it seemed, had recognized him too. 'Why it's Mr Tulver! Are you calling at the house?' Thus challenged, he was lost for a reply. But it didn't matter, because she went on at once, 'I'm so glad that Alicia is feeling better now. We have quite missed her at our meetings. But now she's asked for me. Has she written to ask you to call this afternoon as well?'

She was striding up the path towards the front door as she spoke, and he found himself accompanying her without quite meaning to. But her words had been balm to his humiliated soul. Alicia had not slighted him – she'd simply been unwell.

'I am here on private business,' he said, with conscious pride. He was very glad that he had come this afternoon.

The young woman seized the bell-pull and rang it vigorously, saying as she did so, 'So you are helping, too? Well, let's hope we can find her. I know Alicia's worried, but it's quite thrilling, isn't it?' And before he had time to respond to these mystifying words, Edith had the door open and was ushering them inside.

Two

Alicia Killivant was waiting in the drawing-room, and looked quite startled when she saw Tim come in. She came to greet the woman with her hands outstretched. 'Beth, it is so good of you to come.' Then she turned to him and added, in a civil but distinctly different tone, 'And Mr Tulver! You are here as well! I'm afraid I'm not available for a little while. As you see, I am receiving company just now.'

The other girl gave her cheerful, toothy smile. 'Oh, do not dimiss poor Mr Tulver on my account, Alicia. We came in together. I met him at the gate – although I confess I did not recognize him at first. He was ready to withdraw when he saw that I'd arrived, but I urged him to come in, since of course I know he is a friend of yours and naturally I thought you'd want his help with this.' She laughed. 'Two heads are better than one, they always say, and three are likely to be better still. In fact, I rather fancied that you might have sent for him.'

Alicia was frowning. 'Not at all. Mr Tulver deals with my bank affairs, that's all. I certainly was not expecting him today. But do I understand you are acquainted with Miss Richie, Mr Tulver?'

That was his cue. He said, with dignity, 'We met at the Women's Rally at the hall on Friday night. Perhaps you have forgotten, Miss Killivant, that you suggested that I went?'

Alicia clasped a startled hand to the jabot at her neck, and darted an embarrassed glance towards her friend.

Miss Richie nodded. 'That's right, Alicia. He was enquiring for you – and, as you might expect, I introduced myself to him. And then, of course, you were sadly indisposed and were not able to attend yourself.' She looked archly at them both. 'How disappointing, after the poor man had come to our support.'

Alicia was clearly mortified. 'Of course! I'm sorry, Mr Tulver – Timothy – I did not intend to be discourteous. I'm afraid I'd quite forgotten that I'd half-invited you.'

It was an apology, but Tim still felt aggrieved. He was of such small account that he had simply been forgotten, it appeared. However, it might be forgiven if one were indeed 'indisposed'. He forced a smile. 'I am sorry, Alicia, to hear that you have not been well. It had occurred to me that something might be wrong, since not only were you not at the rally as you hoped, but we have not seen you at the bank this week to claim your monthly money from the trust. I was naturally concerned, and came today on purpose to enquire after you. But now that I am assured that you are in good health, and I see that you have private business with your visitor, I will not intrude upon your patience any more.'

He turned to take his leave, but Alicia called

him back. 'Mr Tulver, I intended no offence. It was kind of you, to call. I regret that I was sharp. The truth is, I had supposed that my brother sent you here – since presumably I can no longer draw money from the trust.'

It was his turn to be startled. 'Why not? What has happened? Is there something wrong? I have heard nothing from Edwin to suggest a change.'

'So you're not aware of what has happened, then?' Alicia looked towards her friend, as if to seek advice.

Miss Richie said slowly, 'I think that he should know. Better that he hears your version of events. And the more people who are looking out for her the better, I suppose. I gather from your note that there may be danger for the girl.'

Alicia still looked doubtful. Tim could bear no more. 'Girl?' he repeated, and then inspiration dawned. 'Do you mean that housemaid ... Fanny, is she called?'

Alicia nodded. 'She was called Fanny in this household, certainly,' she said, with a decided note of wryness in her voice. 'Whatever her name is, she has–' she hesitated for moment '–unexpectedly left my employ.'

So there had been some trouble with the girl. That unfortunate, and no doubt Edwin Killivant would hold him to account, since he had been instrumental in agreeing her appointment. At their next encounter he could expect stern words. But there was a still more important aspect of the whole affair. 'So you will not be calling on the trust again?' He could not keep the note of disappointment from his voice. This would be the end of Alicia's visits to the bank – just when he was hoping that they might be friends. He had another inspiration. 'Although surely you owe Fanny two weeks in arrears?'

Alicia was saying, with a defeated air, 'That's quite true, Timothy, but...' when the other girl broke in.

'If you find her, Alicia, it would only be her due. And if she is in some danger – as your note implies – then a little money might be vital for her, don't you think? It may not be safe for her to come back here, but at least she could buy her fare to somewhere else.'

'You keep mentioning "danger",' Tim muttered in surprise, but the two women were too busy with their own discussion to notice what he said. Alicia was shaking her lovely auburn head, and murmuring to Miss Richie, 'But there's no guarantee that we can find her anyway.'

'Then you can spend the money on the search for her. And there will be expenses, if you really mean to look – if it's only sending Edith out to make enquiries. Expenses that you will somehow have to meet, as I have no doubt that your brother will demand a full account of every farthing that he provides towards expenditure. But he has not countermanded this agreement with the trust. He may do, very soon, of course.' She seemed to notice that Timothy was listening carefully, and she went on, with a little sideways look at him, 'But in the meantime Mr Tulver would be acting properly if he continued to honour the arrangement, as far as I can see.'

Tim heard himself emit a doubtful little noise.

He was getting hot and bothered at the tone of this. Was she suggesting that he broke the rules?

Beth Richie gave him a special knowing smile. 'In fact, I can't see how the bank trustee could well do otherwise. Didn't you tell me once that any change required both signatures? If Edwin has overlooked it, that is his affair.'

'Unless someone writes and tells him,' Alicia remarked, clearly meaning that the 'someone' might be Tim himself.

Miss Richie laughed. 'I'm sure Mr Tulver would be entirely discreet. He's clearly a person of independent thought – otherwise he would not have come to hear the suffragists. Am I not right, Mr Tulver?' And he would have sworn she winked!

He found that he was blushing. 'I'm not sure that I can...'

'You are too modest, Mr Tulver. Of course it's in your power. Did you not say yourself that you had come here to find out why there had been no claim this week? Would you have stopped Alicia drawing it if she had come into the bank? And it is her money, when she comes of age.'

He was about to say something stuffy to the general effect that he could not allow her to access it at will, when Alicia spoke again.

'It is only a few shillings,' she murmured doubtfully. 'And doubtless Edwin will put a stop to even that quite soon. But this month's is already partly for payment in arrears. I suppose one could argue that I was entitled to claim that.' She gave him the little smile that always made his heart turn uncomfortable cartwheels in his chest. 'But I bow to your superior judgement, Timothy, of course.'

It gave him a feeling of importance, suddenly. 'Well, the money was specifically for Fanny, I suppose. And it is overdue. So as long as it is on Fanny that it will be spent...' he said, with what he hoped was a judicial air.

'Alicia wants to find her, to pay her what is owed. Not even Mr Edwin could object to that,' Miss Richie urged. 'And the poor girl may be in some kind of danger too – at least the other maidservant appears to think she is...' She broke off as Alicia shook a warning head, and added teasingly, 'Though perhaps it's best if that is all you know – then no one can accuse you of complicity.' She smiled. 'Thank you, Mr Tulver. You are very good.'

And, somehow, he seemed to have agreed to it. Until Mr Edwin countermanded his instructions, naturally

Strangely, though, he did not feel abashed. On the contrary. He was feeling two feet taller as he left the room, and when he heard Miss Richie saying, as he shut the door, 'What a pleasant man Mr Tulver is. So obviously sensible and helpful and discreet. I knew at once that we could rely on him,' he seemed to float on air: it was a wonder that he didn't knock his head against the chandelier. Two pretty women paying compliments and seeking his support. What would Mater have said, he wondered, if she could have heard?

Not that he was going to tell her, naturally. As

185

Miss Richie had rightly observed, Timothy Tulver knew how to be discreet.

Alicia waited till she heard the front door close, then turned to her companion. 'Beth, you are a wicked tease! He must have overheard.'

Beth gave a knowing grin. 'Well, of course, I intended that he should. The poor little fellow is clearly terrified – but equally clearly he'd do anything for you. Don't look so modest, of course that's how he feels. Why did he come to the meeting otherwise? He's not the sort of person to be sympathetic to the cause, or avid to listen to the speakers. You could tell that on the night. He looked as if he was in purgatory – but I'd put him in the front row and he couldn't get away. Of course, I thought you'd come and rescue him by sitting next to him.' Her eyes were dancing, and she was clearly trying not to laugh.

'Poor Mr Tulver...!' Alicia began, but it was no good. The mental picture was so comical – Mr Tulver, all pomposity, forced to sit and endure boredom among the feathered hats – that it came out as a titter. She caught Beth's eye and that only made it worse. In a moment the pair of them were giggling helplessly, and both of them had to sit down on the chairs and dab their streaming eyes. Most unladylike – especially as Edith chose that moment to come in.

'Excuse me, Miss Alicia, but were you wanting tea?'

With an enormous effort, Liss willed herself to stop, and managed to control herself sufficiently to say, 'Yes, please, Edith, and some buttered

186

toast.' She struggled to quell the tell-tale tremor in her voice.

When the maid had gone she turned to Beth again. 'Poor Mr Tulver. It really isn't fair. He can't help being pompous and he tries so hard to please.'

Beth Richie looked at her with a peculiar smile. 'You shouldn't be unkind to him. He is clearly smitten. I think he's rather sweet. And he's promised to help us – by default at least. Though I'm not quite sure what you intend that we should do.'

Alicia nodded. She was more sober now. 'I'm not quite sure myself. And it's no laughing matter, if Edith is correct. I thought at first that Fanny had simply run away because her father came to find her – and that is naturally what Edwin thinks, and what he blames me for – but Edith has persuaded me that there might be more to it than that.' She outlined the whole story to Elizabeth. 'What do you think, Beth?'

Her friend surprised her. 'I'll do what I can, of course, and very willingly. But I think that you should get your little maid to help. For one thing, she can ask around more easily than us – talk to servants and that sort of thing and go to places that we couldn't go ourselves. And secondly – as you say yourself – she was the one who spotted that something was amiss: she made all the arguments which you've just made to me – which shows she's got a clever brain and sees things logically.' She was leaning forward in the chair and speaking earnestly. 'Pity to waste that, when we're engaged on such a task.'

'You don't mean that you think she's more intelligent than we are?' Alicia was quite affronted.

Beth sat back and laughed. 'Of course not. Though she may be just as quick – only she doesn't have the education that we have had, of course. But perhaps that is the point. She understands the problems of people of her class, better than you and I would – so she's more likely to think of where to look for Fanny Watts. Besides, if it proves that all the fears are wrong – and Fanny isn't really under threat – there's no additional embarrassment for you.'

Alicia found that she was nodding doubtfully. 'I suppose there is a certain truth in what you say. So you propose that I shouldn't be drawn in, but let Edith do the looking? I suppose you're right.' Edwin would have thought so, she reflected bitterly. 'A pity, I had been rather looking forward to it.'

Beth Richie laughed again. 'But of course I'm not suggesting that you shouldn't be involved – merely that it is better to attack this matter in two ways, and some things are better done by servants, that is all. You and I can do the more genteel things – go and ask the police, for instance, if anyone of Fanny's description has been found: and make discreet enquiries of the households that we know to see if anyone has taken on a maid of late.'

'I don't know any households.' Alicia was glum. 'Respectable or otherwise.' She forced a rueful grin.

'Well, I promised that I'd help you,' Beth said

cheerfully. 'And there are all the women at the Movement, for a start. You would be surprised how wide the network spreads. And,' she leaned forward with an excited air, 'if we reach a dead end locally, we could take a trip.'

'Leave Penzance? I couldn't possibly. How could I leave Mother in her state of health?'

'You are not much help to her when you are ill yourself, and everybody knows that you have been unwell of late. Supposing I invited you to go to Launceston – say – as my companion, for a day or two? I'm sure the nurse could cope for that long on her own, and a change of air would be very good for you.'

'The area that Fanny claimed to come from?' Alicia thought a moment. 'But what would Mother say?'

'She wouldn't say anything, I shouldn't think. She doesn't seem to object to your doing as you please: working on brochures at the Movement headquarters half the day, or even going to the evening meetings in the hall.'

Alicia flushed. 'That is probably because she doesn't know. I only mention that I'm going out with a friend. I don't tell her where and she doesn't think to ask. Mother is not interested in much besides her health. I imagine she supposes that I am pleasure-bent.'

'Exactly. And this little jaunt would be the same. And in fact we may not need to go at all. What could be more natural than that we two should make plans, and ask Edith to go up there and look for rooms for us?'

'But...' Alicia said helplessly, 'how could I do

189

that? I haven't any money, and Edwin would never consent to funding such a thing.' And, she thought, with utter helplessness, how would I manage without a maid at all?

Beth gave her toothy grin. 'But of course you have money, you told me so yourself. Four weeks' worth of Fanny's wages are waiting in the bank. What would that add up to? Twelve or fifteen shillings, I suppose? I could put up a similar amount. It isn't a great deal, I am well aware, but it would buy a ticket on the train and pay a few days' rent. You can dock it from her wages if we find her anywhere.'

It did seem feasible, when it was put like that. Alicia shook her head. 'And what about *your* mother? Whatever would she say?'

Beth laughed. 'I told her you'd been ill. If you need a companion for a day or two I don't think she'd object. Especially if we call in on the local suffragists – she's rather in favour of the Movement for the vo—' She broke off as Edith came into the room. 'Ah, and here is the very girl we want.'

Alicia nodded and took a long, slow breath. She found that she was uttering words she never thought she'd say: 'Put the tray down, Edith, and find yourself a chair.' This would have given Edwin an apoplectic fit. Edith was looking pretty scandalized herself. Alicia gave the girl a sympathetic smile. 'Don't worry, Edith, it's perfectly all right. Miss Richie's in agreement. Take a seat. We want to talk to you.'

Edith put the tray down. She could not believe

sort of thinking that we were hoping for. So where would you have walked to, Edith, in her place?'

Edith shook her head. 'Somewhere the opposite of where he'd think to look. Not on the main roads, where somebody could see – one of the field-paths, perhaps, towards Penvarris way. Or the opposite direction – towards Madron and St Ives. Anywhere that took me off the roads and lanes.'

She paused. The two ladies were hanging on her every word. It made her feel important and she racked her brains – and came up with a thought. 'Of course, she wasn't from round here, so she wouldn't know the paths. Take the first one that she came to – that's what I'd have done. Might even have got herself into a room somewhere – just for a night or two. Plenty of places take in people at this time of year. That awful man couldn't check up on them all – even if the same idea occurred to him, though I'd keep away from the station area. Find somewhere with a notice in the window, and go in, ask – and, hey presto, there's your hiding place. She did have a little bit of money, didn't she? That would keep her off the streets and give her time to think. That's what I'd have thought of doing, if I'd been in her shoes.'

She looked up. Miss Alicia was smiling approvingly at her. 'Well done, Edith. That is very good. You have given us a place to start at any rate. The first thing, I think, is to go back to the aunt's – see if anyone knows anything out there. You can go there tomorrow – I'll tell Mrs Pritch-

195

ard that I've sent you out. And, if I should want you to travel somewhere else – Miss Richie has suggested that we take a trip – I assume your family would not object to that?'

Edith stared. 'Me? Go on a journey?' She did not know what to say. No one in her family had ever been further than St Ives – though it was rumoured that Nana's father had been to Truro once.

'It would not be for very long. Just up the county for a day or two. And of course, it isn't certain yet.'

'If you want me to go with you, Miss Alicia, I'm sure they will agree.' She wanted to pinch herself to check she was awake. She'd heard of servants going to far-off places with their employers, naturally – but she'd never thought that anyone would pay for her to go. The idea was so exciting that she wriggled on the stool.

'Splendid, Edith. Then you may serve the tea.'

Three

It was threatening rain next morning when Edith set out on the bus to revisit the place where Fanny's aunt had lived, but no amount of heavy cloud could dim her mood today. It was an adventure, that was what it was. She felt like that Sherlock person she'd heard of in a book: trying to work out what had happened to her friend, and asking questions of the neighbours without them suspecting anything.

Mind, that was not as easy as she thought that it would be. The aunt's old cottage was an isolated one – even the nearest neighbours were out of sight around a bend. The last time Edie had been sent here to enquire, she had simply gone up to the nearest door and knocked, and the woman who answered had been as helpful as could be – told her about the sister dying and Mrs Polcurnooth going to Australia – and had even invited her inside for a glass of strangely bitter home-made lemonade.

So Edith was expecting much the same again. She went straight up to the house – the same tumbledown cottage on the corner of a row, just around the corner from where Fanny's aunt had lived. Not that she was expecting lemonade again, but it seemed a friendly place to start. But as soon as she opened the squealing gate and walked along the path she realized that something was very different. There was a twitching of the upstairs curtains and the window slammed.

She wondered for a moment if she'd come to the right place. Yes, this was certainly the house. It was the right door – she recognized the brighter patches on the faded dark green paint where someone had touched up the blisters which the sun had made – and clearly the same woman was still living here. There was the same brightly coloured rag-bag of mending on the seat inside the porch and the much-worn pair of button-boots placed neatly under it. Smoke was coming from the chimney, too, and there was a smell of baking in the air – but though she hammered on the door until her knuckles hurt, this time no one came to answer it.

She waited for several minutes but there was no reply, and in the end there was nothing for it but to turn and leave. As she was walking uncertainly down to the gate again, idly thinking how Sam would have admired the garden-beds – daffodils and wallflowers in a bold display, interspersed with overwintered onion sets, broad beans and cabbages – she was sure she glimpsed another movement, in the downstairs window now. But when she turned to look, whoever it was had disappeared again and the curtain had been firmly drawn across. There could be no mistake. This was deliberate.

Could it have been Fanny hiding? she wondered, stupidly. But of course it wasn't. The shape at the window had been much too tall and wide. Somebody older, in a cap and pinafore. It looked like the woman she had spoken to last time.

She frowned. This adventure had turned a little sour. The person in the house had obviously seen that she had come, and – presumably – remembered who she was. The woman couldn't spend her life avoiding everyone who called. Yet she'd been so pleasant last time. What had brought about this change? Something must have happened. It didn't take Sherlock to work that out, she thought.

She toyed with the idea of going back up the path, but reason told her it would do no good. So instead she walked along the lane and found the house which used to be the aunt's. It wasn't promising. A glance at the chimney showed that the fires were out, and when she climbed the stone steps up to the upper floor and peered through the dusty glass set in the door – she could see right down the hall into a tiny kitchen area at the rear – the place was clean and tidy but there was no sign of life. She was not surprised to get no answer to her knock.

Bother! There was nothing for it but to go further down the lane, and try to find another house where somebody might help. She was standing hesitating on the topmost step, wondering how far she would have to walk, when a gruff voice from below her made her gasp aloud.

'What you after, missie? Can't you see there's no one in?' An old man in a battered hat was standing by the hedge.

Edith was so startled that she didn't answer

him, simply picked up her skirts and hurried down the granite steps as quickly as she could.

He moved to block her way, and for the first time Edie got a proper look at him. His torn coat and trousers were tied around with string. One of his sleeves was sewn up at the wrist, where his hand was missing, though he seemed to manage well enough: there was a sort of four-pronged pitchfork, the sort that Sammy called an 'eval', in the remaining hand. With his thin hair sprouting in a fringe around his head, and his feet encased in heavy, muddy boots, he looked like the scarecrows you saw out in the fields, except for the piercing eyes and lined, weather-beaten face.

'Well?' he insisted, 'You going to tell me or have piskies got your tongue? What you doing on my property?'

So he was the one who lived here. He must have been working round the side when she came in. He looked so threatening with the pitchfork in his hand that she could hardly speak, but in the end she managed to stammer out, 'There was a lady used to live here' – she searched her memory – 'a Mrs Polcurnooth, or something of the kind...'

He had the four-pronged eval levelled at her now, as though he meant to toss her like a stook of hay. 'Well, what about it? And what is it to you? It don't sound as if you knew 'er very well.'

'She was aunt to my friend Fanny, but now she's gone away – Fanny, that is – and I've lost touch with her. I wondered if anyone might know where she had gone. The aunt, I'm talking about now.' It wasn't a very clear account, but it would have to do.

The man was frowning. 'I don't know what your game is, my maid, but you don't make a fool of me. I told that man who came round 'ere before, I don't knaw nothing about the woman that was 'ere. I rent this cottage from the mine-owners, that is all I knaw. I used to work down there, one time, afore I lost my hand – and I suppose she must've rented from them too. You want any information, I suggest you go down their office in Penzance and ask, instead of coming up 'ere pestering decent folk.'

'The man who came before?' she repeated foolishly. 'Someone's been here asking?'

He nodded. 'I should think they 'ave. I'm big enough and ugly enough to stand up for meself – one-handed or not – and I soon sent him packing with a whole earful of fleas. But that poor woman in the terrace there was in a proper state when he went there banging on her door, shouting and swearing and making such a fuss. 'Tisn't her fault if she doesn't know where Mrs Pol-thingummy went. And when you see him, tell him so from me. I suppose he sent you, since you're nosing round again.'

Edie shook her head. 'No, he jolly didn't – if he's the man I think you mean. Stout man with a beard? A horrid sort of fellow with red veins around his nose – wearing a bowler hat and a coat a size too small?'

'And too free with his great boot stuck in people's doors, so they can't get rid of him?' The

201

old man nodded. 'That's the very one. 'Ad to threaten to call the police, I did, to make him go away and leave the poor old widow in a bit of peace. So you knaw 'im, do 'ee? Thought you must 'ave done. Though it don't sound as if you are so fond of him yourself.'

He'd lowered the eval and looked quite kindly now – so why did she find herself perversely close to tears?

Perhaps it was the kindliness which prompted her to say, 'Came ranting at the house in town where I work as a maid. Looking for that Fanny that I mentioned earlier. Said he was her pa – but I don't believe a word. Why would he wait so long to come here for her, else? Think it would be the first place he'd come looking, wouldn't you?'

The old man shook his head. 'Wasn't a Fanny he was asking for, when he came round here. Some other name he mentioned – Annie, Ellie – something of the sort.'

'Nellie?' Edie ventured.

'Can't remember now. But she was supposed to be this Mrs What-d'you-call-it's niece. Well, one thing I could tell him, there was no girl living here. But 'e wasn't giving up. Seemed to think the widow woman might know where she had gone. Didn't want to tell him, she told me afterwards, because she didn't trust him further than she could throw a stick, but she did knaw something: and he went on and on at such a rate – bawling and 'ollering with his foot stuck in the door – he frightened her to death. Seems he bullied it out of her at last.'

Edith winced. 'So that was how he found out where to come and look! And it was my fault, too. I came here once before to try to find the aunt, and told that woman then that I'd been sent to ask questions on the Killivants' behalf. Just like I am today. Only this time the woman would not even answer when I knocked.'

'Been afraid of her soul of answering the door to strangers ever since,' the man replied. 'Nice woman, she is, too. Only wish I gone round earlier – but I didn't knaw her to speak to, till that day, you see. Not a one for neighbours as a general rule – don't care for comp'ny since I lost my wife, and it keeps me busy growing what I eat, and a little bit extra that I take around to sell. But that afternoon there was such an awful row – you could hear 'im blinding and hollering from here. Wondered if I ought to go round earlier – only you don't like to interfere – but his language was getting something terrible and in the end I went.' He smiled, showing a row of snaggled teeth. 'She turned out very grateful, and I'm glad I did. She's started coming now and then to give the place a clean. I give her a few vegetables and she makes me a pie.'

Edith was impatient of these hints of elderly romance. 'Well, I won't keep you talking. You've got work to do. And so have I. Have to find out where Fanny has got to, if I can, before that dreadful man catches up with her. So, thank you for your help. You've given me something to start with anyway – the mine-office in Penzance. I'm sorry that Mr Rouse – or whatever his proper name is – came out asking and bullying your friend. I'm not surprised that she was terrified. I've never been so scared of anyone in all my life.' She met his eyes and added, candidly, 'Not until you came here with that fork at any rate.'

That made him laugh aloud. 'Well, you won't be afeared of me another time, my maid. Old Tommy's never used a fork in anger except for lifting soil. And I'd best get back to it. Going to plant some carrots for next winter's store.'

'Double-digging to a tilth, and adding a bit of seaweed to the drill?' Edie said, and when he looked surprised, she added proudly, 'My young man's a gardener.' The widow woman was not the only one with a romance! She smiled. 'Well, goodbye, Mr...?'

'Hoskins. Tommy 'Oskins.' He put down the eval, spat on his good hand and wiped it on his trousers before he offered it.

But she didn't take it. She was too surprised. 'Tommy Hoskins? From the carpenter's shop down at Penvarris mine? I'm sure I've heard my father speak of you. His name is Edward Trewin. Have you 'eard of him?'

He pushed his hat back with an eval prong. 'Well, I'm damded! Teddy Trewin's maid? How didn't you say so to begin with, then? 'Course I know Teddy. How's that cough of his?'

She only wished that she could give him better news.

He heard her out and then the old face wrinkled into a thoughtful frown. 'Well, perhaps there's something else that I can help you with, my maid. Your friend Fanny now. You say you don't believe this fellow that came here is her pa. Well, I can't swear to anything, but I think you might be right. Up to no good, he was, as far as I can see. I only had to mention policemen and he turned a different man – all oily and smiling and anxious to be gone. And – from something that he said – though I don't knaw for certain-sure, I shouldn't wonder if that Mrs Pol-what's-her-name is dead.'

She stared at him. 'You don't think he killed her?' This was too much like Sherlock to be comfortable.

He gave a little laugh. 'No, 'course I aren't saying anything like that. Wouldn't have been so careless if he was a murderer. But he did say something about "when she was alive" – then tried to pretend he meant to say "when she was living 'ere". But 'tisn't the same thing – as any fool can see. If your Miss Killi-what's-it wants to come and talk to me, I'll tell her the same. And if I should hear anything 'bout where that Fanny might have gone, I'll be sure and let you know. Seeing as 'ow it turns out you're Teddy Trewin's maid.'

Edith could hardly wait to get home and tell Miss Alicia. But Miss Killivant had news for her as well.

It had been a tiring and interesting day. Miss Richie had called in early on – before eleven o'clock – when Edith, dependent on the horse-bus, had already left. So it had fallen to Mrs Pritchard to let the caller in and bring up a tray of tea and buttered toast. Beth was in an excited frame of mind: her greeting to Alicia was very warm but brisk, and it was clear that she could hardly wait for Cook to leave the room.

'Now,' she said, almost before the door had closed again, 'I have been thinking. If we are to find Fanny, we need a proper plan.' She reached into her reticule and produced a little tasselled notebook, with a special little pencil fitted down the spine. She took that out and tapped her lips with it. 'I've made a start for you. I've already been to headquarters' – she meant the suffragists – 'and made a list of the supporters of the cause who might have taken on new servants recently. I thought that you and I might call on them.' She opened the notebook to reveal a page of closely written names.

Alicia blanched. 'But almost everyone keeps staff! One cannot simply go round asking every house in town.'

'I have thought of that. I asked the ladies who were addressing envelopes, and the names with stars beside them are the wealthier ones. There are only six of those. Fanny would be likely to try a bigger house – so as not to draw attention to herself. I know that you employed her as a housemaid, but without a written character she couldn't count on that. She would be more likely to apply as something like a pot-girl or a scullery-hand. Or, if the house was big enough, she might have found a post helping in the laundry or the dairy, I suppose.' She tore the page carefully along the edge and handed it to Liss. 'You could start with those.'

Alicia stared blankly at the list of names. 'But

I don't know these people. We cannot simply call.'

Her friend gave her a gleeful, sideways glance. 'I thought of that as well. I've found you a reason to visit the addresses. You can deliver these.' She reached into her reticule again and produced half a dozen envelopes. 'The latest copy of the circular. Not only does it give you an excuse to ring the bell, it saves headquarters the cost of postage stamps.' She beamed, clearly delighted at her own enterprise.

Alicia sighed. This was in danger of getting out of hand. 'We had agreed, Elizabeth, that we must be discreet. I cannot march up and ask the lady of the house, on no acquaintance, whether she has taken on a maid.' She did not take the proffered circulars.

Her friend was unabashed. 'But of course you won't have to do anything of the kind. It will be a servant who answers when you ring. It is not difficult to remark to them that you understand there's been a new appointment recently. You could even tell them that you were wanting somebody yourself and were looking for a source.'

'And be overrun with unsuitable enquiries, I suppose? Or have employers thinking that I want to lure away their staff?' Alicia pulled her skirts more firmly round her knees.

Beth thought for a moment. 'I suppose you're right. You'd have to make it clear that there was no intention to lure anyone away.' Her face broke into a cheerful grin again. 'But it might lead somewhere, and it's a start at least. When I asked the ladies at headquarters earlier (I did that, of course, in case any of them had taken on new staff, but none of them had done so, or knew of anyone who had) no one thought it odd that I was enquiring. I simply told them you were looking for a maid, and they were inclined to help, if anything. There were several suggestions, not a bit unsuitable.'

'I'm surprised you stooped to telling such untruths,' Alicia said. She sounded ungracious, even to herself. She tried to soften her gruffness with a smile.

Beth looked a bit affronted. 'I don't see why you call it an untruth. You can't have poor Mrs Pritchard doing everything, as she was today. I imagined you would be on the lookout for somebody to take Fanny's place, by now.'

'How can I do that? You know my brother's views.'

'Of course!' Her friend was instantly contrite. 'I had forgotten that. But all the more reason why you have to act.' She tapped the notebook as if to stress the point. 'If you can prove that Fanny was in danger when she left, not even your brother could blame you for her flight. Nor call it a misjudgement that you appointed her.'

'You don't know Edwin,' Alicia replied, but somehow the argument must have swayed her all the same, because she found herself saying, 'I suppose that we could try. Though it seems a fairly hopeless scheme to me. I had simply thought of calling in the police.'

'There is nothing to prevent us doing that as well.' Beth sounded dubious. 'But, after all, what are the police to do? The girl is not a criminal.'

'I could tell them I was anxious for her safety, I suppose. That's what I'd thought of doing. They are more likely than we are to discover where she's gone.'

Beth closed the notebook with a little snap. 'I suppose you're right. They have better ways of finding out these things.' She sounded disappointed. 'A policeman can question anyone he likes. It's not the same for us.'

'All the same' – Alicia got abruptly to her feet – 'let's see what we can do.' Perversely, just as her friend seemed ready to abandon the whole scheme, it suddenly seemed much more attractive than before. 'We'd better call in at the police station first, and then we'll try these houses that you've marked out with a star.' She glanced at the list which she still held in her hand. 'Though some of these addresses are a long distance apart.' She didn't add, 'And without Edwin's agreement I can't afford to take a cab,' but this time Beth seemed to read her thoughts.

'Well, you go to the police station then. It is probably better if I don't go too. Several of the policemen know me by sight – they've moved me on for selling "Votes for Women" in the street.' (So that was why she had been so unwilling to involve the police, Alicia thought!) 'Meanwhile, I'll find a hansom cab and deliver the circulars at the houses furthest out, and you can have the envelopes and do the nearer ones. I'll meet you later on this afternoon – back here again perhaps – and we can see if either of us has

209

anything to report.'

'You are suggesting that I call upon these strangers on my own?' Alicia was startled. 'But I thought...' She had only envisaged doing such a thing in company.

Beth waved an airy hand. 'It doesn't need two of us to deliver an envelope. In fact it might seem odd if both of us appeared. And this way we can cover twice as much. I'll take four envelopes and you can do the other two when you have finished talking to the police. That shouldn't take above half an hour. Then you can go calling, as I said before – it won't be difficult, just a matter of talking to the servants at the door.'

The visit to the police took less than half an hour. The sergeant at the desk was courteous and listened to her tale, but when he came to write the details down his manner changed a bit.

It began when he enquired, 'What did you say this missing girl was called?'

'Fanny Watts,' she answered. 'Or, possibly, Nellie Rouse.'

He was clearly unimpressed. 'Well, make your mind up, miss. How can we look for someone, if we don't know who they are?'

Alicia shook her head. 'I knew her as Fanny, the fellow called her Nellie. Or of course she might be calling herself something else by now.'

He closed the book and put his pencil down. 'We'll keep a lookout. That's all we can do. But there've not been any signs of trouble round here, lately, miss. No bodies found or anything like that.'

she said so more than once. No, I'm sure the family's dead. In fact, the neighbour said so, when I went to find the aunt.' She frowned, trying to recollect the incident. 'Leastways, I believe so. I can't e'zactly think.'

'Well,' said Miss Richie, joining in again, 'perhaps that's the first thing that we ought to check. But we want you to do it – it would be too strange for Miss Killivant and I to suddenly appear and start asking questions in the neighbourhood. If you go back and simply tell them that the girl's a friend of yours, but that she's left her employment and you don't know where she is, no one will think there's anything surprising about that. And perhaps you can ask the tradesmen when they call, as well, if any of them saw her after she left here.'

Edie said slowly, 'I already have, and there isn't one of them's seen hide nor hair of her. Wonder where she went? Wouldn't be likely to go and take a train – not that same day anyway, for fear of running into him. He came from up-country, told us so himself.'

'Would she catch a horse-bus, then?'

'Where to, though? That's the thing. Bus wouldn't take you very far at all – and the driver would be sure to notice you. Too easy to check up on, and then she'd have that fellow after her again. Leastways, that's what I'd decide if it was me. She might have walked somewhere, that's all I can think.' She saw the two ladies exchanging a quick glance, and added quickly, ''Course, I could be wrong.'

Miss Richie said, smiling, 'No, this is just the

194

'No, Edith, that's the sort of thing that we can do ourselves. What we want from you is the servant's point of view. Where would a girl like Fanny go to hide, if she was running from a relative?'

Edith eased her other buttock up on to the stool, so that she was no longer sitting so uncomfortably. 'I've been asking myself that question, ever since she left. And I don't know the answer.' Almost without thinking she pushed her fingers underneath her frilly cap and scratched her head – the way Pa always did. 'If I was in trouble, I would run straight 'ome – but she's got no 'ome to go to, poor thing, anyway.'

Miss Richie had leaned back in her chair and clasped her hands together as she said, 'So she claimed. Perhaps that is another thing that we should check. Your mistress is willing to believe that her account was accurate – but you have to be prepared to face the truth, whatever it might be. So you must realize, Edith, it is feasible that the man who came here was her father after all.'

'But, in that case, why would she want to run away?' She turned to Miss Alicia, who was staring at the floor.

Her mistress glanced up, and looked away again. 'It's possible, I suppose, that he was mistreating her at home. You do read of dreadful beatings and that sort of thing. Not every family is as happy as your own.'

Edith tried to imagine being terrified of Pa, but she couldn't do it. 'Well, I don't believe it. What about her ma? Her mother would put a stop to anything like that. And Fan adored her mother,

193

her ears. A servant sitting down, when there was company? But Miss Alicia seemed to be quite serious.

She fetched out a stool and balanced the corner of a buttock on one edge. 'If this is about this morning...' she began, wondering if Mrs Pritchard had complained. It had been almost five past six when she had got downstairs.

The mistress shook her head. 'This is not a reprimand. We want to ask your help.' She glanced towards her guest. 'There are one or two things we'd like you to assist us with.'

Edith let out the breath that she'd been holding in. Things would be all right. This was just some kind of errand, and she was used to that – though it must be something funny for them to sit her down like this. 'I'm here to be of service, Miss Alicia,' she said, and rather wished she hadn't. She sounded like that Mr Tulver or somebody, she thought.

Silence. Miss Alicia was looking at the visitor again, as if she might find inspiration about what to say, and after a moment Miss Richie herself spoke. 'It's about your fears for Fanny. Miss Killivant has told me what you said – no, don't look so worried, it's in confidence, of course. And having thought it over, we believe you might be right. She may be in danger. We want you to help us to find out where she's gone – even if only to make sure she is safe, and see that she gets the money she is owed.'

Miss Alicia nodded. 'It's not just the money that you found up in her room. There are several weeks' wages owing in arrears. Quite a lot of

191

money to a girl like that.'

Edith was startled. 'She wouldn't be due the extra really, would she, though?' Nobody working in a household would, she thought. If you don't give proper notice, then they stop your pay in lieu. It's the very least that anybody would expect. Leave alone what would happen if you simply ran away. She thought that was probably a criminal offence. 'Isn't there something called a "breeches of contract" in the law?'

To her amazement both the women laughed. 'Yes, there is, Edith,' Miss Alicia said, quite kindly. 'Or something very like. But that is about marriage – when the fellow lets you down. Fanny didn't have a proper contract with the house – we'd simply agreed that I'd extend her trial and pay her from now on – and she didn't leave with any money that she hadn't earned, so I don't think there's anything illegal in her going. This isn't slavery – she has a right to leave.' She frowned. 'Though it might be interesting to go and ask the police.'

Edith shook her head. 'I 'ope you aren't going to ask me to go down and do that. Terrified of policemen, I have always been.' She flushed. She shouldn't have spoken to Miss Alicia like that, but she had vivid recollections of one awful day, when she'd been scrumping apples with Reuben after school, and the local constable had caught them in the act. Gave them a clip across the ear that they would not forget – though he hadn't told Father, as he'd threatened to. Her ears were stinging at the memory.

But it was all right. Miss Alicia only laughed.

'I wasn't suggesting that the girl was dead.' Alicia was shocked. 'Only that she might be in danger of some kind. You won't begin a search?'

'Pardon me, miss, but if that was her father – as you say – I don't see how we can. If he had come in asking for her, that's a different thing. She would be a missing person, then. But looks like she went off of her own accord. You say you haven't paid her for the month, so you've got no grievance there, and you aren't bringing charges?'

Alicia shook her head.

'Then, I can't see quite what you hope that we can do. Though if we hear of anything, we'll be sure and let you know.'

Alicia felt foolish as she went back to the street. She fared a little better at the first house on her list. It was a longish walk, but when she reached the door a housemaid answered it at once.

Alicia handed her the envelope. 'I'm Alicia Killivant. I was asked to bring you this.' It was hard to think of what else she could say and she was conscious that the maid was staring at her. She blurted out, 'Have you worked here long? Only I wondered if your mistress had taken on new staff.'

It sounded awkward, but the girl seemed unsurprised. 'Oh, you mean Gladys? Yes, she left last year. They took me on instead. Been here three months, I have. Sorry if I should have recognized your name, Miss Killivant. But it's always hard when you're the newest in the place. I'll be sure and know you if you call again.'

Alicia was buoyed up by this effortless success and she hurried to the second house with much more confidence. There was a bell-pull this time, and she pulled on it, rehearsing the words which had worked so well before. There was a distant ring, and after a long pause the door creaked open to reveal a chubby maid.

'Yes?' the apparition said, suspiciously. Not the usual greeting, but after a moment she added, 'Can I help you, Miss?'

'A letter for Miss Halligan,' Alicia replied, quoting the name on the envelope, and preparing to launch upon her little speech.

'Who is that?' A man's voice came from the interior. Alicia could see his shadow in the hall behind.

'It's a lady come for Miss Doris,' the plump maid supplied. 'One of they circular things from those suffragists of hers.'

'Well, tell her...' the young man began, then seemed to change his mind. 'Or perhaps on second thoughts I'll speak to her myself.' He came out on to the doorstep and stood confronting Liss. He proved to be a youngish man – though obviously a few years older than herself – incongruously dressed in shirtsleeves, waistcoat, stiff collar and no tie – evidently in the process of changing to go out. He looked somewhat athletic, with his broad shoulders and his mop of fairish hair, but he sported the affectation of an ivory-topped cane. He looked at Alicia.

'Now, look here, young lady. This is not the time. If you're from the women's Movement, you must know where Doris is.'

Alicia shook her head, a little foolishly. 'Then I assume she isn't here?'

'You assume correctly. My sister is in jail. Arrested last week for throwing stones through windows, thanks to your famous Movement. It is causing my poor mother a great deal of distress – she is already frail and failing in her wits. I don't know what my sister can be thinking of. I have made written representations to the court on her behalf, but it seems that she intends to plead guilty to the charge, and if they imprison her she says she will not eat. You understand what that implies, of course?'

'Oh, that's terrible, you can't let her do that,' Alicia cried, genuinely horrified. 'They do such awful things to girls on hunger strike. I couldn't stand up to it, not for a single day.'

He looked at her coolly. His eyes were very blue. 'I thought that you were an adherent of the cause?'

'Well, so I am,' Alicia stumbled, 'but I don't agree with everything they do. Not with breaking windows. It's against the law.'

'But you think it is acceptable that she should do the rest – go off to London to march about the streets shouting slogans, and heckling the police? No wonder they arrested her for disturbance of the peace. An educated, well-brought-up, intelligent young woman like my sister, behaving like the drunken owner of a public house.'

He sounded like Edwin, or she would not have snapped, 'And you find it more acceptable that an educated, well-brought-up, intelligent young

213

woman like your sister should count for less in choosing a government than the same drunken owner of a public house? That, after all, is what the protest is about.' It was not quite original, she had heard the argument at one of the rallies in the town, but she produced it with an air of confidence. It had struck her as very impressive at the time.

It seemed to have impressed the fair-haired young man as well. He looked at her again, more appraisingly this time. 'A firebrand, then? And quite an orator. But you must understand, Miss...?'

'Killivant,' Alicia supplied.

He paused, frowning. 'Killivant? Did you say Killivant? I know the name. Have you a brother?'

Alicia's heart went plunging through her boots. As an accident of fate this could not be worse. News of her exploits would reach her brother now for sure. 'You are acquainted with Edwin, then?' she asked.

He shook his head. 'I don't know an Edwin. Must be a different branch of Killivants, I suppose. Fellow that I'm thinking of is a Charlie Killivant. We were together in the regiment, until I took that dratted tumble from a horse and made such a confounded mess of things.' He gestured to his leg. 'After that I was invalided out, and we sold the house in Devon and came down here to live. This used to be my mother's home when she was young.'

But Alicia wasn't really listening. She was remembering her unkind thoughts about the walking-cane. Clearly it was not an affectation after all. She coloured. 'Was it very serious? Your wound?'

He gave a short dismissive little laugh. 'Took me a year before I walked again and by that time I'd rather lost touch, I'm afraid. But if your brother's Edwin, it isn't the same chap. Quite a coincidence, though – you're having the same name. It's not a common name. And you look not unlike him – the red hair and everything. Pity, I should have liked to get in touch with him again.'

She found her voice. 'It is no coincidence, Mr Halligan. Edwin is the second son. Charles was my eldest brother.'

He said, sharply, 'Was? You mean poor Charlie's dead?'

She nodded, aware of the tears that pricked her lids. 'Killed on duty in South Africa.'

'I didn't know. I'm sorry.' The voice was gentle now. 'You must miss him, sorely. He was a splendid chap. '

'He was. It's awful. I was very fond of him.'

'You can't be the little sister he used to talk about? But of course you are. Even little sisters grow up, I suppose. So you're Alicia – I'm delighted to meet you after all these years.'

'And I you.' She met his glance. He had such piercing eyes. They were scarcely even acquaintances, of course, so she was unable to explain why she felt the sudden urge to add, 'And you must come and meet my mother. She isn't very well, but she would be delighted to talk to someone who knew Charles.'

If it was inappropriate, he didn't seem to mind. 'I should regard it as an honour, Miss Killivant,' he said. 'Just as I would deem it a favour, now, if you would permit me to drive you where you want to go. My coachman will be waiting to take me into town, and the weather is threatening to turn wet again.'

Given such courtesy, how could she refuse? And even though she had little to report – beyond the fact that Fanny's father clearly hadn't asked the police to search – she could hardly wait to see Beth Richie and Edie and tell them everything.

Except, perhaps, her feelings. She'd keep those to herself. Yes, altogether a tiring and exciting day.

It was Sammy, of all people, who brought back to Holvean House the only real clue as to Fanny's whereabouts. He had been down at the seashore with the barrow half the day, ferrying loads of seaweed for the 'pile', and chatting to a local farmer who was doing the same thing – ready to mulch the flower fields for next year's crop, he said. A garrulous old fellow, the man was shovelling up the wrack, stopping from time to time to rest his aching back, though he never seemed to feel the need to rest his tongue at all.

They were nearly finished picking, he said. The itinerants were already starting to move on. Always had a cartload of them; came down to pick the blooms – the early daffodils and the anemones – pack them into boxes and get them to the train. Fetch a good price in Covent Garden the next day, fresh flowers would, you know, if you could get the pickers. And he allus did. Same ones very often, from one year to the next – slept in the barn, and worked from dawn to dusk in return for a few pennies and a hearty meal. Next best thing to gypsies, they were, most of them. Rough as rats, and spent their pay on drink, but it was surprising how gentle they could be handling dainty blossom, when it came to it. Accustomed to it, see. Most of the casuals weren't a half as good.

'Though you do get people now and then who seem to 'ave a flair. Had one just ten days or so ago. Skinny little creature, turned up at the gate and seemed so willing that I took her on. Came down this way looking for her aunt, she said, and found that she'd moved on, so she was trying to find something to earn her fare back 'ome. Good little worker, but she didn't last. They don't, these casuals. It's harder than you'd think.'

'What did this girl look like?' Sammy asked at once.

The farmer stopped talking, and gave Sam a shifty look. 'Think you knaw her, do 'ee? Well, I dunno what she's said, but she's got nothing to complain of. She agreed the terms. Bread and soup, and bedding in the barn – and a penny an hour from the goodness of my 'eart.'

'If you cheated her on wages, that's your affair,' Sam said. 'What did she look like? That's what I'm asking you.'

The description fitted Fanny to a T, and when he took his barrow home and saw Edie on the step, he naturally told her everything he'd heard. Next thing, of course, she'd told Miss Alicia, and he was summoned in – upstairs to the drawing-room, where he'd never been before. As if he was gentry, he said afterwards. Made him so nervous that his mouth went dry.

But they heard him very kindly – Miss Alicia and that ladyfriend of hers – and seemed excited by what he had to say. So much so, they sent him down again, this time to call in at the farm and find out more, but of course the farmer wasn't keen to talk. Even the remaining pickers weren't a lot of use. Seemed she hadn't spoken to other people much – just seemed grateful for a rough bed and a meal – and after a day or two she'd simply moved on. It was not surprising: pay was by the box, and lots of casuals found they couldn't stand the pace.

No one had any real idea where she had gone.

Four

'Where's our Edie to, then?' Teddy Trewin asked his wife. 'Some awful late today.' He spread his bread carefully with Minnie's home-made rhubarb jam. Abel, beside him, watched him with a grin.

'Have some butter, Father!' the boy said. 'Big birthday, after all' – meaning that he had turned fourteen today, and was now old enough to leave school and go to work. Teddy had put a word in, as he'd promised Minnie that he would, and they'd found a place for Abel up surface, with his pa. They'd been down to the mine already, and it was all arranged. Abel was nearly bursting with the pride of it. He offered his father the butter with a grin.

Teddy shook his head. 'Jam'll do for me.' Either jam or butter was the family rule – unless it was Christmas or a big day like today, when you could have both, though Teddy never did. 'Waste of a treat to have two things at once. And here's our Edie, come.' He turned as his daughter hurried through the door.

She stooped to embrace him, stripping off her cloak. 'I'm some sorry, everyone, but I had to walk halfway. Miss Alicia kept me and I missed the bus. I'd have been even later if Crowdie hadn't seen me on the road and given me a lift in his farm cart the rest of the way home.' She hugged the little ones and slipped into her seat.

Minnie took the plate of stew that she'd been keeping warm and put it in front of her daughter with a frown. 'Well, I hope she had good reason for keeping you tonight, with it being Abel's last day as a boy. And your meal will be ruined and dried up as it is.'

'Couldn't really help it,' Edie said, tucking in without delay. 'Wanted me to be there when that Miss Richie came – and that new gentleman that she's so taken with. Captain Halligan, or something, he is called. Anyway, they've got a plan and they want me to help. Told me to ask you if you would agree. You'll never guess what she is wanting me to do. Only asked me to go up to Launceston on the train.'

'She never!' Teddy almost choked on his rhubarb jam. 'She's going herself, I suppose.'

Edie nodded. 'Her and that Miss Richie. Going first class they are, but they're going to send me up a day or two before, find somewhere nice for them to stay.'

Minnie scowled. 'Should have thought that Miss Alicia would have written up and leased a proper place, like people of her kind generally b'long to do.'

Edie shook her head. 'Poor Miss Alicia could not manage that – it would mean hiring a cook and everything. No, they've decided to find a lodging-house. Somewhere comfortable which has rooms to let, and serves a meal and all. Captain Halligan has been there lots of times, and he's told me where to look – and when I find a place, I'm to book into it myself and wire them the address.' She wiped the platter with a piece of bread, then pushed the plate away and grinned around the table at them all. 'Imagine me staying in a boarding-house, being waited on from dawn till night!'

Teddy heard Minnie give a sharp intake of breath. 'I'm not sure that it's a good idea. A young girl like you going all that way alone – to a strange town where there is nobody you know. Anything could happen. What is she thinking of?'

He cut another slice of bread, and ate it slowly, saving the jammy bit till last. He didn't want to voice what he was thinking – that if he went on coughing the way he did these days, Minnie might be dependent on Edie's wages very soon. Thank goodness Abel was going to earn at last – though of course he wouldn't be bringing in very much at first. 'If your employer asks you, I think you ought to go,' he said carefully. 'I'm sure Miss Killivant won't send you anywhere it isn't safe for you to go.'

Minnie had clearly been expecting his support. She looked furious – but it could not be helped. Better to have her mad at him than have her worried sick – he had persuaded her the cough was passing off.

Edie, though, nodded through a mouthful of bread. 'That's why she's relying on Captain Halligan. He's the brother of one of those Suffering people from the movement in Penzance, and seems he was in the army with that Mr Charles who died. He knows where the better places are, and people who take visitors from London now and then. Respectable sorts of houses. Apparently there is also a temperance hotel but Miss Alicia thinks a boarding-house would be most suitable.'

'Temperance hotel, my foot.' Minnie glared at Teddy. 'You'd still be traipsing in a strange town on your own. I think your father's soft to say that you can go.' She slammed the teapot down. 'But there you are. I suppose he's your father and what he says goes.'

Teddy gave her a warning frown, and shook his head. 'Of course your mother's right to worry, Edie. But you're sensible. If Miss Alicia trusts you to do this for her, then I shan't say no. And it is quite a chance for you, going all the way by train. I've never been further than Hayle in all my life.' He grinned. 'Give you ideas above your station, if we don't look out. You'll be charging money to talk to people next.'

'Why would she get ideas above the station?' Donny asked. 'Are there lots of books, like there are in school?'

It eased the tension and made everybody laugh, and Teddy seized the moment to turn the talk to something else. He raised his teacup. 'Here's to Abel starting at the mine. Mind you get some proper sleep tonight, my lad – you'll be up first thing tomorrow.'

Abel turned scarlet, but looked so proud that they thought he might burst. 'Going to start off helping in the blacksmith's shop,' the boy explained, for Edith's benefit. 'Only fetching and carrying at first, and maybe working the bellows for the fire: but if I suit they've promised I can start to learn the trade.'

Teddy bit his tongue. He didn't want to damp the boy's hopes before the start, but he could see how it would be. There wouldn't be the money for an apprenticeship, and Abel – and Reuben when he came along – would have to settle for the old ways in the end, and go back underground. Not that Teddy would mind that at all – that was proper mining, and he'd be proud of it – but Minnie would be worried every blessed day. Though she would no doubt come around to it, when the household depended on what they were bringing home.

He was so busy with his thoughts that he did not catch what Edie said, until she repeated, 'Tommy Hoskins, from the mine – he only had one hand.'

Teddy nodded. 'Got it caught in some contraption and had to have it off. 'Tisn't all safety, just 'cause you're up to grass.' That was for Minnie's benefit. He glanced across but she was glowering, and he added, more pacifically, 'What's all this 'bout Tommy Hoskins, then?'

'Like I say, I met him. Must think a lot of you. Turned out very civil when I mentioned who I was. Promised to do anything he could to help,' she said.

'I should think so too, a pretty girl like you,' he said gruffly, helping himself to another slice of bread. He had butter on it this time. It was the third piece of that 'andsome loaf he'd scoffed, but after all – as Abel said – it was a special day.

* * *

Timothy Tulver was feeling rather piqued. Not that he had reason, as he told himself. It was perfectly in order for a gentleman to call at Holvean House, especially a gentlemen who had known a member of the family – as it appeared that this Captain Halligan had done. Mrs Killivant had risen from her bed and ventured downstairs to the drawing-room in order to greet the visitor. So it was she who had met Timothy when he was ushered in himself.

He had sent his card up, so she was expecting him, but he had never seen the lady of the house before, and it had been a shock to him to find her sitting there, pale as funeral lilies, and as fragile too, though she had clearly taken pains to wear her best.

She held out a thin veined hand for him to press. She did not attempt to rise. 'Mr Tulver. So we meet at last. Alicia has often mentioned you to me.' Her voice was wavering and uncertain, like a ghost's, but the words were comforting. He was pleased that Alicia had seen fit to mention him.

'Has she indeed?' he smiled and sat down on the chair as Mrs Killivant was indicating that he should.

'I imagine that you have called to see Alicia, now?'

It was clearly a question, so he hastened to explain. 'I was hoping she would spare me a moment if she could. I have some ... information which she asked me to report.' Not very much information, in fact, only that he had enquired

224

among his own acquaintances and none of them had taken on any household help which could possibly be Fanny – but he felt that it afforded him an excuse to call. However, he could not say that to Mrs Killivant, who was looking at him expectantly now. He hesitated, not certain how much Alicia had told her mother about the whole affair. Certainly Edwin was not being kept informed. 'Do I take it that Miss Alicia is not here?'

'She will be shortly. She has gone up to change. We are expecting company,' the old woman said.

Not such an old woman, he realized, with surprise. She could not be much older than his own mama – though one would never have guessed it from a casual glance.

'Indeed?' he said, politely, trying to suppress a private sense of pique. The caller must be someone of consequence, he thought. 'A friend of yours, no doubt? They will be very pleased to see you so improved. Unless...' He broke off, as a panic-stricken thought occurred to him. 'You are not expecting Edwin?'

But she shook her head. 'Not Edwin, no – though of course I had forgotten you are a friend of his. This is a Captain Halligan. I have not had the pleasure of his acquaintance yet, but believe he used to be in the army with my elder son.' There was a sudden gleam of amusement in the eyes. 'Alicia met him and invited him to call.'

The pique had expanded into a tightness in his throat and he found that it was difficult to speak. 'You must be delighted.' It came out as a croak.

225

'Indeed we are, Mr Tulver. It has done me good – though my nurse was concerned that it would be too much for me. I got out Charles's letters and read them through last night, and I found a mention of this Philip Halligan. It makes me feel as if I had a link with Charles. And I am sure Alicia thinks the same. She has been quite animated ever since they met, and I'm sure that she has changed her mind about her dress three times today. He will be here before her if she does not make haste.'

Timothy stood up. 'Then I must not detain you, since he will be here so soon, and obviously his visit means so much. Perhaps you would be good enough to let your daughter know I came.'

The pale eyes glimmered with what might have been a smile. 'But you have something for her, do I understand? Would you care to leave it here? I will see she gets it, Mr Tulver, if you wish.' He noticed that she did not urge that he should stay and wait.

He shook his head. 'It is only information. I will call again. If Miss Alicia would care to contact me, perhaps I could arrange a more convenient time.'

If that was slightly impolite she did not notice it. 'Thank you, Mr Tulver. Of course I'll tell her that. I'm sorry that you've had a wasted visit here this afternoon. But of course, you could not know what was arranged, and I believe you call quite often to see Alicia.' She offered him the blue-veined hand again, and there was nothing he could do but press it in goodbye. 'She will be sorry to have missed you, this afternoon,

226

I'm sure.'

He only wished that he could be as positive of that. It was a sober Tim Tulver that walked back down the drive. Sober and a little jealous, if the truth were told. To change her mind about her dress three times! Alicia had never gone to change her clothes on his account.

But of course that had nothing at all to do with his decision, later on that night, to write a note to Edwin about the day's events. After all, if Mrs Killivant was getting well again, surely it was only proper that her son should know?

And if he mentioned Fanny, it was only once, just to say she was no longer at the house and that Alicia was set on finding her. That was no more than was sensible, he told himself – if Mrs Killivant felt well enough to write, she was certain to mention that the maid had gone.

It was nothing to do with Captain Halligan at all.

The trip up to Launceston was every bit as exciting as Edith could have hoped. Miss Alicia and Miss Richie came and saw her on the train – as though she were the lady and they were attending her. They helped her find her carriage and showed her how to put her little package on the rack, and found the guard and told him to help her to get off.

Then, just a moment before the whistle blew, down came that Captain Halligan, limping on his stick.

'Glad that I managed to get here before you went. I don't know that I ought to be encouraging this escapade,' he said, though his eyes were twinkling wickedly as he spoke. 'But it makes a fellow feel a bit less useless, doing what he can, so I've got this for you.' He'd drawn a little sketch-map for her – with his own hand, by the look of it. 'Used to know Launceston, when I was a boy. Had a chum at school whose family lived up there, and I stayed with them sometimes in the holidays. 'Course, it may have changed a lot since I was there – but you might find this of help.'

Edith thanked him gratefully, and put the map away into the envelope where she already had his list.

He turned to Miss Alicia. 'Occurs to me the family might still live in the town – you might care to call on them when you go up yourself. Lillywhite, the name was, lived in a big house halfway up the hill – I've marked it on the map. The parents may still be there, though I dare say my friend's moved on. Going to be a lawyer when I last heard of him.'

Pity the people didn't keep a guest-house, Edie thought. Might have been nice to find a room with somebody you knew. She folded the en-velope and put it carefully away, inside the inner pocket of her skirt. She'd look out for the house, although of course she couldn't call in there herself – wouldn't be expected, a servant-girl like her. But it was nice of Captain Halligan to draw the map like this, and give her the list of lodgings. Though it was less on her account than on Miss Alicia's, she knew. It was clear that he was smitten. Look at him chatting to the ladies

228

now, and looking up to wave as the guard gave the signal and the carriage pulled away. Mr Tulver would have a rival if he didn't look out – and a good thing too.

Some nice gentleman, the Captain was, Edie thought as she settled back into the seat – and he'd made such a difference to Mrs Killivant. Like as if the old lady had come to life again – except that she had taken to prowling round the house, finding fault with the way that everything was done. Why weren't there vases of flowers in the hall, and why had so many of the rooms been closed with dust-covers over all the furniture? Drove Mrs Pritchard wild. And then Nurse Morgan coming afterwards, grumbling that the mistress ought to go and rest and not try to start doing everything at once, and Mrs Killivant insisting that she was perfectly all right. It had been quite hard on Miss Alicia as well, who was used to having her own way with things by now. There'd been raised voices on the subject once or twice – it was almost a pleasure to be leaving it behind.

It was certainly a pleasure to be sitting on the train, with nothing to do but watch the world go by. Edith could not remember such an idle day, not since she was tiny – and there was so much to see. Little granite villages, farmyards, wagons, lots of cows and sheep, people cutting cabbages and running after dogs – then great towns like Truro, with a glimpse of crowded streets, and suburbs of houses that seemed to stretch for miles. And London was even bigger, everybody said. It was almost impossible to imagine it! Then more streams and woodland, and they were back to farms again, and then the sweep of a huge river and a handsome bridge. She was actually out of her native county. 'Plymouth!' Her heart was thumping so hard she thought that they must be able to hear it back at home.

Almost too soon, they were chugging to a stop, and the guard came to tell her that it was time to get off and change trains. It was so big and confusing that she felt a little lost, but a kindly porter pointed out the platform that she needed next. This time she knew what to expect, and when she found the train she settled herself and her luggage like a seasoned traveller.

She even closed her eyes a little as the afternoon drew on and dreamed of Sammy and what he would think of this.

Five

Launceston was a revelation in itself, once the ticket inspector at the gate had pointed out the way to get into the town. A great hill in the middle, and a castle at the top. Not like the 'rock castles' on Penvarris cliffs, or a castle people lived in, like St Michael's Mount – this was a proper castle, like you saw in books.

The first task was to find a suitable place to stay, and she set about locating the suggestions on the Captain's list. The first place she called at was already full, but the second was much bigger and they still had rooms.

'Two best bedrooms and a small one at the back? That would be possible,' and she went up to look. Even the small one was better than she'd dreamed. It was clean and comfy looking – there was a little bath next door, with a proper geyser over for hot water any time, though you had to put a penny in the slot. The front ones had lacy curtains and a chest of drawers, a lovely washstand with a bowl and jug, and – unheard-of luxury, a carpet on the floor. She thought it was lovely, and when she went downstairs there was a proper dining-room with fancy table-cloths, where they served the meals – 'Breakfast and evening. Lunchtime extra by arrangement', as the notice said.

'Well?' the woman demanded impatiently. 'Do you want the rooms or not?'

Edith hesitated. It was very well for her – this was more comfort than she'd dreamed of in her life. But what would Miss Richie and Miss Alicia think? It wasn't half so smart as Holvean House, of course. But, surely, if Captain Halligan thought that it would do...?

She was still havering when someone came marching through the door – an older man with such a military air that she was not surprised to hear the woman say, 'Good afternoon, Major. And how are you today?'

Major! That was all that Edith had to hear. If there was a major, it had to be all right.

'I'll take the rooms,' she said, with such confidence that she surprised herself.

The woman looked suspiciously at her, eyeing her best Sunday skirt and coat in a way that suggested that she was wondering if it was wise to let her stay. 'Your mistress and her friend will be here very soon?'

'As soon as I have telegraphed to let them know I've found a place.'

The woman sniffed. 'We'll make it from tonight then. I can't keep them otherwise. And staying for a week. I shall want paying in advance, of course. Just in case that mistress of yours changes her mind and doesn't come. Three days, let's say,' she said, and named a sum that made Edith feel quite weak.

No one had budgeted for spending quite so much straight off, but she did have enough money in that little purse which Miss Alicia had given her. After she'd paid the woman there was not a great deal left, but there ought to be enough to send the promised wire. She left her luggage in the bedroom – the little one, of course, though it was tempting to at least go and sit in one of the bigger rooms, since it was being paid for tonight in any case. Obviously you couldn't use the sheets, but there was no harm in admiring the view – but it seemed disrespectful and after a minute she went back to her own. She locked it, as instructed, and took the key downstairs, then set off to find the office for the post and tele-graph. It was late, but she should just have time to send a wire.

She sent it, bold as brass, as though she'd done it all her life, although she could not help but watch the woman tapping it all out, on the little Morse key in the office at the back.

'Marvellous, isn't it?' she said, when the telegraphist looked enquiringly at her. 'To think of all that going down the wires, and they get it in Penzance.'

'Won't even need the wires, very soon, they say. Wireless telegraphy, that's the coming thing, thanks to that Mr Marconi and his experiments. Able to communicate with ships at sea, and all. Soon won't be anywhere for criminals to hide.' She had finished with her tapping now and come back out again. 'Thank you, dear, the message has been sent. That should be delivered in an hour or so.'

Edie shook her head in disbelief. 'And to think of all that long way in the train ... Some clever, isn't it?'

The woman smiled. 'Not so clever as a telephone. Heard of them, have you? Wonderful they are. You talk into a machine and folk can hear you miles away. Next thing we know we'll have public ones of those – one on the corner of every street, I shouldn't be surprised, like they have pumps and taps for water now. That'll be the way of it a hundred years from now. Just you think of that – instead of sending them a telegraph you'd be able to talk to them instead. Sending home, are you? Because you're not from round here, I can tell it from your voice and I've not seen you before. Tend to know most people, in a job like this.'

Edith shook her head. 'I'm just here visiting. I'm looking for a friend.'

She went as if to go, but at the door she turned. The telegraph woman had just given her an idea. 'The trouble is, I don't have an address. I suppose you wouldn't know of anyone called Rouse?' The post office would know, she thought, if anybody did. 'Or,' she added as an afterthought, 'a family called Watts who perished in a fire? Either of those names might be a relative.'

The telegraphist made a little face and shook her head. 'Lots of people of those names hereabouts. And I don't remember hearing anything about a fatal fire. How long ago was this?'

Edith felt rather foolish. 'I'm not exactly sure. Six months or so, I think. But it's only a rumour, it may not be true.' It was the first time she'd admitted that, even to herself.

The woman was busy with some papers now, but she looked up and smiled. 'Well, I'm sorry I can't help you. I hope you find your friend.'

Edith swallowed. 'There is another thing. There was an aunt who used to live down near Penzance. A Mrs Polcurnooth, or some strange name like that. I don't suppose you ever...'

The woman stared at her. 'Now, wait a minute! I do remember that – nice little woman used to come in here, now and then – and buy a postage stamp, sending a letter to someone of that name, and I believe the address was somewhere near Penzance. Never got a letter back, though – far as I recall. Come to think of it, I'm sure her name was Rouse. Wife of a builder out Trewendron way – though I did hear tell she had died in some awful accident and he had taken another wife. But he's still there, I think. Might be a place for you to start, at least.'

Edith shut her eyes. This would be something to tell Miss Alicia. 'How do I find Trewendron?'

The woman smiled again. 'You would have to walk. Trewendron's a mile or two along the road to Callington.' She took the sorted papers and filed them on a spike. 'Though I'm not so sure I should be sending you out there. He's not an easy fellow, from all accounts. That poor soul used to come in here, afraid of her life that he would find her out – and I know she had her answers sent to somewhere else in case he learned of them. She was terrified of him, and he sounds the sort of man to bear a grudge. So, if you call there, don't go saying that you heard of him from me.'

'I won't,' Edith promised, and went out into the street. Fanny's story was all beginning to make a kind of sense. Her proper name was Nellie Rouse, that much seemed certain now – though Edie couldn't think of her by that name at all – and that man who'd come calling was probably her pa. But the tale about her mother and the aunt was wholly true – and it seemed that Fanny really had something to be terrified about!

It was closing time by now, and the shops were turning out. She went back slowly to the lodging-house. The landlady, when she got there, was superior and chill but the rooms were warm and cosy, and the meal – when Edie plucked up courage to go down in answer to the gong – was delicious, almost more than she could eat. There was hot water to wash in brought up to the room, and afterwards she snuggled down beneath the covers of a lovely feather bed, feeling like a princess in a story-book.

Trewendron, she thought as she drifted off to sleep. Tomorrow she would go out there and see what she could find.

'You all right, Teddy?' Cap'n Maddox's voice behind him made him turn. 'What you doing out here, this time of the day?'

Teddy couldn't answer. Hadn't got his breath back from that last attack. He was still panting and his chest was hurting cruel, so he simply shook his head and tried to summon up a smile.

He'd been working on the tables when the coughing bout began. He'd been moved there

236

lately and it suited him – none of the humping pails of stuff around, or dealing with the sweepings, which always made him cough. All he had to do was watch the settling grooves and check the mucky liquid that ran down over them – the tin-heavy 'washings' pumped in from elsewhere. The principle was simple – the heavier the deposit the earlier it fell, while the sludge was carried out into the sluices underneath – but not everyone could do it. You had to choose the moment to divert the flow, so the tin was separated from the rest of it, but Teddy had quickly got the hang of it.

So it had been an awful business when he'd doubled up, so busy coughing that he couldn't move, and if it hadn't been for Jimmy Rowe who spotted what was up, all the ore would have gone down the wrong sluice and had to go round the system and be done again. But he couldn't help it. He had come outside, still coughing, and sat down on a wall. He thought his lungs were bursting, the pain had been that bad, and even now he was shaking and could feel cold sweat on his brow.

'All right, are you?' Maddox said again.

This time Teddy had breath enough to speak. 'Shall be directly.' He attempted to stand up, but the ground had an alarming tendancy to tilt. He sat down again. 'Don't know what's the matter. I'm as weak as school-treat tea.'

'Ought to go home and go to bed, it looks to me.'

Teddy gave him what Minnie called 'the look'. 'Can't do that, can I? I got mouths to feed.'

Maddox gave him a glare to match his own. 'Aren't going to do it if you're up the graveyard though. What you want to do is go home and shake this off. With the Miners' Friendly, you'll get ten bob a week – that's what you've been paying your subscriptions for. Even pay for a doctor, if it comes to it, they will – if you have been a member long enough.'

Teddy found the strength to haul himself upright. 'Ah – won't come to that,' he said. 'Put a poultice on me chest and I'll be right as rain. Just seems to get a bit of something on me lungs, and I can't shift it no-how – that is all it is.' He was about to volunteer that he would get straight back to work, but a wave of weakness made him change his mind. 'But perhaps you're right. Perhaps I won't go back into the sheds today. Can you let them know? I'll only lose an hour, it's nearly home-time now. I'll just sit here a minute, get a breath of air. No need to go home early, worrying my wife. I'll just wait for Abel.'

Maddox nodded. 'All right, Teddy, if that is what you want. But you think serious about what I just said. And if you mean to wait for Abel, I should go outside the gates – have people coming otherwise to ask you why you're here. And if you decide tomorrow that you're going to stay at home, send him to see me. I'll see the Friendly knows and that you get everything you are entitled to.'

Teddy touched his forelock. 'Thank 'ee, Cap'n Maddox.' He watched the fellow walk away. Captain he might be but he still had the common touch. If they were all like Maddox, wouldn't

238

life be grand?

He was still thinking about Maddox as he walked out through the gates and out on to the miner's path along the cliffs. Stop and wait for Abel at the stile, perhaps – there would be no Edie come to look for him today. She was gone up Launceston – only think of that!

It was costing him a great deal more effort than he wished, and by the time he reached the stile he was grateful to sit down, and perhaps he even drifted off a little bit, because he was not aware of anyone until he heard the voice.

'That's never Teddy Trewin? I believe it is.'

He looked up sharply, startled from his dream. A tall man, like a scarecrow, stood in front of him carrying a sack across his shoulder with his one good arm. 'Why, it's Tommy Hoskins, as I'm alive!' he cried. 'However are you, Tommy? I hear you've got a cottage down Nanvarris way?'

Hoskins wrinkled up his weather-beaten face and showed a row of ugly-looking teeth. 'Hear that from your maid Edith? Yes, I'm lucky there. Got a little bit of this here compensation from the mine, and some from the Friendly, and that pays the rent. With that and me bit of pension, I can make ends meet.' He dropped the sack, spat on his hand as if it ached, and wiped it in his coat.

'That's that old-age pension that they brought in last year?'

Hoskins did his snaggled grin again. 'I should say it is. Lucky I was seventy and could qualify. Don't know however I could have managed else.

Not like my poor brother – though he's the older one. He went on the parish for a month or two – makes him a pauper, see, so he don't qualify. Gone in the workhouse up to Madron, he has – and I can't help him out. I habn't got enough to keep the pair of us, though I try and go and see him any time I can, now they let the inmates have visitors a bit. Take him some baccy or something, if I've a penny spare. Though if they'll let him have it is another thing. Not allowed possessions except his clothes and bed – you take up fruit or anything, they won't give it them. Too rich for their stomachs, with what they get to eat, and when they have it, it gives them you-know-what.'

Teddy could imagine. He didn't dwell on it. 'What you doing here in any case?'

Hoskins shrugged his shoulder. 'Brought some stuff to sell. Captain Maddox from the mine buys from me now and then, and one or two others that I used to knaw. But, come to that, I could ask you the same thing. What you doing out 'ere at this time of day? Don't you belong to be down underground?'

'Up in the sheds these days,' Teddy admitted. 'Got a boy there too. Waiting for him this minute, so we can walk back home.'

'Oh,' Hoskins said, and picked up his sack again. 'Well, if your boy is half as good-looking as your maid, you're a lucky fellow, Teddy Trewin. Real nice girl, she is. And you can tell her I habn't forgotten what I said. If I hear anything at all I'll let her knaw. Now, don't suppose you want to buy a cabbage for your tea? Two for a penny, seeing as it's you. Pick up the money on my way past, if you like.'

And though he had just lost at least an hour's pay, somehow Teddy found that he'd agreed.

'Is that you, Edwin?' Claire came running out into the hall to welcome him. 'I am glad you're home. Do you wish to come upstairs and see the nursemaid giving little Caroline her tea?'

Strange to think that at one time he would have flinched from such a thing. Of course his daughter was almost sitting up by now and could take things from a spoon, instead of only sucking at a shaped glass bottle with a teat. (That he had always found a bit embarrassing – the thing was very reminiscent of a woman's breast and it never seemed quite proper for a man to see.) But he had made it a habit to go up every day and spend at least a quarter of an hour with the child – and the way she chuckled and gurgled when he came gave him a warm feeling which nothing else had ever done. Besides, Claire seemed to like it. She was smiling at him now.

'Have you had a good day, Edwin?' She took his hat from him and carefully brushed it before she hung it up.

It had been a very gratifying day indeed, in fact: two wretched prostitutes delivered from the streets. They had been brought to the mission, where they were fed and washed and given some cast-off clothing and a place to sleep. They would start tomorrow in a job that he'd arranged, packing biscuits in a factory. 'A good day,

yes. Two young women came to seek our help.'
He didn't say what kind of women, and she
didn't ask.

She was intent on brushing down his coat and
scarf as if she were the maid, but she must have
been listening because she murmured doubtfully, 'I sometimes wish you did not have to go
to these awful places quite so much. And meet
these dreadful people. They could have some
disease.'

'My dear!' he said, quite sharply. 'It is the
function of the mission to reach these very souls.
We do not look upon the outward man, but only
on the heart. Besides,' he went on in a more
normal tone, 'I only talk to them. We have a
special woman who takes care of the rest –
makes sure they strip off and have a disinfectant
bath, and combs their hair for nits and all that
sort of thing.'

She hung the hat and scarf up and turned round
to look at him. 'Oh, don't be silly, dearest. Of
course I was not suggesting that you were going
to do more than shake their hands. It's only – I
know you and the other missioners go to seek
them out, and so you visit the sorts of places
where they live, and I wish you didn't have to.
For the baby's sake. I've seen where they come
from – you took me there yourself – and I know
how terrible it is. There's so much squalor
there's bound to be disease, and the nursemaid
tells me there are these things called "germs"
that live in stench – you could pick one up and
bring it home with you. And there are lots of
them about. Even the King has got infectious

242

pneumonia, they say, and has taken to his bed.'

So that was why she was careful with his clothes, he thought. 'Don't worry, Claire, that's why we have the disinfectant bath.' He smiled placatingly. But perhaps his wife was right. One of those girls today had had an awful rash. Suppose that it was catching, and he'd brought it home, and Caroline should be infected with it? It was a dreadful thought. He would take more care in future to wash his hands before he left: the clergy washroom was equipped with strong carbolic soap. Perhaps it was even time to think of moving on – take a parish, possibly, like anybody else.

He went to the bathroom now and scrubbed his hands – one couldn't be too careful dealing with a child – and then he went upstairs with Claire to watch his daughter fed. It was a messy business but it made him smile, and she cooed and dribbled rice at him. When it was over and her face was duly washed he held her for a while. He was glad he'd scrubbed his fingers when he did, because Caroline reached out for one and curled her hand round it, before the nurse took her and bore her off to her bath.

That was not a proper ritual for fathers to attend, so he went back to the drawing-room and sat beside the fire with a glass of whisky and a newspaper, waiting for Claire to come and dinner to be served. A pleasant ending to a fulfilling day.

Claire came down shortly, still happily aglow. 'Isn't she growing? And her hair's so curly now.' She paused by the bureau. 'Did you see the

243

catalogue? It's the one I sent for – children's furniture. We shall need a bed for her very soon. I don't suppose you've had a chance to look at it – came in the last delivery late this afternoon.'

He stretched out a hand for it. 'Anything else of interest?'

'Nothing very much. Oh, except a letter from that bank-man in Penzance. Do you want to see it now?'

He shook his head and took another measured sip of drink. 'It can wait till after dinner. Just a statement about Alicia's account, as usual, I expect. He always provides me with one at the beginning of the month. Now what have we for supper? Did you promise me lamb chops?'

'With soup and fish to start with, and then some apple pie, and of course some cheese and fruit to finish with. All of your favourites, but quite a simple meal. We don't need very much, when there are just the two of us to dine.'

And he knew that she basked in his approving smile.

Part Four

May – June 1910

One

The letter from Edwin was so furious that you could almost feel the heat rising from the cramped lines of script. Every page was pulsing with a wave of righteous wrath that left Alicia shaken for an hour afterwards. Phrases like 'utterly irresponsible' and 'foolhardy behaviour' were no more than she expected and possibly deserved – given that he'd found out about Fanny's running off and her own attempts to trace her – but the final paragraphs had shocked her to the core.

It pains me to have to say this, Alicia, but sometimes I wonder how a girl like you – with every blessing that good family, position and education can provide – can find it in her heart to act in such a way. It was bad enough to bring this girl into our mother's house, without recommendation or a written character, but I was prepared to overlook that and forgive your foolishness as the product of an over-trusting nature (coupled perhaps with an urgent wish to have some extra help). Events have doubtless taught you the folly of your ways. 'Folly', however, is too polite a word to describe your current activities. Your involvement with the

Women's Suffragists I cannot approve – as presumably you realized, since I note you have not seen fit to mention it to me at any time. Understand that I forbid you to attend again. And as to inviting a young man back to the house (to whom, I understand, you have not even been properly introduced), inflicting him on Mother and on other guests, and then conspiring with him to search the county for the wretched girl who left – these are acts of rashness that I do not understand, and absolutely decline to condone in any way.

Therefore, I regret that with immediate effect I am removing the management of Holvean House from you. I will no longer issue you with any housekeeping, and all bills for services and servants must be sent to me. Fortunately, dear Mama has made good progress recently, so in good time I hope to deal with her direct – since it is clear that Papa was right in the provisions of his will and you are not a fit person to handle such affairs. Further, I am writing to Mr Tulver (to whom I am indebted for the truth about all this) to cancel the allowance which was made from your account. If in future you require a dress, or boot repairs, or money for the church, kindly do not apply to Mother, although I know she has a little money of her own, but put your needs to me in writing. I shall require receipts.

On the subject of Mama, I confess I am dismayed. I know that she has not been well enough to take account of everywhere you go and what you do, but I fear she is encouraging you in welcoming this man and she seems not to realize the impropriety. Yet you know no more about him than you knew about the maid. Have you learned nothing from that unfortunate affair? In the first instance, therefore, I see no alternative. I shall come down myself, next weekend – though clearly with a baby this is inconvenient, and it will mean unwelcome separation from my family and home. All the same, I know where duty lies. Please tell Mrs Pritchard to prepare my room.

More in grief than anger, I remain,
Your loving brother,
Edwin

He had underlined his signature with a flourish of the pen.

Alicia read the missive for the umpteenth time, but no amount of reading changed a word of it. Edwin had reduced her to the status of a child. She was cut off without a penny, not even enough for the collection plate at church; and the running of the household – which she had secretly enjoyed – had been taken from her. Her gleeful plans for going to Launceston with Miss Richie were in ruins – and they had been due to travel up this very day. Beth would doubtless be here soon, packed and ready and looking forward to the trip. Whatever was she going to say to her?

She sat down at the dressing-table and found to her fury that she had begun to weep: but they were hot tears of anger, there was no grief in them. Anger against Edwin, and Tim Tulver too.

Tim Tulver most of all. Had he not led her to suppose that he was fond of her? She'd even taken him into her confidence. And then to write and betray her, as he had clearly done!

How dare they – Edwin and Tim Tulver – treat her in this way? She thumped her fists against the dressing-table top.

It made the mirror tremble and she glimpsed her face. She looked what Edie would have called 'a sight': the red hair tumbling from its fashionable chignon – she could not pin it nicely the way that Edie did – her dress dishevelled and her face all streaked and red. And Beth Richie was expected in an hour or so. Well, Edwin might be giving her the status of a child, but she would have the satisfaction of dignity at least. She took out a handkerchief and dabbed her eyes and cheeks, splashed her face with cold water from the wash-jug on the stand, and then patted on some eau-de-Cologne to cool her cheeks and neck. That was a little better.

She was suddenly aware of a movement in the glass, and Nurse Morgan was behind her, having hurried up the stairs. 'I'm to tell you, Miss Alicia, that your visitor's arrived,' she said. 'Mrs Pritchard's busy bringing in some tea, and there's no one else to bring the message up to you.' She sounded less than happy at being used as errand-girl.

Alicia managed a rather tight-lipped smile. 'Thank you, Nurse Morgan. Please tell Miss Richie I will be down very soon.' She wondered about asking the nurse to help her dress, but the woman looked resentful at her mission as it was, so Alicia merely watched her as she went down-stairs again.

So it had happened. Elizabeth had come, and now it was time to break the news to her. She should have sent a message to Beth's house earlier, but with Edith gone there was no staff to send and, humiliatingly, she did not have the cash to send a casual urchin with a note.

She had stopped crying now. She shook her hair loose, ran a brush through it, and – knowing that it was impossible to dress it well oneself – pulled it tightly backwards from her face, twisted it into a single coil and pinned and netted it firmly into a savage bun. With the dark dress, it made her look exactly like a governess, she thought – severe and humourless and limited of means – but even governesses had some role to occupy, and a degree of independence. Why should these things be denied to her? She picked up Edwin's letter, and with thoughtful care tore it into pieces and dropped it in the grate. Lest Cook should read it when she came to light the fire, she took up the poker and hid the letter under the coal and wood that were already laid. Then she raised her chin and walked firmly down the stairs.

At the door of the drawing-room she had to pause again, but the problem must be faced. She squared her shoulders and walked into the room. 'Elizabeth, I'm very sorry...' she began.

'But it was not Beth Richie who was awaiting her. 'Captain Halligan?' she stammered.

He came towards her, his face concerned and kind. 'My dear Miss Killivant, whatever is

251

amiss? I understood from Miss Ritchie that you were travelling today, and I came to offer to accompany you both as far as the station to help you with your bags. I have my carriage waiting...' he broke off. 'Why do you shake your head?'

She found that it was difficult to frame the words. Her voice insisted on betraying her by trembling. 'It is nothing, Captain Halligan, except that I cannot go. I have been obliged ... that is ... there's been a sudden change of plan.'

'But not one of your choosing?' He was standing very close and every nerve in her body was aware of it.

She dropped her head and would not meet his gaze. 'It is nothing, Captain. Truly. Merely that my brother is expected to arrive, and I must be here to greet him. Nothing more than that.'

'Nothing?'

It was said so gently that she betrayed herself. She turned away. 'There is always a problem with Edwin, I'm afraid – he disapproves so much, especially of me. No doubt he would tell you that he has ample cause. He was angry that I had taken Fanny on at all, and he's even more angry that I want to look for her – and now he will be angry that Edith isn't here and there won't be proper servants to look after him. My fault, of course, for sending her away, as Edwin will doubtless point out when he arrives. And now Nurse Morgan is unhappy too – it isn't really the poor woman's place to undertake the duties of a maid, but honestly there is becoming less and less for her to do – what with Mother getting up and getting dressed these days, and even remembering to take her medicines. She's been a different person since you came to the house.'

'And your brother will not at least be pleased at that?'

She could not tell him what the letter said. She looked away. 'Oh, you don't know Edwin. He'll give Nurse Morgan notice, and Mama will be upset – because she has taken a great liking to the nurse. He'll ban you from the house, and she'll go back to bed again, and that will be my fault as well because I brought you here. Just as it is my fault that he's coming here at all, when he doesn't want to – he has a daughter now, and he dotes upon her. So you see, I am responsible for everyone's unhappiness.'

'You don't make me unhappy, Miss Killivant,' he said. 'Quite the contrary.'

The gentle kindness was too much for her. A sob escaped her, and though she pressed her eyelids shut she could feel the shaming tears escape and run in hot trickles down her cheeks.

'My dear Miss Killivant – Alicia – my dear. Whatever is the matter?'

She shook her head. 'It is nothing, Captain Halligan. I must apologize.' With an effort she had controlled herself. 'I have no business to burst out in that way, and as for behaving in this shaming fashion...' She met his eyes. 'My brother is quite right. I am foolish and thoughtless.'

He placed a finger underneath her chin and tipped her head, so that she was looking directly

253

into his eyes. 'You are not thoughtless, and you could never be a fool. You have too much spirit and intelligence for that. A little headstrong, maybe. I have a sister – as you are aware – and she has behaved a great deal worse than you, getting herself arrested for throwing stones, and of course I have made it clear that I do not approve. But I would never consider taking the tone your brother takes. I have done my best to help her, in my humble way, whatever opinions I might have of what she's done. But to make you so unhappy and distressed! And why should he want to ban me from the house? I cannot imagine what possesses him to treat you in this way.'

'Perhaps because my presence is a charge on him. I do have money, but it is not mine to use till I am thirty years of age. Not unless...' She stopped again. It would sound as if she were suggesting that she should marry somebody, simply so that she could get her hands on the account. 'I had a small allowance, but he has cut it off, and I am to apply to him direct for everything – even for the house. Just when I've given Edith money for this Launceston trip as well. I can only imagine what he'll say to that.'

'If you have need of money, Alicia, I should be happy to assist. Do not be affronted. You can pay me back when you are thirty, if you insist on it.' He was still looking intently in her face and for a moment she thought – she hoped – that he would take her in his arms, but they were interrupted by a sharp cough at the door.

'Excuse me, Miss Alicia,' Mrs Pritchard said.

254

back, barking and growling something terrible.

Edie shook her head. This was bewildering. 'I only hoped to have a word with him. It's about someone that I think might be his child. He came to our house once...'

'Well, if he got you in trouble, that's your lookout, not mine. I got my hands full looking after what I got,' the woman said. She turned in the doorway and called to someone in the house. 'Freddie! Get out the back and untie that stupid dog and let it loose. It'll see this girl off. Might as well earn its dinner for once in its damned life.'

There was a scuttling in the hall behind her, and what seemed to be a child ran in the direction of the back door and the yard. That was enough for Edie. 'It's all right, I'm leaving!' she said, hastily backing out on to the street. She thought of trying to shout and leave a message that she'd called, and that it was about Fanny – or rather Nellie Rouse – but the sight of a large and snarling dog dissuaded her from that. In any case, she thought, it might be better just to leave. Rouse was unlikely to tell her anything – perhaps she should have thought things out more carefully before she came.

She retreated, walking backwards, still keeping her eyes fixed firmly on the dog, which was now in the doorway straining at the leash, held by a smallish boy in ragged clothes who looked as if he might easily be tugged away with it.

'Here, look out, my 'andsome.' Something bumped her back. She turned. A bent old woman with a basket was peering up at her. 'Near as

nothing walked right into me and knocked me shopping clean out of me 'and.'

'I'm some sorry, missus,' Edie said at once. 'I was that worried by the dog, I wasn't looking where I went. Never hurt you, did I?'

The woman shook her head. 'Trod on me skirt, that's all. Though I am not surprised. Wretched dog's a menace – and that new wife's the same. Brought it with her – and that skinny kid. Spoil the place they do. Used to be a real nice neighbourhood round here.'

Edith said quickly, 'You knew the other wife?'

The woman nodded. 'Well, not to say knew her. Saw her in the street. I don't know of anyone who knew her properly. Kept hersel' apart, as you might say – not unfriendly, ju didn't get out much, or have the neighbours Nice sort of woman though– not a bit like *h* She gestured to the end house, where the w with the baby had slammed the door 'Terrible what 'appened to her in the en hitched the basket up on to her hip. 'Bu stand here gossiping, this 'ere basket ton.'

Edith said quickly, 'Can I carry i She took the shopping – it was heav

'Kind of you, my 'andsome. M aren't what they used to be.' The her toothless gums in a deligh show you the way,' and she hust more sprightly without her he

Edie hurried after her. She h additional information abo Rouse, but the old woman which seemed to hold the food – the rest of the wall space was completely covered with hooks and shelves and nails, from which dangled every imaginable household article: boots and cups and candles: saucepans, brooms and herbs: coats and sieves and strings of onions and enamel jugs. The woman moved a pile of knitting from a chair, and motioned Edith to sit down in it, while she placed the basket on the table-top and carefully took out her precious purchases: a big bag of flour, potatoes, sugar, swede, four eggs carefully wrapped up in newspaper, and – from the butcher's – a big piece of suet and some off-cuts in a paper bag.

The evidence of such a meagre diet made Edie wish that she had not agreed to come inside. She was ready to make some excuse and hurry off, but the back door was opened and an ancient man came in – even more bent and wizened than his wife – struggling under the weight of water in a pail. 'Heard you coming, brought this from the well.' He squinted at Edie with moist, faded eyes. 'Who's this to, then?'

'Found her getting bawled at by that Rouse woman and her dog,' his wife replied. 'And then she was good enough to bring my shopping 'ome. Thought she deserved a drop of tay. This is my 'usband, Walter Carter, by the by.' She took the pail and set it on the floor, and then ladled some of its contents into a kettle which she hung over the fire. 'Don't know your name to tell him who you are.'

'Edith Trewin, from Penzance.' Edie held out a hand.

He spat on his and wiped it on his sleeve, before he proffered it. 'Glad to meet you.' He emptied the other chair, sat down on it and pulled a pipe out of his pocket. 'What you wanting with those Rouses then?' He took a twist of baccy from a tin and began to tamp it down into the bowl, looking at Edie questioningly all the while.

'I think I knew the eldest daughter – I was looking for the house,' Edith said, giving as little away as possible.

He nodded. 'Ah! I said to Patience that there was an older girl as well. Used to see her sometimes going off to the school, and then we heard she went off working, or something of the kind. Wonder they never said so in the newspapers. You heard about all that business with the cart?'

It was her turn to explain now. 'Your wife has just told me, but I didn't know the rest of the family at all. Except I think I might have met the father once.' The old man said nothing and she added, hopefully, 'Bit of a rascal, I thought, from what I saw of him.'

The old man chuckled. 'No "bit" about it, he's a caution, that one is. The way he gets round people, it allus makes me laugh.'

Mrs Carter poked the fire, and said savagely, 'I don't know why it should. He's a proper rogue. How he gets away with it is more than I can see.'

Walter Carter took a spill and lit it from the fire, and spent a long moment puffing at his pipe. Only when he had it burning did he speak again. 'Now, now, Patience, don't start that again. He's done no harm to us. I say he did a good job when he fixed the roof for us. He's a handy workman, when he puts his mind to it.'

'Which isn't very often,' his wife said tartly. 'Too busy getting up to sneaky tricks.'

Her husband sucked his pipe. 'And where would we have been if he had not put out that fire?'

At the mention of a fire, Edie's ears pricked up. 'Fire?'

Patience Carter nodded. 'Fire in the chimney – that was all it was. Just when he'd finished putting back the slates – my Walter used to do it, but he gets giddy now. Anyhow – no sooner had Rouse done it, than he's knocking on my door. "Oh, Mrs Carter, you should have swept your flue. Your chimney's afire, shall I put it out for you?" Well, of course I panicked and I told him yes and gave him a shilling for his pains – it wasn't till afterwards I came to think. We'd had the sweep here only weeks before –how did the chimney come to be on fire, just when Rouse was up there with his ladders on the roof? And how did he put it out so quick as that? It's my belief he started it himself.'

'Surely he didn't?' Edith was appalled. 'That would be dishonest – and dangerous as well.'

The woman wrapped a piece of cloth around her hand, picked up the kettle and poured water from it to swill the teapot round. 'Wouldn't put it past 'un. He's allus up to tricks. Walter won't have it that he played one on us – seeing how we're nearly neighbours – but I'm damty sure of it.' Having warmed the pot, she measured out the leaves and made the tea. 'He used to boast of playing that pasty trick on folk.'

Walter puffed contented smoke at her. 'That ain't the same at all!' He turned to Edith. 'Just a bit of fun. Be on a job, see – at a farm or anywhere they kept a dog or two – and round about dinner-time he'd turn up in the yard, flapping his cap and swearing like a coot – "Get off, you beggar" or something of the sort – until the woman came out the door to see. Then he'd come over all pathetic.' He put on a comic voice. ' "It's nothing, missus, only your old dog. Blessed thing jumped up at me – stole my bit of pasty that I'd brought for lunch. But no matter, missus, don't you worry about me, I'll just do without." The poor soul would feel that sorry she'd give him something else, often a pasty if she had one on the go – but of course he'd never brought his lunch in any case. I've heard him tell that tale himself, at least a dozen times. Used to laugh, and say it never failed.' He slapped his thigh and chuckled. 'Old dog very often got a hiding though.'

'Just so Rouse could get a bite to eat?' Edith said. 'Poor creature! That's not fair.'

Mrs Carter looked approvingly at her as she poured the tea out into three enamel cups. 'That's what I say, my 'andsome. If a man's a cheating liar, he will lie and cheat to us – but Walter won't have it, and there's an end of it. Doesn't like to think that he's been made to look a fool, and Rouse is somewhere poking fun at him. Which he will be, Walter – don't you think he won't. And people will be laughing and thinking it's all fun – just like you do, when it's other folks.' She was fetching plates and splits and butter as she spoke. 'Trouble is, Rouse can be charming, when he wants to be. Persuade the pope that black is white, if he'd a mind to. But enough of that. You tuck in, my 'andsome. Would you like some jam?'

Edie knew better by this time than to accept the food, but she took the cup of tea with gratitude. 'Did you know Fan ... Nellie, the eldest girl?' she said.

The woman shook her head. 'Like Walter said, we only saw her in the street. I believe I did hear that she went off to work for some big house in the town, and after the others died her father fetched her home – to look after that blessed infant, I suppose. If so, she wasn't there for very long, because we never saw her after, and next thing this new woman came and set up house with him. No better than she should be, by the looks of it – already had a child.'

'I tell you, woman, you always think the worst of things.' The old man blew on the surface of his tea. 'How you know she wasn't wed before?'

The woman sniffed. 'Well, she's slow to say so, if that is the case. And now there is another baby on the way. She must have been months gone when she first married him!'

'My dear!' The man spoke sharply. 'Be careful of young ears!' He turned to Edie. 'Sure you won't join us in a bit of split?'

Edie swallowed the remainder of her tea. 'No, honestly. That's very kind of you, but I'll be expected back. I've taken up too much of your time as it is.' She got to her feet. 'Thank you for the tea.'

She was quietly excited as she walked back to the lodging-house. Excited and rather proud of what she'd found out today. There was so much to tell Miss Alicia when she arrived – and that ought to be tomorrow on the later train. There would probably be a letter or something when she got in.

But it was not a letter. It was a telegram. The lodging-house lady came out to give it to her, with a sniff, and the sight of the yellow envelope gave Edie quite a fright.

But not as much of a fright as the message inside: 'Plans unavoidably cancelled. Return at once. Edwin expected Saturday. Alicia Killivant.'

Captain Halligan had been wonderful. He had driven her in his carriage to the post office to send the telegram, quietly insisted on paying for it himself and then entertained herself and Beth to a delightful tea in a charming teashop on the Marazion road where they could see the sea. 'Since you are to miss out on your little expedition up the county,' he'd explained.

Beth was disappointed, there was no hiding it, and a little impatient of Alicia's distress. 'Well, I should think you could have kept a prior engagement with a friend!' she had grumbled. But then Philip – Captain Halligan – had whispered something in her ear. Alicia could not hear what he said but it seemed to do the trick, because afterwards her friend was all concern and sympathy.

264

'I'm sorry, Liss, of course you're disappointed too. It must be quite frightful to live as you do, dear – quite like a marionette, with horrid Edwin pulling all the strings,' she murmured as they stopped outside her home and the Captain carried her suitcase to the door. 'Mama and the boys will be surprised to see me back!' She got out of the carriage and stood at the door of it. 'Shall you be coming to the meeting this weekend?'

Alicia shook her head, too mortified to speak.

'Oh, Edwin forbids it. I had forgotten that. Well, I promise I will come and see you very soon. But I won't bring "Votes for Women" until he's gone! And when we are thirty – if you haven't married first – and you come into your money, we shall go away, and not just to Launceston. To London, or even to Paris if you like. I'll save up and we'll make a point of it.'

Her friend's attempts to make amends were so transparently absurd that Alicia almost felt like laughing, for the first time that day. 'Thank you, Beth, but I'm quite sure you will have found a husband long before then.'

Beth twinkled at her. 'Me? I doubt it very much. We don't all have dashing admirers, you know. But you, now...' She actually leaned forward and kissed Alicia's cheek. 'I hope that your wretched brother does not come between you, that is all.' And, waving cheerfully, she went into the house.

Alicia felt herself turn scarlet to her ears. What could Beth possibly have meant by that? And when Captain Halligan came back to the coach and ordered the coachman to drive to Holvean House, somehow Alicia found it hard to talk to him.

'I'm sorry you've been disappointed over your trip,' he said as they drew up at the gate and he helped her down. 'I do not like to see you looking so distressed.' Her hand was still resting lightly on his arm, and he placed his own upon it and squeezed her fingers hard. 'You've got so much spirit, it's as if there's a light inside you. Don't let your brother Edwin put it out. Don't let Edwin win, in fact.'

It was something that Charles used to say to her, when they joined forces in their childhood long ago, and in her present frame of mind the familiar jest was too much for her. 'I think his victory's complete this time, thanks to Mr Tulver,' she said bitterly.

'What's Mr Tulver done?'

So she told him, and as she spoke she watched his face. She saw it change from concern to anger. 'How dare he!' he exclaimed.

She shook her head. 'It's my fault, I suppose. I thought Mr Tulver was rather fond of me. It did not occur to me that he'd betray my trust. You know he'd asked me to a concert in his company? And I told him that I couldn't go with him, because there was a women's rally in the town. I'm afraid I suggested that he could find me there, never supposing for a moment that he'd go, but I understand he did, though as it turned out I was unable to attend myself.'

'I see!' His face wore an expression of en-lightenment. 'So that is why he wrote to your brother as he did. It would seem he resented my attentions. I can't say I'm surprised. I would have felt the same in his shoes, I am sure.' He smiled at her.

'Jealous of your attentions?' she repeated in disbelief. Was it possible that Beth had been correct? 'Forgive me, Captain Halligan, I had not realized...'

'But surely, Miss Killivant ... Alicia ... you must be aware...? I did not think it proper, on such slight acquaintance, to presume – but I had supposed that you were not completely indifferent to me.'

She stared at him, a flow of pleasure starting at her toes. 'I ... no ... that is...'

'I liked you from the very moment that we met,' he went on eagerly, 'almost as if your brother Charles was a link. Of course, he'd often spoken of you when you were a child. I felt I almost knew you from the start. And when you invited me to come back to your house and meet your mother, I thought it must mean that you did not dislike me.'

She shook her head, flustered. 'I had no idea you felt like that.' Immediately she could have bitten her tongue as she saw how hurt he looked.

'I am sorry if I misinterpreted, Miss Killivant,' he said. 'I was sure you must have known the way I felt for you.' He gave a rueful smile. 'I thought my behaviour made it evident.'

'Perhaps it did, to others,' she murmured stupidly.

She was thinking of Beth Richie, but he misunderstood. 'I'm sure that Mr Tulver, for exam-

267

ple, was in no doubt at all. But it seems I have misread your simple kindliness as something more, and I fear I have affronted him. And he is the person for whom you really care. I've been a fool. I'm sorry.'

'Oh, no, no, no!' she cried. 'You are not at all a fool. If anyone was foolish, it seems that it was me. I did not realize that I'd signalled to the world how much I ... that I...' She stopped in confusion and added breathlessly, 'It is not Tim Tulver that I have feelings for.'

'Then you do care something for me? Is that what you mean?' They were still standing by the carriage, so everyone could see, and he was still holding her hand in both of his. He squeezed her fingers. 'Can I hope for that, Alicia?'

She met his eyes, and did not try to move her hand away. 'Edwin tells me that I'm forward, and perhaps I am. But, yes, Captain Halligan, you may hope for that.'

'Then you will call me Philip?'

She nodded speechlessly.

'And I'll call you Alicia. I already do. And you will let me meet your brother while he's here?'

She found that she was smiling through unexpected tears. 'You don't know him, Philip! But I suppose I must.' She glanced towards the house. 'And now, I think, we had better go inside, before Queenie falls out of the upstairs window in her attempts to gape at us.'

Two

Edwin was supervising the packing of his bag. His new man had done it – and not very well.

'I shall require my collar box, and garters for my socks. And one pair of braces should be quite enough...' He broke off as Claire came hurrying into the room. 'What, my dear? What is the matter?'

She looked shocked and distraught. 'Edwin, I'm sorry, but you can't go this weekend. I've just...'

He held his hand up to signal her to stop. 'Claire, my dear, we've been through this before,' he said, outwardly patient – but with an inward sigh. 'I understand it isn't practical for you to go yourself. I would not expect it, with little Caroline. You are afraid of germs. Holvean House is not a place for infants, I'm aware, since Mama has been so sick. In fact, although she'd be enchanted to meet her granddaughter, I fear she is not really well enough to cope with all the strain.'

Those were the reasons for going alone, he told himself. Not because he did not want to share his child with anyone – although the thought of Alicia and Mother cooing over her and talking about 'my grandchild' or 'my niece' had reconciled him somewhat to leaving her behind. 'There's nothing to discuss.'

Claire looked as if she wanted to say something all the same.

He shook his head. 'Alicia has clearly been behaving like a fool. This one-legged adventurer has got his claws in her, telling her tales about the regiment and worming his way into Mother's confidence as well, and we know absolutely nothing about his family except that his mother is mad and his sister is in jail. I suppose this recommends him to Alicia!' He shook his head. 'Just when I had hopes of Tim Tulver from the bank. You know that she had encouraged him, as well? Agreed to let him take her to a concert very soon? And then this man arrives, and Mama is so enamoured of his having known Charles that she is incapable of seeing through his wiles. No doubt he's heard that Alicia will have money when she weds.'

'But, Edwin...'

He sighed – outwardly this time, and quite deliberately. Claire could be horribly persistent when she chose. 'Of course I don't wish to leave you, or Caroline,' he said. 'I won't be a moment longer than I need. I'll call in on Monday and arrange things with the bank and I'll come back as soon as possible. But it must be done at once. Alicia is spending Father's hard-earned cash on madcap schemes to find this maid of hers, on some footling pretence that there's danger for the girl – simply because her father wants her to come home. Mama seems powerless to intervene. The house is obviously in total disarray and the sooner I can sort it out the better for us all.'

'But, Edwin,' Claire said, in the sharp tone he had not heard for months, 'I am trying to tell you! You can't go to Penzance. At least not for the moment. There may not be a train. Or cabs or anything. I am sure your sister is of great concern, but there are some things which take precedence, even over that.'

'Why? What is it?'

'I have just heard it from the baker. It's the King. He's dead. At a quarter to twelve last night, apparently. It's posted on a notice at the palace gates. The country is in mourning, and businesses are closed, and thousands are turning out into the streets.'

He nodded. This was clearly different. There would be special services in every church and meeting-hall, no doubt, and he'd be wanted at the mission this weekend. Already a sermon was forming in his mind, about the germs of evil and the seeds of hope. 'You are right, dearest,' he murmured, gracious in defeat. 'I must delay my trip. I'll write to Alicia.' He frowned his thoughtful, contemplative frown. 'Or should I send a wire? I wonder, with all this, whether there'll be post.'

Holvean House seemed awful empty when Edie wasn't there. She'd only been gone a day or two, but it already seemed a month. Sammy went about his tasks as usual, but collecting eggs had turned into a chore, now that there was only Queenie to take them to the house. Mr Gribbens seemed to grumble more than usual, besides, and when he came upon Sammy turning over one of the front beds, ready to put the summer bedding out, his rebuke was sharp.

'Put your back into that digging, lad. Never make a gardener of you, if you slouch about. Never been the same since you was asked into the house.' And he stumped off to pot up more of his precious seedlings.

Sam took out his feelings on the clods of earth. He knew better than to speak his thoughts, but he pretended each lump was a devil's face and thumped it with a will.

It did the trick, though, because next time Mr Gribbens happened by, he nodded. 'That's a bit more like. And when you've finished that, you can hoe the rest of it, and then go and give that pile of yourn a turn.' He sniffed. 'Can't put in a word for you if you don't pull your weight.'

Sam jammed his spade into the pile of earth, and straightened up. 'Put a word in, where?'

Mr Gribbens ran a grimy hand along his nose. 'Thing is, I might know of someone looking for a boy to bring along, make him up to be an under-gardener soon. 'Course, they need someone who knows a dock leaf from a bean and isn't afraid of hard work now and then. Thought it might suit, if you was looking to be wed.' He leered at Sammy. 'You're starting to shape up. Supposing you aren't daydreaming about that girl of yours and manage to keep your mind on what you're doing.'

Sammy swallowed. He knew it was ungrateful but he wasn't altogether thrilled. Only a year ago he would have leaped at this, but now there was Edie, and leaving Holvean House meant leaving her as well. It had always been the plan to try to find a place where he could rise to be in charge – perhaps somewhere with a gardener's cottage, where he could take a wife – but somehow they had never thought that it would mean they would be apart. This was a conundrum, that's what it was.

'Where's this to, then?' he said, with something like alarm.

But Gribbens only made a wicked face and rubbed his nose again. 'Can't tell 'ee that, lad, not till I've spoke to them again. And it's not definite. But I'll put a word in for you, when the times comes, if you like. Be a chance for you to make something of yourself – and a bit extra in your pay each week, I shouldn't be surprised.'

Sammy sighed and picked up the spade again. 'I aren't sure I'm so keen on moving anywhere,' he said, slowly. 'All depends, I suppose. Don't want to go a million miles away. And, in any case, how would you manage here? You can't be doing everything yourself.'

Gribbens gave his rare wheezing laugh. 'Ah, don't you go worrying about that, old son. I trained you, didn't I? If I can do that, I can train anyone. Now, you going to get on with what you're doing, Sammy Hern, or are you going to stand there chattering all day? Ruddy beds won't dig themselves, you know.' He went off, chuckling.

Sammy stood there, staring after him. The old man was enjoying this, he thought – teasing him on purpose with only half a tale. He sighed. If only Edith had been here, he could have talked to her; found out what she thought about his going away. She might think it was worth it, even, if it meant that they could eventually wed. They could have free days together now and again – it might be easier if he was working somewhere else and there was no one to see that she had a 'follower'. He made a little face. Could work out, perhaps, if it was not too far away. But, on the other hand...

He raised the spade and began to dig again, taking comfort in the rhythmic nature of the task. He didn't hear about the King till after tea.

Edith had spent a miserable night since her summons to go home. Here was a pickle and no mistake. She didn't have a train ticket to go back straight away – and no wherewithal to buy one. The payment for the room had used up all the money that she had, and she couldn't even wire or write to ask for more. Now what on earth was she going to do? She was ready to break down and cry at her predicament – but, as Pa would say, 'If bawling doesn't solve a problem it's a waste of tears.'

Well, she told herself – at least she wouldn't starve. Her breakfast and dinner had been paid for, for the next two days. Worry had taken away her appetite for food, but the meals were good and she would try to make the most of them – just in case she was obliged to walk the nigh-on-a-hundred weary miles back home.

Then, tossing and turning, sleepless in that

comfortable bed, she had at last devised a sort of plan. She would write a letter to Miss Alicia. She could pawn something, if necessary, to buy a stamp for it. There was writing paper and some envelopes laid out on a table in the lodgers' sitting-room, together with a dip-pen and some ink, though she wasn't sure if she would have to pay for using them as well. She didn't want to ask the landlady (who was looking at her very suspiciously by now, as if she might have guessed that there had been bad news) but she did seek out the Major, who was eating breakfast too.

'No, my dear girl, they're complimentary.' He laughed, and then – obviously seeing that she didn't understand – added, 'You don't have to pay.'

She wondered why that was a 'compliment', but she thanked him for his help. She was still nervous though, and she took good care that no one was about when – a little later – she went into the sitting-room and sat down at the desk. She selected a piece of paper from the rack, and very gingerly took up the pen. She was no great writer, though she had learned at school. They taught you copperplate with a slate-pencil and slate and you moved on to pen and ink when you were good enough, but she had always been too hasty and inclined to blot her work. If she took it slowly she might do a better job, though she was not accustomed to this kind of fancy nib.

It took her two attempts to write a letter she could send, but in the end she was quite pleased with it.

Dear Miss Alissier [*had she spelled that right?*],

I beg to bring the following to your esteemed attention [*she knew that was what you said, because she'd copied it from the landlady's account*]. I have had to pay for several days lodgings in advance, and I haven't got the money for a ticket home. If you could send some I will come at once. I have found out some interesting things.

I remain, your obedient servant,
Edith Trewin

That would have to do. There were fancy, pre-made envelopes, and she took one of them and folded the letter carefully inside. She hoped it would reach Miss Killivant safely by next day, though there was no sealing-wax to stick down the flap – and she did not have a signet ring, even if there had been. Then, still taking care to avoid the landlady, she fetched her cape and hat and set off down the street in search of the pawnbroker she had seen the day before.

There were a great many people in the street – a good deal more than she was used to in Penzance. Perhaps Launceston was always busy on a Saturday. She was so intent upon her errand that she did not pay very much attention to anything else, and it was not until she reached the building with the three brass balls outside that she realized it was shut. A scrawny youth in a brown apron was putting up the shutters even as she arrived.

'You closing?'

He turned to scowl at her. 'What does it look like? Yes, of course we are.'

She frowned. 'But aren't you busiest on a Saturday?' She had visited a pawnbroker once or twice before, when there had been that stoppage at the mine, and she had seen the crush: church- and chapel-goers queueing to redeem their Sunday clothes (which had not been needed in the week) while what Ma would call 'the heathen' were scrabbling to 'pop' anything that would buy their weekend pint – and never mind how they would pay the money back.

'Well, so it might be busy, as a general rule, but the governor says we're closing as a gesture of respect. Cost me a day's pay, I shouldn't wonder, too.'

She ignored the grumbling. 'Respect? What's happened?'

'Can't you read? I should have thought you'd have seen the notices.' He took a step backwards and revealed what she had not seen before, a black-bordered handwritten sign displayed on the door: 'Closed till further notice as a token of respect, following the death of His Majesty the King'. 'We heard about it from the people who came down from London on the train, and one of the businesses has got a telephone and they rang through to the capital to check. It's the King. He's dead. Just before midnight yesterday, it seems.'

'The King?' she echoed, as though it were impossible for royalty to die, like ordinary people. Though of course she could remember, if she put her mind to it, when the Old Queen had passed away. It had seemed more exciting than anything, at the time: bands and solemn marches and a day off school and wreaths of black bunting hanging in all the shops.

She looked around. It was happening again. Many of the shopkeepers had closed their doors – only the food shops were half-open and serving customers – and all the wares had been brought in from the street. There were no saucepans, racks of shoes or piles of cabbages, and if the drifting crowds were gazing into shop windows as they passed, it was at displays of crêpe ribbons and pictures of the King.

So how was she ever going to buy a stamp and be in touch with Miss Alicia? She found a granite window-sill and sat down hard on it. The pre-payment for her lodging was only for tonight. And, drat it – she was going to cry, as though that was going to help. She fished into her pocket for a handkerchief and her fingers closed around a piece of folded paper there. It was the map that Captain Halligan had drawn and given her. And there, in the middle, marked with a large cross, was the house he used to visit when he was a boy.

It was worth a try. She could go and ask them if they could spare a stamp and, if so, she could still send that letter to Miss Alicia. She'd have to promise to repay them by and by, but in a big house like that they really wouldn't miss the price of it. Of course, it was a rather forward thing to do – they might send her off with a cuff around the ear, or the people might have left and moved on long ago, but it was the only strategy she had. It made her feel better to have a plan at all.

She got to her feet and walked slowly up the street. It wasn't difficult to find the house. It was a large, imposing one, taking up nearly a whole block to itself, and it had a little flight of steps and a big brass doorknocker shaped like a lion's head, and an even bigger doorknob, also made of brass, right in the centre of the green-painted door. There was a plaque beside the door, set up on the wall. It read 'John Lillywhite and Son, Solicitors'.

Lillywhite – the name was still the same. That was a start. She walked up to the entrance and, taking a deep breath, was just about to raise the gleaming lion's head and knock, when a plump girl in a gingham uniform and cap opened the door and came out on to the step.

She stared at Edie. 'What you doing here?' She did not stop to hear the answer, but began to signal to someone in the window of the house who was trying to place a notice where it could best be seen.

'I wondered if I could speak to Mr Lillywhite. It's an important matter.'

'You can't do that. You'll need an appointment, like anybody else. Anyway, we're closed until the funeral.' The plump girl made a final signal to the house, and nodded to the notice. 'All the courts and everything are shutting down till then, and Mr Lillywhite is going to go away. Like it says up there – you can read it for yourself.' She turned to Edith and looked her up and down. 'What do you want to see him for in any case? Cost you a guinea just to talk to him.'

'Oh, this isn't business. Or not the kind you mean.' Edie was flustered. 'It's about a stamp. I think Mr Lillywhite might know a friend of mine.'

'Well, I've told you, you can't see him, and that's the end of that.' The plump girl looked as if she meant to shut the door.

Desperation drove Edie to sudden recklessness and, taking a lesson from the awful Mr Rouse, she put her foot into the aperture. 'I've got a map my friend drew me,' she said urgently. 'He marked out the house and all. It's on this piece of paper. I can show you if you like.'

She had spoken too loudly. A man's voice boomed from within. 'What is going on, Matilda? What's the fuss about?'

'There's a girl here wants to see you, sir, and she won't be told.' The plump girl tried to shut the door again.

Edith flinched, but did not move her foot. 'It really is important. Tell him I've come from Captain Halligan,' she said, knowing the dratted tears were brimming in her eyes.

The plump girl looked scornful, and called out over her shoulder once again. 'She's got her foot stuck in the doorway, sir, and will not go away. Claims to know a friend of yours, but doesn't look the type. Do you want to send someone for the police?'

Edith raised her own voice deliberately loud, so that the person in the house could hear. 'I've come from Captain Halligan, in Penzance. He

280

says he sometimes used to visit this house when he was young.'

The owner of the voice came into sight. He was an old man – older than Edie's ma and pa – with thinning hair and a distinguished look. He wore a dark suit, white starched collars and an old-fashioned tie and had a pince-nez balanced on his nose. Edie's spirits sank. This couldn't possibly be the Captain's friend.

But the man was speaking and his voice was not unkind. 'Now, what's all this, young lady? You are Philip's friend?'

It took her a moment to work out who 'Philip' was, but she moved her foot away and said politely, 'Well, he isn't my friend – naturally – though I think a lot of him. It's my mistress really, Miss Alicia Killivant.' She looked expectantly at him, but it was clear the name meant nothing, and she hurried on. 'The thing is, she sent me here and now she wants me home, and I haven't got a ticket and I can't let her know. I had to pay our lodgings in advance and she'd not allowed for that. I've written her a letter, but I couldn't post it on. I was going to hock my purse to buy a stamp for it, but the pawnbroker is shut. I didn't know about the King, you see.'

For an awful moment he did not respond. He just stood and looked her up and down. 'What do you want from me?'

'I wondered if you could let me have a stamp, sir. Just for a day or two. Once my mistress sends me the money, I'll pay you back, of course. I'm sorry about putting my foot into the door, but I was desperate. I'm honest, truly,' she

281

pleaded through her tears. 'Captain Halligan would speak for me, I'm sure. Look, here's the piece of paper with his writing on.'

His face twitched with something that might have been a smile. 'In that case, young lady, you'd better come inside.'

Three

Edie looked around her. The house was very big, quite as sizable as Holvean House inside – although the two front rooms downstairs were clearly offices, and there was a sort of waiting area further down the hall. But Mr Lillywhite – if that was who it was – led her straight past these rooms and up a flight of stairs into a light and airy sitting-room, where a grey-haired woman with spectacles was stitching by the fire.

'We have an unexpected visitor, my dear. You remember Philip Halligan, that friend of Jeremy's who used to stay with us?'

The woman in the armchair put her sewing down. 'This is not his sister, surely?' She seemed about to rise.

Her husband made a gesture which prevented her. 'No, this – it appears – is merely the servant of a friend. She's on business in Launceston for her mistress for a day or two. It seems that Philip was kind enough to have remembered us, and mentioned our address. She came to us to ask us for a stamp. I thought we could oblige.' He seemed to be amused at something, from his tone of voice.

'A stamp?' the woman echoed, sounding equally amused. 'Why does she want a stamp?'

283

'That's what she can tell us, while she drinks some tea.' He rang a little bell and the plump girl in gingham answered it at once. 'We'll have some tea, Matilda. And some muffins, too. No, my dear,' he added to his wife, 'I know the girl's a servant, but she is in distress and we'll entertain her properly – for Philip's sake, at least. Jeremy would say the same, if he were here, I am sure. Now, then!' He turned to Edie. 'I'm John Lillywhite and this is my wife Joan.'

Edith was not sure how to answer this, but she sketched a curtsey. It seemed the proper thing. 'Pleased to meet you both, I'm sure. I'm Edith Trewin, ma'am.'

Mr Lillywhite motioned to her to take a chair, She did so gingerly. 'Well,' he said heartily, 'what's this all about?' And when she hesitated, he went on, 'Start from the beginning. That makes it easier.'

So Edith gave him a potted version of events – how she'd come to look for Fanny, who'd run away from home, and how her employer and her employer's friend had planned to come as well – while the plump servant brought tea and the most delicious buttered muffins in a dish. (There was jam, as well, but Edie was afraid of slipping that – it was hard enough balancing the fragile china cup, and trying not to spill the crumbs of muffin on the rug.) 'So there you are,' she finished. 'Miss Alicia's brother's going to come, so she isn't coming.' She realized that she hadn't put that very well. 'She wants me to go home.'

'But you've paid the lodgings, so you haven't got the fare?'

She nodded. 'That's right, Mr Lillywhite. Just when I had found out something about Fanny, too – or Nellie Rouse, as I suppose that I should say.'

'But surely, you had a ticket to come up...' the woman said, but her husband interrupted.

'Just a moment! Did you say Nellie Rouse? Eleanor Rouse, would that be? From Trewendron, possibly?'

Edith's mouth was full of muffin by this time, but it did not seem proper not to answer him. She said indistinctly, 'I suppose she might be Eleanor by rights – though I never heard that name. I knew her as Fanny and her father calls her Nell or Nellie. But the family comes from Trewendron right enough. The father is a builder, and he lives there still. The mother and three of the children were killed in a cart last year – though it seems he's got another family now.'

Mr Lillywhite was looking at her very hard indeed. 'And you say this Nellie came to work with you? How did that happen? That was in Penzance.'

Edith had swallowed her muffin, and could say, 'She'd come down looking for an aunt of hers. Her mother's sister, by the sound of it – but when Fanny got there, the aunt had moved away.'

He was still staring at her in a most peculiar way. 'Did you know the aunt?'

Why was he asking all these questions about Fanny, Edith thought? All this fuss about a postage stamp. But he was a gentleman and you had to answer him. 'I never met her, though I do know where she lived – a little village. Her name was Mrs Polcurnooth, I believe.'

'But she had moved, you say?' He was exchanging knowing glances with his wife.'

'Gone out to Australia to be with her son.' Edie was mystified. 'But nobody had so much as an address, so Fanny was stuck there – like I'm stuck up here now. That's how she came looking for a job.'

He clapped his hands together with a sudden sound. 'Then it is the same person. I knew it had to be. Wait here, young lady! 'And he disappeared. She could hear his footsteps clattering downstairs.

Mrs Lillywhite had picked up her work again, and she looked at Edith through her spectacles. 'What were you doing, visiting the aunt if you didn't know her?'

'Fanny – or Nellie, as I should be calling her I s'pose – came to us without a character. Said she had been given one, but had lost it in a fire.' Edith felt uncomfortable as she spoke the words. Like a lot of things that Fanny had said, it might have been a lie. ''Course, we don't know if that was true.'

The woman nodded. 'Well, she was given one, certainly. Eleanor was servant to a friend of mine – and very satisfactory she seemed to be as well. And then there was that dreadful business with the cart, and the father came up to the house and took her home with him. I believe there was an infant who had survived the accident. There was quite a scene, I think. Eleanor was pleading not to be sent back – but when her father wanted her, what was my friend to do? She was a bit uneasy, I do remember that, but there seemed to be no reason for refusing him. She gave the girl a written character – and said that she would always put in a word for her. But she never heard again.'

Edith said eagerly, 'Then, would she speak to me? I know my mistress would be much obliged. Her older brother was very cross, you see, when she took Fanny on without a reference, and it would make her feel much better if we had one – even now.'

But she was disappointed. The woman shook her head. 'My friend no longer lives here, they have moved to Callistock. But if you wish it, I could give you the address. Your mistress could apply to her in writing, if she chose. Ah, but here's my husband. Did you find it, dear?'

'Yes.' Mr Lillywhite had a paper in his hand and he consulted it. '"The estate of Mrs Fanny Polcurnooth, born Fanny Constance Watts of the parish of St Just."' He turned to Edith. 'That is where your friend derived her name from, I assume.'

Edith nodded glumly. It did seem probable.

'Then it seems we have been looking for your friend Fanny, too.'

'We approached my friend in the first instance, naturally, but she did not know where Eleanor had gone,' his wife put in. 'Perhaps you could help us? There may be a small reward.'

Edie swallowed hard. 'So she was in trouble? I was afraid of that, when her father came to us.

Well, I'm sorry, Mr Lillywhite, I don't know where she is.'

'Her father came to you? How long ago was this?' And there were a host of other questions,too, about Mr Rouse's visit to Holvean House.

She gave a full account, and then said stoutly, in her friend's defence, 'But Fanny only ran away because she saw him at the door. I'm sure she would never have left us otherwise. She was terrified of him – and I'm not surprised. He seemed a proper ruffian to me. I'm almost sure he beat her – though she would never say.'

She saw the Lillywhites exchange that glance again. The old man shook his head. 'It does seem that something of the kind is possible, and there may be other things she wasn't telling you. It is rumoured that his wife was fleeing from the house and taking the children with her, when the accident occurred.'

Edith felt a chill of fear run down her back. 'Fleeing where? Only be the workhouse for her, wouldn't it? Seeing that her sister'd gone abroad. But of course she didn't know that...' She tailed off in dismay.

The solicitor was nodding. 'Very likely not. Our enquiries suggest that they were not in constant touch. It seems the husband made it difficult. Though it appears that there was fondness between the sisters, all the same. The provisions of the will seem to suggest as much.'

'The will?' Edith was startled. 'Fanny's mother left a will?'

'Her sister did,' the man said solemnly. 'And

your friend is not in trouble – as you seem to think. Quite the contrary, in fact. It appears that the aunt's estate should pass to her. Her father tried to claim it, when we traced the house, but the terms of the bequest exclude him quite specifically. Let me explain...'

Edith learned a lot of things that afternoon. Fanny's cousin – as Mrs Polcurnooth's son had been, of course – had been successful in Australia. He had gone prospecting, as many people did, and being a miner...

'You're never going to tell me that he struck gold, and is worth a fortune?' Edith said.

'Not gold, but copper and an opal seam. And it was not a fortune, but a substantial amount. Enough to keep a person comfortably for life. That was why he wrote to ask his mother to come out; he could provide a handsome house for her. But only a few weeks after she arrived, he got himself into an argument – some drunken struggle about another claim – in which he was hit with a shovel and was killed. A nasty business – quite a lot of blood. It was too much for his mother, she had a heart attack and died a few days later in the local hospital.'

'And young Mr Polcurnooth never had a wife?'

The lawyer shook his head. 'As his next of kin, his mother inherited everything he had. Of course, she only survived him by a day or two. But among her effects they found a proper will – it seems she was so nervous about the sea voyage that she'd been persuaded to make one before she left. Everything was to go first to her

289

son, of course, but if that failed, then to her sister, Mabel Rouse – and to any of her children, specified by name, with the proviso that the father should never benefit. "On account of his unspeakable behaviour to his wife and to his eldest daughter", I believe was the wording.'

'Can you do that sort of thing?' Edie was amazed. Wills and inheritance were a closed book to her. No one she knew had very much to leave.

'It might be disputed, but it would hold in law, unless a court decided otherwise. And since Mabel and the other named children are all dead, that leaves Eleanor as beneficiary. That's why we want to find her.'

'Only think of that.' Edith was frowning. 'And all this here money is in Australia? It must be costing fortunes to go looking for her here.'

He nodded. 'There is the house, of course, and that has value too – but, yes, there is a danger that the estate will dissipate, or go to Chancery. That's why the executors are offering a reward. The father is still attempting to make a claim on it, but I doubt he has the means to pursue it very far or that he would wish the exclusion terms to come to court. No doubt that's why he told us that the girl was dead.'

'He never did! He knew she was alive!'

'All the same he swore a statement saying that to the best of his belief his eldest daughter Eleanor was dead. He then tried to make a claim on his youngest child's behalf – on the grounds that the aunt had not known that he was born, but that he was her nephew, and her nearest relative. Of course, if he could have produced the girl herself...'

Edie whistled softly. 'So that's why he turned up! He wanted to force her to come back home with him, so she could claim the money he already knew about...'

'And as she is his daughter, he could wrench it out of her, no matter what the provisions of the will? I suspect that you are right. From what you say, I'll want to talk to him. It's clear he was attempting to pervert the law.'

Edie put her cup down. It rattled on the saucer, she was trembling so much. 'But if we could find Fanny, we could tell her that she's rich! Isn't it some shame we don't know where she's to? But we've already looked everywhere and found no sign of her. Except we found a farm where she had worked a day or two.'

'Did you now?' he said, in a peculiar tone of voice. 'I would be interested to speak to them myself. And to your mistress too. I'll send her a letter and arrange to meet. We could prove, at least, that the father's telling lies, and that the girl was still alive when he was swearing other-wise.' He smiled. 'Now, in the meantime, there is the question of this stamp.'

Mrs Lillywhite looked up from her work. 'John, don't be so absurd. We must buy the girl a ticket, and put her on the train. Though I can't imagine why her mistress did not buy her a return.'

'Oh, she did do,' Edie said at once. 'But it's booked for Wednesday afternoon. And it's only Saturday.'

So that was another thing that Edie learned that afternoon – that tickets could be altered, which she hadn't known. Then, since by this time she'd missed the last connecting train and Mr and Mrs Lillywhite were travelling to Plymouth the next day (as the notice at the door had advertised), they promised to take her to the station there, make sure there was a down train running, and put her on to it.

Mr Lillywhite even took her back to the lodging-house that night, in his own carriage, though it was only half a mile. And after he had spoken to the landlady – in an impressive voice – Edie also discovered that she'd been overcharged, and should only have paid deposits for the extra rooms. So she'd go home with money in her purse.

She would travel like a lady to Plymouth station too, in a proper two-horse carriage with comfy leather seats, and little mirrors you could see your hair-do in. And there was still dinner, that lovely bed, and then breakfast to come. This time she would make the most of her night of luxury.

Timothy Tulver walked down Market Jew Street with the careful expression of mournful gravitas he felt was appropriate on such a day as this, though inwardly he was almost smiling with relief. He would not now have to accompany Mama to that dreadful recital in the Town Hall tonight. All theatres and concert halls were closed as a mark of mourning, and public entertainments had been cancelled until further notice. So the dreadful soprano with the screechy voice would not, after all, be boring him to death, and he would not have to endure his cousin's company.

He had only agreed to buy a ticket in a fit of pique, when it had become clear that his dreams of escorting Alicia anywhere were doomed to failure now. Since Captain snooty Halligan had inveigled his way in, her old friends (by which he meant himself) had been forgotten, and she had eyes for no one else. It was as well that he'd warned Edwin of what was afoot.

He did feel a tiny twinge of guilt on that account. The letter he'd sent had not, of course, contained anything untrue – he would not condescend to do anything like that – but he was aware that he might have conjured an impression that was not wholly just. He had no compuction about some of the letter: Halligan's mother *was* batty and the sister was undoubtedly in jail – he'd had that information from Alicia's own lips. But his description of the Captain, for instance, was perhaps a little cruel. It was true that Halligan was literally a 'cripple with a limp', but arguably he need not have expressed it quite like that. On the question of the Halligan credentials, too, what he had written had been less than frank: 'No one I have spoken to has ever heard of them, and in the course of my enquiries I have not been able to ascertain that the family has any assets or pedigree of note.' Every word of that was literally the truth, he told himself; he'd simply neglected to mention how few people he had asked.

And here – dammit – was the gentleman himself, walking up the pavement with Miss Richie on his arm. Tim had his hat off in a moment. 'Good afternoon to you.'

Halligan had to juggle with his stick in order to take his hat off too. 'A very sad one, I'm afraid. Though everyone appears to have come out in the street.'

Beth Richie gave Tim a melancholy smile. 'I went to headquarters – I'd promised to deliver some leaflets this weekend – but even that was closed, so I went down to the bandstand to listen to the band, and there was Captain Halligan, listening to them too. The Salvation Army had got a programme up of hymns and solemn music. It was very good, and afterwards the Captain was kind enough to walk me into town. The tributes in the shops are so moving, we have been reading them.' She sighed. 'Such a tragic loss.'

'He will be sorely missed,' Tim muttered piously. It was doubtless true, as well, though only a few short years ago, when the Old Queen was alive, the Prince of Wales – as King Edward had been then – had been a byword for fast living, with his trail of mistresses. 'The King was such a–' he hesitated '–manly sort of man.'

'Meaning that he was a devil with the girls?' Halligan said, twinkling.

It was, of course, exactly what he'd meant, but this was not the time to voice such thoughts aloud. Tim scowled reprovingly. 'Really, Captain Halligan, we have a lady here! Though, come to think of it, Miss Richie, were you not supposed to be in Launceston with Miss Killivant today? I trust that you were not in some way indisposed?'

Beth Richie looked flustered and turned slightly pink. 'Perhaps you have not heard. Mr Edwin is expected, so Alicia could not go. We had sent Edith on ahead of us, and she has wired us back – she has information, by the sound of it, but we have had to ask her to return. It is quite a disappointment, I assure you, Mr Tulver, to be deprived of our little adventure in this way.'

And Mr Tulver, who knew himself to be responsible for the disappointment, could only smile and say, 'So Miss Killivant has not gone either, she is still at home?'

'She is, but you must not think of calling. Not today. I went in this morning and was snapped at for my pains. I rather think her brother causes her dismay.' She broke off as a party of women crossed the street, including a figure that he recognized – a fright of a woman with a nest of wild red hair, and an appearance of having been picked up by a gale and blown into her clothes. He stepped into a doorway so that he could not be seen.

Beth, though, was delighted. 'Ah! There is the lady that I came to town to see. If you will excuse me, gentlemen, I must catch up with her. Good afternoon, Captain, thank you for your company. And, Mr Tulver, I hope I see you soon.' She waved a small gloved hand at them and darted down the street.

So Tim was left alone with Captain Halligan, and trapped in the doorway, too, so he could not decently escape. There was an awkward pause.

'I'm afraid Miss Richie's right, Miss Killivant is very much distressed,' the Captain said, at last.

'Now, look here.' Tim was belligerent. 'If you think I've upset her, you can think again. I work in her best interests, and her family's, that is all.'

The Captain looked closely at him. 'You ... admire ... Miss Killivant, do you not, Mr Tulver?'

It was true, of course it was, but Tim was not about to give the man the satisfaction of proving to be right. 'Miss Killivant is quite safe from my attentions, sir. I have purely a business relationship with her, that's all. I deal with her financial affairs. You doubtless know she has a little money in the bank, but that she can't touch it till she's thirty years of age?' He didn't mention the other provision of the will.

'I'd heard her mention something of the kind. And you are one of the trustees on this account?'

Tim nodded. 'Her brother, in particular, has shown great faith in me.'

Halligan waited a moment, for more pedestrians to pass, and then stepped into the entrance-way with Tim. 'Then, may I tell you this in confidence? Since you are concerned, as I am, for her happiness,' he said, in a low voice. 'If she has need of money, simply let me know. I have offered her in person, but she will not hear of it. Perhaps I could arrange to filter it through you? She need not even know the provenance. I fear that her brother Edwin keeps the purse-strings, and I would not wish her to want for anything.'

He looked at Tim. His eyes were piercing blue. 'You understand the way I feel, I think.'

Tim felt a wave of jealous anger starting at his feet. Anger and a feeling of dismay as well. The wretch did have money after all, it seemed. What was Mr Edwin going to think of that? But he kept his decorum. 'If you call in at the bank, next time it is open, I will see what can be done.' Keep relations formal, that was the trick of it.

The man he had called a limping cripple smiled. 'Thank you, Mr Tulver, I know you'll be discreet. Alicia respects you very much, you know. If she felt you had betrayed her trust she would be very hurt.'

He knew about the letter! Or, at least, he'd guessed. The devil of it! Tim forced himself to smile. 'I try to work in her best interests, as I said before.'

'Of course.' An answering smile from the Captain. 'And perhaps it is as well that you are not too fond of her. It might be the cause of some friction otherwise, I think.'

'Cause of friction?' Tim stared at him. Was Halligan threatening him in some way?

But the Captain merely juggled with his stick, and put his hat back firmly on his head. 'But, my dear chap, you must have noticed the way Miss Richie looks at you.'

'Miss Richie?' He was beginning to echo everything like a parrot in a cage.

The Captain shook his head. 'I thought – since it appears your relationship with Alicia is purely professional, after all ... But perhaps I am speaking out of turn. Now, here's my coachman come to pick me up. Can I get him to drive you any-where?'

Tim was gazing vaguely down the street, where Beth Richie and her red-haired friend were standing by a shop, looking at the memorial displays. If he sauntered that way, he would catch them up. It would mean a conversation with the frightful woman too, but if Halligan was right...? Beth Richie was charming, and she was always nice to him. Indeed, she was looking in his direction now.

'Thank you, Captain Halligan,' he murmured with a smile. 'That is gentlemanly of you. But the afternoon is fine, and I think – after all – I would prefer to walk.'

'Now then, young shaver,' Mr Gribbens got up from his seat and put his hand on Sammy's shoulder as he passed, 'what you fixing to do this afternoon?'

Sammy was still finishing his plate of lunch, at the lopsided table in the little downstairs room of Gribbens's cottage in the grounds of Holvean House. He looked up in surprise. It was true that he sometimes worked a Sunday now and then – especially if he wanted to meet Edie in the week – but he took it as his regular free day as a rule. It was generally expected, that was what you did – you couldn't have servants working outside in full view when it was the Sabbath. What would the neighbours think? 'Course, there were always jobs that wanted doing if you had to work in lieu – like washing plant pots or sharpening the tools, or even planting up, this time of year – but that was always in the greenhouse, safely out of sight.

But, with Edith up country, he hadn't asked to change his day. So what did old Gribbens have in mind for him?

He hadn't long to wonder. Gribbens cleared his throat. 'Only, seeing you're still wearing your clothes for going to church, wondered if you'd care to take a stroll down to the town. Going to be a concert in the bandstand, I believe, down the Morrab Gardens – in honour of the King. And they say there's no end of shops got wreaths and things displayed. Shouldn't mind to see them. Shan't have another chance. Wondered if you would care to come along.'

Sammy stared at him. Had the old man lost his wits? Never in all the years he'd worked at Holvean House had Gribbens ever suggested anything like this. He was the gardener and Sammy was the boy, and there was a great gulf between them.

'Why's that, then?' he said doubtfully.

Gribbens was wheezing. 'Bit of education for 'ee. Bit of history. Besides,' he tapped his nose, 'want to have a bit of a talk to 'ee, where there aren't so many ears. Now, you take these plates back to the kitchen in the house, and tell Mrs Pritchard thank you very much, and then we'll get our coats and go out for an hour. I've spoken to the mistress and she's agreed that we can go. She'll want some flowers for the house, she says, but that can wait till morning now.' He looked at Sammy hard. 'Hadn't got anything else to do this afternoon, had you?'

All the same if he did have, Sammy thought ungraciously. He could see what was coming. Gribbens was going to press him about this job of his. And he had been wondering about taking a long walk, going to see Edie's father – have a talk to him. But now he wasn't going to have a chance.

He was right, of course. That was precisely what Gribbens had in mind. They'd hardly walked five minutes down along the road before the old man said, 'Thought any more about that post I talked to you about? Only the people are quite anxious to find somebody soon. Be a chance for you, Sammy. I wouldn't urge you else. Always thought you'd come to take my job on, by and by, but – chance like this, you didn't ought to let it slip. Not if you are serious about that girl of yours. She won't wait for ever, while you work your way up. Handsome great maid like that, there'll be others after her. You take my word for it. Don't want to end up like I did, on your own.'

He'd never heard Gribbens utter so many words at once – and never a syllable that suggested that he might have private feelings and regrets. Sammy turned to stare, but Gribbens had run out of talk, it seemed.

After a while, the gardener prompted, with some impatience, 'Well, what do you say? Am I to tell them that you'll come and talk to them or not? Only he was up here asking me the other day.'

Sammy was embarrassed. 'How can I say yes? I don't know where it is or anything.'

300

Gribbens pulled his cap down further on his ears. 'Soon find out, though, won't you? I haven't seen the place, so I can't tell you rightly, but it isn't miles away, it's only in the town.'

'I ought to talk to Edie. I wonder what she'd think.' Or whether I could manage, he added silently. Or even if I'd suit.

'Just you make sure that you don't miss your chance. I was talking to the fellow that used to do the job – had him pointed out to me down the nurseryman's. He's been there ever since the owners bought the house, but he's getting old now, and it's too much for him. With this here new pension they've brought in he's thinking to retire. His daughter's got a place and she's got room for him, so there's a gardener's cottage will come vacant when he leaves – soon as the new man's up to working on his own.'

Sammy swallowed. 'You think I'm up to it? Sounds more responsibility than I'm accustomed to.'

Gribbens gave him the sort of look he gave the 'pile'. 'Well, when you going to start? There'll be a year or so to learn the ropes, he says, and get the hang of how the garden's planned. Then it's up to you – or to whoever they take on. No guarantee they'd take you, if you do apply. Still, wouldn't do you any harm to go and talk to them.'

'No,' Sammy said slowly, 'I suppose you're right. Edie'd wait for me a year or two, I'm sure. Though it's a bit alarming, starting somewhere new, and everything hanging on your shoulders all at once.' Gribbens had started

301

walking smartly down the street, and Sammy had to hurry to keep up with him. 'How did you come to hear about this job in any case?'

Gribbens gave a horrid leer. 'One of they young gentlemen who comes up to the house. He was asking me. Friend of Miss Alicia's – or he'd like to be. Lives with his mother, the other side of town, he says. His mother is a trial, by the sound of it, but that shouldn't be a problem if you aren't working in the house.'

So it was Mr Tulver. That was not too bad. Not a person to have peculiar ideas. Sammy nodded. 'I know the chap, I think.'

The grin was wicked now. ''Course, if he succeeded with Miss Alicia...'

'She might take Edith with her?' Sammy laughed. 'No chance of that, I think.' He'd learned a lot from Edie about Miss Killivant, and how she poked fun at the pompous little man, and then was sorry afterwards because he tried so hard. Not an easy man to work for, but was it worth it in the end?

He wished he knew what Edie would have thought of it.

'I might call in and see him,' he said thoughtfully. 'Like you say, it can't do any harm.'

Gribbens nodded gruffly. 'I should think so, too. I'll tell him what you said. He'll call you up to see him in a week or two, I 'spect. Now, you coming to hear this band, or aren't you? We'll be missing the parade.'

Four

Edwin's sermon had been a conspicuous success. Perhaps he had gone on a little longer than he'd meant, but the congregation (which had been particularly large since everyone connected with the mission had been there, including those two poor wretches who had recently been saved) had been unanimous, when he asked them afterwards, that it had been a truly fitting tribute to the King. Moving, too, with heartfelt singing in the hymns, and appropriate sombre music on the harmonium. And then to come out and hear the solemn pealing of the bells, all over London by the sound of it! The King could not have had a more proper requiem in any place of worship in the Empire, he felt.

It was almost a pity not to mark the day with some other token of patriotic zeal, so he had suggested this post-prandial stroll to walk off the effects of lunch and join the throngs of mourning citizens mingling in the park. Claire had been glad to accompany him, though she was too afraid of germs to allow the nursemaid to bring Caroline out in her perambulator, as he'd really hoped. All the same it was a pleasant afternoon. The park was full of people, of every kind and class, but even some of the humblest wore appropriate dark dress – quite as if they'd lost somebody of their own – and perfect strangers doffed their caps, and said 'Bad business' or something as they passed, as though the whole city had become acquaintances.

So, when there was a sudden rumour in the crowd that the new king was on his way to take the oath, Edwin consented to join the jostling throng and watch the carriage pass.

'There you are, my dear,' he said to Claire. 'That was King George the Fifth. And we were among the first to see him in that capacity.'

She was standing on tiptoe to try to get another glimpse, and she did not turn to look at him but simply said, 'Does he count as King, then, before he takes the oath?'

Really! When he had wanted to give the moment some real significance! Claire could be irritatingly literal sometimes. He said, rather crossly, 'Well, whether he is King or not, there's no point standing here. You have just seen him, which is what you hoped to do, and we've had our little consitutional. I think it's time we went back home to change for evensong. And I'll look in on little Caroline for half an hour. If I have the time, that is.'

He meant it to be rebuffing, but she was not snubbed at all. 'Well, of course, my dearest, if that is what you'd like. But if you have lots of preparation for tonight, then don't concern yourself. Caroline and I will manage very well. After all,' she smiled up at him, 'we were not expecting that you'd be here at all. It is only that the poor Queen's loss has been our gain, otherwise you would be at Holvean House by now.'

'Yes,' he said grimly. 'Yes, I should have been. And it's essential that I get there as soon as possible. You've not forgotten that?'

She put a tentative gloved hand upon his arm. 'But not until after the poor King's funeral? They say that it is likely to be sometime next week. And obviously, Edwin, you can't be somewhere else. All the crowned heads of Europe will be here, and representatives from all the Empire – except of course the ones that cannot get here in the time. And all the senior clergy will be taking part – and there'll be dozens of services and vigils taking place. I'm sure that your bishop would wish you to be here.'

He frowned at her a little. 'Well, of course, I should be back by then.'

She gave a silly, tinkling laugh. 'But, Edwin, you can't go down before the funeral. You've read the paper and seen the notices. Banks and insurance houses have closed their doors to private customers, until after the funeral – as a gesture of respect. They're only dealing with business of national concern. If you were down in Penzance, there would be nothing you could do. You can't see Mr Tulver if the bank is shut, and you can't do anything about Alicia's account.'

He was about to say something furious, but it occurred to him that if he could not make representations to the bank, then his sister couldn't either – which improved his mood. Though it didn't solve the problem of this adventurer who had designs upon her money, though she would not face the fact. That much was evident from what Tim Tulver had said.

'Then I shall go down immediately afterwards,' he said. 'I shall reserve a ticket as soon as the date of the funeral is announced. Understand me, I shall not delay again.'

He wrote another scorching letter to Alicia when he got in, telling her the same. And he did spend ten minutes in the nursery, after all.

Alicia was upstairs with Mrs Pritchard, in the absence of Edith, who had not yet come home. They had decided to make up Edwin's room. The King's death had delayed him – but you never knew. It would be like Edwin to turn up any time. And with Nurse Morgan busy, and Queenie scrubbing floors, there was nobody to help Cook with the linen but Alicia herself. It didn't please her to be doing this, but she amused herself by thinking of how furious Edwin would have been, if he could have seen her sorting pillowslips.

'Like a servant,' he would say, and of course he was quite right. Edith should have done it, but Edith wasn't here. And that was the worry. It was upsetting too. Surely the girl had got the telegram? But she hadn't come back on the down train yesterday. And there had been no explanatory wire.

Alicia found a lace-edged bolster-case and put it on the pile. She refused to admit the possibility that the danger to Fanny had proved to be too real, and that Edith wasn't coming home at all.

But what was that? There seemed to be a noise, and suddenly there were pounding footsteps on the stairs, and there was Edie – breathless and red-faced – still in her cape and bonnet and with her holdall in her hand.

'Oh, thank heavens!' Alicia cried aloud, with more emotion than she'd meant to show. 'I thought something had happened to you. Are you quite all right?' She went across and might have taken Edith in her arms if she had not recalled herself in time. She took a step backwards. 'We were worried for you. Wherever have you been?'

Edie looked startled at this outburst of concern. 'Oh, Miss Alicia, there you are. Nurse Morgan told me I would find you here. I've got such a lot to tell you, you would not believe. Fanny's worth a fortune, only she don't know – and if we can find her there may be a reward. Oh, and I've got a letter from the Lillywhites. Wait till I get my breath back from carrying this bag.' She put down her parcels and stood there panting hard.

'Edith...' Alicia began sternly. But suddenly she realized what the girl had said. 'Did you say a fortune?'

'Not like you and Captain Halligan, of course, Miss Killivant, but what the man called a "considerable sum". Enough to have them looking, from Australia. And there's a house as well. And I've found out the people that Fanny worked for first, and they'll give her a written character – so you can tell Mr Edwin to put that in his pipe!'

'Edith!' Alicia said again, but she could not repress a smile. 'You forget yourself.'

Edith grinned at her. 'Sorry, Miss Alicia, but it's no wonder if I did. You'll never guess what I've been doing, all this time. Drinking tea from china cups with proper gentlemen, and riding in carriages like someone in a book. I was half afraid to pinch myself in case of waking up! And I've still got a bit of money in my purse to give you back.'

'Edith,' Cook said, in a commanding voice, 'pull yourself together. Don't just stand there, babbling like a brook. Go upstairs and change, and if you've got something to tell Miss Killivant you can do it presently, and coolly, when she sends for you. In the meantime, come and lend a hand. We've got work to do. Queenie's done the walls and windows and I've washed the floors, but there's all the bedding that we've got to air. Poor Miss Alicia's made a start on it, since you hadn't come, but I couldn't ask the mistress to turn the mattress with me, too. I was just about to send for that Sammy from outside, but now you're here so you can take an end.'

Edith said, 'Yes, Cook,' and disappeared upstairs.

Alicia looked at the mattress doubtfully. It looked very heavy – and a little damp. 'Edith will be able to lift that, I suppose?' She wasn't sure she could have lifted it herself. 'She seems such a little thing.'

Mrs Pritchard made a clucking noise. 'I should hope so, Miss Alicia. We do yours every week. Used to be her and Fanny did it – save my poor old back – but now it's just the two of us, we manage as a rule.' She took a clean blanket from the cedar box. 'We'll get this aired, as well. Light the fire and get the room warmed up. Well, that's it, Miss Alicia. I've got Edith now, we'll do it in a twinkling. Thank you for your help. Just as well that Mr Edwin was delayed, the way he was – we would never have been ready for him, if he'd come yesterday.'

'Thank you, Mrs Pritchard. Send Edith to me when you've turned the bed.'

Alicia went downstairs. It had never struck her how much the servants did. Even sorting the linen was surprisingly hard work – though the stuff was ironed ready and all neatly put away. It had taken ages to sort out a proper set, and put what wasn't wanted back on the shelf again – in a way that Mrs Pritchard was content with. Alicia reflected that she probably hadn't really been much help at all, but she had come and offered because she couldn't bear to sit doing nothing in the drawing-room, and worrying what had happened to Edith all the time.

She went back to her papers. She would have Edith down and hear the full story from the girl. It sounded marvellous. In fact, she decided, picking up the pen, she'd make a note of every-thing to confront Edwin with. There was the question of the written reference – that would deal with one complaint. And Fanny, it seemed, was not a helpless soul, or any kind of petty criminal, but a potential heiress of a 'consider-able sum'. That would be another thing that he could 'put into his pipe'. Good for Edith, she murmured to herself.

She was so busy scribbling in her notebook that she did not hear the girl in question at the door. 'You wanted me, Miss Killivant?'

She turned around, and on an impulse – as she had done once before, when Beth Richie had been with her in the drawing-room – motioned Edith to sit down on the stool. Edith looked uncomfortable, but she did obey. 'If you've been sipping tea with gentlemen, you can sit down with me. And tell me all about it – nice and slowly now.'

The story Edith told her was so remarkable that she wrote a letter to Philip Halligan right away, and – on reflection – another one to Beth. And then she sent Edith to deliver them.

Sammy was wishing he hadn't worn his Sunday boots. Or at least that he hadn't decided to walk out all that way to talk to Edie's pa. It was further than he'd thought, and though he hadn't stopped for tea, it was getting late by now. And it was damty hard to walk on country lanes when it was getting dark. Hard enough to work out which way you had to take – let alone trying to save your Sunday boots.

He was glad he'd had a chance to chat to Mr Trewin, though. Edie's pa had made it quite clear that he did not object to Sammy asking for her hand. 'If Edie will have you, you can marry her. Just you make sure that you take care of her.' They were down in the back garden, staring at the rows, to be a bit private.

'That's why I've come to see you. There's a

post, you see.' And he told Edie's pa all about it. 'I aren't that keen on having Mr Tulver as a boss, and I hear his mother is a handful too, but if I suit all right, it's more than likely that in a year or two there'll be a gardener's job and a cottage to go with it. We two could get wed. Mr Gribbens thinks that it's too good a chance to miss.'

''Course it is, my 'andsome,' Teddy Trewin said and clapped him on the back, but there was something in his manner that made Sammy pause.

'You don't really think so. I can tell it from your voice.'

'Of course I really think so. And Edie'd say the same. It's only...' He shook his head. 'It's nothing. Don't you worry. I'm just being soft.' He cleared his throat. 'You see those cabbages? That stuff you gave me did the trick all right. Not half as many caterpillars as there used to be.'

He was changing the subject but Sammy wouldn't let it go. 'There's something on your mind. What is it, Mr Trewin? I can't marry Edie if you don't feel it's right.'

Trewin went on gazing at the cabbages. 'Nothing 't all, really. Only hope it all works out. And I'm sure it will. Don't know how Minnie would manage, without Edie's bit of money coming in – that's all I was thinking – you know, if anything should happen and I couldn't work. Which of course it won't do. Don't know why ever I should think of such a thing.'

Sammy looked at him, suddenly remembering

311

the dreadful cough which had racked the poor
man earlier, when he'd tried to laugh. And how
hadn't he noticed how pale and strained he
looked? 'You still thinking that you'd like to
work outside?' A sudden thought struck him.
'You aren't thinking that you'd rather take this
post yourself? Might just suit you – never
thought of that.'

'My dear life, Sammy, I could never manage
that. Fellow that's doing it can't keep up with it
– you just said so – and he's done it all his life.
How would I get on? A gardener needs proper
training, like Gribbens's given you. No, you take
it, my handsome – if they'll have you – and good
luck to you. I wonder if the Killivants will take
on someone new? Might be an opening for
Reuben, if they do. Mind, he's a bit young yet
for leaving school – though they aren't so fussy
if your family needs your wage.' He shook his
head. 'But, like I say, I don't expect that it will
come to that. Now, coming in to have a cup of
tea, are you?'

It had all given Sammy much to think about.
Suppose he gave up working for the Killivants,
and then he couldn't marry Edie after all? Or not
for years and years, till some of the rest were
earning and her ma could do without Edie's bit
of contribution every week? Only a pity that
Miss Alicia had set her mind against that Mr
Tulver. It was like Gribbens said: if she was Mrs
Tulver, and took Edith as her maid, then the two
of them could work there – that would be the
trick. Proper married couple, with a house and
all. In that case Edie could still send money

312

home – if her father was as poorly as he seemed to think he was.

That, of course, was an awful lot of ifs. He'd have to talk to Edie when she got home again. Supposing that he ever got home again himself. He was awfully late. They'd have his guts for garters when he did get in. And he'd just trodden in something horrible in his best Sunday boots.

Five

It was a Wednesday evening and Teddy was just home – earlier than usual, if the truth were told. 'Left our Abel at the mine,' he said, and leaned, breathless, on the wall.

It hadn't been the best of days and Minnie seemed to know. Took one look at his ashen face and said, 'My dear life, Teddy – when you going to learn? You're greener than that cabbage you brought home the other day, and limper than a boiled leaf of it, besides. Well, I aren't going to have it. You get off to bed, and I'll bring you up your tea. And you mind you eat it – you need to build your strength.' She was grumbling at him, but her voice was full of tears. She turned back to the stove.

He came up behind her and took her by the waist. 'Here now, what's all this for? I shall be all right. Just got a bit of something on my chest. I was saying to Cap'n Maddox just the other day – do with a bit of poultice, help to clear 'un up.' He did feel better, now that he was home.

She turned towards him and buried her face against his chest. 'Can't have a poultice if you're working at that mine. Need you to have a day in bed for that.' She pulled her head away. 'And you damty need it. I can hear you wheezing like

314

an organ-pipe with every breath you take. You got to get better. You're the only one I got.'

'I can think of some others,' he said, grinning, and nodded towards the garden at the back, where the children's squabbling and laughing could be clearly heard.

'Oh, go on with you!' She made a tutting noise. 'Sent them out there to bring the sheets inside – give me a few minutes to talk to you and get you to see sense. Lovely day for washing, all that breeze and sun. Done your flannel nightshirt too, so I will see to that – get it aired off and ironed and you can put it on.' She fended him off gently. 'And don't go starting that. I got more than enough to see to as it is. Get off to bed with you, you silly thing. I'll be up directly, bring you up some tea. And Edie'll be here before so very long, no doubt. Hope she hasn't gone waiting for you by that damty stile. Though Abel will tell her that you've gone on home. I suppose he knows?'

Teddy nodded grimly. Abel knew all right. It would be halfway round the mine by now – even his old friends underground would know that Teddy Trewin had been taken bad. Coughed so much he had that pain again, and very nearly fallen in the slimes. No two ways about it, they'd sent him home this time, and the man from the Miners' Friendly was going to come and call. He would have to tell Minnie, though perhaps she would be pleased, knowing he would have a day or two at home in bed. Funny people, women.

He was just about to tell her, when the knock

315

came at the door. 'That'll be the Friendly,' he said, but he was wrong.

'This Teddy Trewin's house?' a voice enquired. 'I've come to see him. Hoskins is the name.'

Teddy had been halfway to the stairs but he turned back. 'Tommy Hoskins, is it? What you doing here?' He came to the doorway. The man was standing there, with his sack of bits and pieces slung across his back and his coat tied round him with a piece of string, his one empty sleeve pinned up. Meg and the younger ones were crowding round behind, the washing forgotten, staring at this apparition standing on the step.

'Who is it, Pa?' said Donny. 'Is he some kind of tramp?'

'No, he damty isn't,' Teddy said. 'He's a friend of mine. Worked down the mine until he had an accident. Stop your gawping and get your mother's washing in. Come on inside, Tommy, and have a cup of tea. Minnie was just about to make a pot for me.'

Minnie looked startled but she stood aside and let the man come in. 'Sorry, Mr Hoskins. I know the name, of course. I've heard our Edie mention it, I think. You're the one that sells the cabbages.'

He looked at Teddy. 'Though I see you got a handsome crop of them yourself.'

Teddy nodded. 'Can't have too many, with all these mouths to feed. But you aren't here to sell them – or is that why you came?' If so, he thought, it was a bad lookout today. Boughten vegetables were not a luxury a sick man could afford. Be the leftovers from market, more than likely, from now on – what they sold off cheaply, penny for a bag – and what the family could produce themselves.

But Hoskins was shaking his half-balding head, with its extraordinary fringe of greying hair. 'Came about your Edith. You know where she is?'

Teddy looked at Minnie and made a doubtful face. 'Up to Holvean, working, or on her way back here. Far as I know, any road. You got different news?'

Tommy put his sack down on the kitchen floor, and looked as if he'd shed two burdens at one time. 'That's a mercy then. Can't be the same one. I was up Madron at the workhouse and I heard them call her name while I was waiting in the reception yard. I'd gone to see my brother, like I belong to do – now they let you do it – and he said yes he'd seen her on the lists. Girl called Edith Trewin been up there for weeks.' He hesitated. 'And then, when I heard that you'd been taken bad...'

Minnie had been busy with the kettle and the pot, but she slammed them down and whirled round from the range. 'You thought it was our Edie? Well, it hasn't come to that. And it won't do either, while I live and breathe...'

Teddy shook his head at her. 'It is a funny thing though,' he said peaceably. 'Not a common name. Not many Trewins round these parts that aren't some kind of kin. And there aren't any Ediths among them as I knows on. She was named for me. Edward Daniel – E.D. Trewin,

317

see. Sounds like Edie – short for Edith – that's how we called her that. And now there's this one. Wonder who she is?' But he was already quite certain in his mind.

Tommy clearly had the same idea. He sat down, uninvited, on the corner of the bench. ''Course, it could be a coincidence, but it seems to me...'

Minnie was pouring milk into the cups. ''Tisn't a coincidence and you know it's not. Bet it's that Fanny at her tricks again.'

Hoskins nodded. 'Just what I thought myself. Better tell Edith when she comes in, do you think? I suppose Miss Killivant is going to have to know. Though I don't know that the girl is wanting to be found.'

Teddy gave a laugh that turned into a cough, and it was a few minutes before he caught his breath. 'More to this story that you know about. There's money due her – might be a reward. Could come your way if it proves to be the girl.'

Tommy Hoskins took his cup and had a sip of tea. 'I couldn't tell you if it was or not. Never clapped on the creature in my life. Have to be Edie who went up to see. Oh, and here she comes – and all the others too.'

So what with Hoskins and the washing and what Edie had to tell, there was quite a lot of talking before Teddy went upstairs at last and put himself to bed. When Minnie took his supper up he was already fast asleep.

Edith could hardly wait to tell Miss Alicia the

news. 'It has got to be Fanny. Who else could it be?'

Her mistress looked delightedly at her. 'Wonderful, Edith. Then go up and see. If it is Fanny, tell her she can return here if she likes. I'll give you a letter for the authorities to say that I will take responsibility for giving her a home. A position, if she wants one, till she sorts matters out and can secure a ticket to Australia, as I imagine she will do. I will not return her to her father, you can assure her of that.'

'But Mr Edwin...?' Edith blurted. 'Whatever will he say? He'll be here tomorrow, won't he?'

Miss Alicia laughed. 'I'm afraid my brother has a surprise or two in store. For instance, I propose to hold a dinner party when he comes.'

Edith thought her chin might hit the floor. 'A dinner? Here? Does Mrs Pritchard know?'

'She does. I decided this last evening, and I talked to her first thing. Just a dinner party. Quite a small affair. Mother's helped me choose the menu – she is thrilled to bits. I intend to asked Miss Richie to join us if she will, and Mr Tulver too, if he would care to come. And of course, Mr Lillywhite from Launceston and his wife. I've invited them already, and Captain Halligan, and they will be glad to come. In fact it was he who gave me the idea.'

'Mr and Mrs Lillywhite! You mean the ones I met? But they live up the county!' Edith said, amazed. 'You're never going to offer them a bed at Holvean House?' Whatever next? Dinner parties and asking visitors to stay? And Mr Edwin coming? The familiar world she lived in had gone stark staring mad.

Miss Alicia chuckled. 'No, of course I shan't offer them accommodation here. They do not require it in any case. They are staying a few days with Captain Halligan – I understand they've been in correspondence since you called up there, and are renewing their acquaintance. You know that Mr Lillywhite had sent a note to me. I replied by letter and invited him to call, if he ever found himself in town. He came last evening, while you were away. Philip – Captain Halligan – sent to ask if I'd consent to see him, at that hour, and I'm glad that I agreed. Mr Lillywhite has told me a great deal that I did not know.'

'You mean about Fanny?' Edith said, a little mortified. 'I thought I'd told you everything. And now we think we've found her, isn't that enough?'

'Edith, you have been a perfect rock,' her mistress said. 'Without you none of this would have been possible at all. But there are things which Mr Lillywhite told me that he may not have told you. Partly about why Fanny was so frightened of her father. It appears there was a note that her mother wrote to her and which her former mistress found when she was moving house. It was hidden in the maid's room, stuffed into a crack. Fanny must have put it there before she was dragged home.'

Edith was bursting with curiosity. 'What did he do? Beat her? I thought it must have been that.'

Miss Alicia bit her lower lip. 'Well, not that
320

exactly. Better if it had been that, in fact. But it isn't very delicate and nothing has been proved – though he might go to prison if it ever came to light. Mr Lillywhite may not have thought it proper to tell you about that, and I shall say no more myself. Fanny herself will tell you if she wants to, I expect, but if she doesn't you should not be upset. It isn't the sort of thing you really want to hear.'

Edith could not make head nor tail of this, and she was feeling rather snubbed. She said, quite primly, 'Shall I go up there, to the workhouse, then? Only I'll want that letter to them, if that's what I'm to do.'

'Of course you will, Edith.' Miss Alicia smiled. 'And thank you for your help. Oh, and don't be late. I shall want you to run down to the butcher's later on, and the greengrocer and grocer, I expect, to get some provisions for tomorrow night. Mrs Pritchard will give you a list.' She gave a peculiar little smirk. 'You can tell them to put it on the bill. Edwin can deal with it when he arrives.'

So it was a startled Edie who set out to walk up to Madron Workhouse a little later on. Whatever had got into Miss Alicia? She was all pent-up excitement, like a child on Christmas Eve, and Mrs Pritchard was as bad: thrilled to bits to have a 'proper dinner to make, for once, just like the old days when the Colonel was alive', and rushing round the kitchen like a demented goose, happily scolding Queenie and everyone in sight. Edith was quite glad of the excuse to get away.

She looked out for Sammy as she went but

there was no sign of him. Gone down to see about that post today, of course. Gribbens had promised to set it up for him, and was going to get the address and everything. And suppose he got the place? That was another thing. It wouldn't be the same at all at Holvean House if Sammy wasn't there. But if he did get that cottage, what would she do then? She couldn't leave her job and go and marry him – much as she realized that she wanted to. It would be better than all the fortune in the world to have her Sammy coming home each night, to put his arms around her and give her a kiss – just like he'd done the other morning when she had just come back.

Worth going away for, she'd told him at the time. And she'd meant it too. But it was no good putting her head beneath the sheets and pretending that everything was going to be all right, because it was clear that it wasn't. Pa was very ill, and 'getting iller by the day', as Tommy Hoskins said. Even Pa himself was talking of having the doctor come to look – though he clearly didn't want to. It was not the cost – the Miners' Friendly was going to see to that – but having the doctor was the next best thing to calling the undertaker in to measure up – or that's how Pa had always looked at it.

Still, you couldn't wish Sammy anything but luck. And there was no point in standing moping, she had work to do. Go up the workhouse and see if Fanny was there. She set her face grimly and walked on up the hill.

* * *

Sammy had been practising his manners all the way. Go round to the back door – 'course, he'd have to do – and ask politely if the master was in. Gribbens had drummed it into him that's what he must do, though it seemed irregular. Wasn't Mr Tulver's mother still living in the house, and wasn't there a present gardener who was in charge of things?

'It's the master wants to see you, personal,' old Gribbens had said, when Sammy questioned it. 'Told me to tell you to go and ask for him. Now, you going to go and do it, or keep on jawing here?'

So here was Sammy, standing at the gate, twisting his best cap between his fingers like a child starting school. He could already see the garden through the hedge. A great big place it was, as well – much larger than he had expected. Imagine being in charge of all of that! It was enough to make you nervous, supposing that you weren't already. All those roses. You would never cope. Let alone with Mr Tulver breathing down your neck – like a pompous penguin, as Edie always said.

He was almost ready to turn tail and flee, when a pleasant voice behind him cut across his thoughts. 'Hello, Sammy.'

He whirled around. 'Why, Captain Halligan. What are you doing 'ere? You're never calling on Mr Tulver too?'

'Mr Tulver?' The Captain seemed surprised. 'What has Mr Tulver got to do with it? No, I simply had some business in the town that took a little longer than I thought it would. I'm sorry

323

if I kept you waiting at the gate. I know that I told Mr Gribbens three o'clock.'

Sammy stared at him. 'You mean this is your house? This is where you live?'

The Captain was still smiling, in a puzzled way. 'But of course I live here, Sammy. What did you suppose? Surely Mr Gribbens...'

Sammy forgot himself enough to interrupt. 'Why, that old devil! He knew all the time, and he let me go on thinking...' He used his cap to slap his knee and laughed. 'Well, never mind all that. You are the one that's wanting a new gardener, sir?'

'I am indeed.' Captain Halligan pushed open the gate, and ushered Sam inside. 'As you can see, we have substantial grounds and our present gardener is retiring next year.'

'But you have a boy, sir, surely? Pretty much like me?'

The other man smiled. 'Yes, of course we do. But we also have another property in Devonshire, which we have let of late. My sister, bless her, is planning to move back.'

'Your sister?' Sammy said. 'Wasn't she...?' He stopped himself in time. What Edie had told him about Miss Halligan wasn't what you said out loud, especially when her brother might be about to offer you a job.

But the Captain simply laughed. 'Yes, she was in prison – I suppose you heard? – on account of some nonsense with the suffragists. I found a lawyer for her, my old schoolfriend young Lillywhite in fact, and she repays me now by writing to say she is in love with him.' He said it lightly and was clearly not at all displeased. 'She'll have the house in Devon, half of which would have come to her in any case, and has agreed to take my mother back to live with them. That will be a blessing, as she is quite confused, and will certainly be happier in an old familiar place – and the same thing applies to old familiar staff. Hence the current garden vacancy.'

Sam stood looking around himself. 'It is a lovely place. Any young gardener would dream of working here.' Any young *head* gardener, he thought wonderingly, to himself. 'So it is your sister that I have to thank for this?'

Halligan laughed. 'Well, not entirely – no. Miss Killivant suggested that I might talk to you. She seems to think you have some interest in her maid – and since she has consented today to be my wife, it seemed that this might be convenient all round.'

Sammy gasped. 'She could bring Edith with her, do you mean?' He knew his cheeks were burning with embarrassment.

'Alicia seemed to feel there was more chance the girl would stay with her and come, if you were already on the premises. She seems to think you may have marriage plans yourself.'

Sammy shook his head. 'We might have done, and all. But it isn't going to happen, for a while at least. Edie's family need her earning, with her father ill.'

Halligan looked at him, long and hard and searching, until at last he said, 'I understand, from a note that I had from Alicia earlier, that Edith is going to look for Fanny Watts today.

You had heard, had you, that there might be a reward? Not a great fortune – some thirty pounds or so – but if Edith is successful, I imagine that would help? If she were to benefit by the reward, that is? Thirty pounds would make a little difference, I suppose?'

Sammy stared at him. 'My lor'! As much as that? More than two years' wages for a girl like her, that is. Make a difference? I should say it would. Especially if I had a job that had a house as well...' He broke off, flummoxed. 'In the end, of course. I don't mean straight away.'

The Captain chuckled. 'Most likely around next Easter – if I can persuade Alicia to marry me by then. You'd work your way up, till you know the ropes, and finally take over when the head gardener leaves. In the meantime you would start here in four weeks' time. That's soon enough for you? You'll have to work your notice at your present place.' He looked at Sammy who was nodding frantically. 'Then I take it you are likely to accept the post? In which case, perhaps you'd care to come and see what it involves.'

And a shamefaced Sammy was shown around the grounds, and found himself nodding like an automaton as he was introduced not only to the plants, but to the people too. He kept on nodding, but he'd have to ask again. Tomorrow, he knew, he would not recall a word. All he could think of was getting home and telling Edith the amazing news.

Six

Edith was standing outside the workhouse now. A grim old place. And worse inside, from all she'd heard of it. People starved to death before they would come in here, and the very name was enough to make you pale, but she forced herself to it and went in through the arch. A very old man in a bowler hat was sweeping out the yard.

'Reception ward is that way.' He gestured with his chin. 'Or do you want the officers?'

She didn't know the answer. 'I've come to see a resident,' she said reluctantly. 'She's not expecting me, but I've got information to get her out of here. Girl about my age.'

'Huh!' The man resumed his sweeping. 'Be able-bodied then. Be working at this time. Laundry, I should think. But you can't go in there. You'll have to see the officers. Through that door over there.'

It was daunting, that was the only word for it, and the woman she spoke to was more daunting still: a woman in a grey uniform with a great starched triangle of a nurse's hat, and a face that was so hard you could have quarried it.

She listened to Edie's tentative request, and glanced at Miss Alicia's letterhead. 'This is most irregular. There's a proper time for visitors – but

327

I suppose I must. Name?' she demanded.

'Edith Trewin, ma'am.'

'Not the name of the inmate. I mean your own, of course. Or are you a relative?'

'We are not related, but that is my name. I think she borrowed it.'

The stone-faced woman was not amused at all. 'If you're suggesting that this girl has misled the union authorities, then that is serious. I'm not sure I can permit you to see her after all.'

'I don't believe she used the name to get anything she was not entitled to, only to protect herself.' An inspiration seized her and she added suddenly, 'There is a solicitor in town who could explain it if you like. Better'n I could. Shall I send for him?' She saw the look that crossed the woman's face, and she pressed her advantage. 'The poor girl has got money owed to her, but there's someone after her who's stopped her getting it. She should never have been forced to come in here at all. I've been sent to tell her that it's all been sorted out. It's all in that letter.'

She had no idea what Miss Alicia had written, naturally, but the mention of solicitors had clearly done the trick. 'Very well, then. I will make an exception, in the circumstances. If you wait in the female dayroom, I will send her through. She does have the right to discharge herself, of course, given reasonable notice. That is three hours, so she can expect to be leaving here tonight. There will, of course, be forms and things to do.' She sounded as if the idea of release had been proposed on purpose to make extra work for her.

'Yes, ma'am,' Edie said humbly, and was led along a bare stone corridor into a bare stone room where she was to wait. There was a fireplace and a bench around the wall – too narrow to sit very comfortably on – and nothing else at all except a pile of battered books. 'You'll have the dayroom to yourself for half an hour,' the woman said. 'The infirm and elderly are taking exercise. We let them walk around the female yard when it is fine.' And she was gone.

Edie went over and leafed through the books. Dreary moral stories, by the look of them, and not a single illustration, but they'd been read to death. Perhaps when there was absolutely nothing else to do...? She was trying to imagine what such a fate was like, when the woman put her head around the door again, 'Here she is, then,' she said and pushed Fanny in.

At least, it must be Fanny, though for a moment Edith did not recognize her friend. Fanny had always been so pale and thin and neat, but this girl in the shapeless blue and white striped uniform was stout and pasty-faced.

'So you found me, Edie?' She did not sound happy, though. 'I'm sorry I used your name, I didn't know what else to say. Had to think of something, and if someone asked for me...'

'I know. It worked. We asked for you ourselves. I tried to look for you. Miss Alicia has been worried half to death.'

Fanny gestured at her bulk. 'Well, you can see the problem. What else could I do? I hoped past hoping that it wouldn't come to this – tried jumping up and down and all that sort of thing.

But it didn't do no good. And it's no use Miss Alicia hoping I'll come back, because there's not the slightest chance of that, as you can see.'

'But Fanny...'

'I'm not Fanny. My name is Nellie Rouse. And that was my father came calling at the house. But I'd have had to leave you, sometime, if he hadn't come. I'd just hoped to put by a little more, that's all – perhaps even have the baby somewhere comfortable, and give it up for adoption. Pretend I was married. I don't know what I thought.'

'Baby!' Edie stared at her, aghast. She knew about babies, or she thought she did. Ma'd had an awful lot of them, when all was said and done – though Edith wasn't certain how it came about. She and the others were somehow never there. They went off to Nana's for a day or so, and when they came back home, there was the baby in a crib. Nana had told her that it was brought by a stork – it apparently left the baby underneath a bush outside – but she doubted that. There weren't any bushes outside their house. Perhaps her parents had arranged some other way.

Though come to think of it, Ma did get fat sometimes. She was beginning to have an inkling of a different idea. 'How do you get a baby, any case?' she said.

'Oh, my dear Edie,' Fanny said, in a despairing voice, 'don't you know anything at all? You'd better ask your mother – I can't tell you now. But, yes, there's a baby – or there's going to be. And that's why I can't discharge myself from

here. You'd better go back and tell Miss Killivant all this. Tell her I thank her from the bottom
of my heart, and I'm only sorry that I had to tell
so many fibs.'

'Wasn't all fibs though, was it?' Edie said. 'It
was true that your mother and your family was
all dead – only for a little baby that survived.
Only it wasn't a fire, was it, it was in a cart?
Why didn't you say that?'

Fanny looked away. 'I didn't really say so.
Miss Alicia thought I did. I said I'd had a written
character but I'd lost it in the fire – and it's quite
true, that is exactly what I did. My father took it
from me, tore it into pieces and put it in the
flames. Said I'd never get a job without it, and
I'd have to stay with him. But I couldn't stand it,
and I ran away. Not quick enough though ... He
had me there a week. Used to hold me down
and...' She shuddered. 'I wouldn't have stood it
that long, if it wasn't for the baby that survived
the crash, but I couldn't just leave it and run
away. And then I heard that Father had a woman
somewhere else, so I left the child on her doorstep and I caught the train down here. I'd saved
a bit of money from wages earlier, and had it
hidden in my skirts. It was just enough to get me
down here. And the rest you know.'

'Well, you have got a written character again.
Miss Alicia has written to the household where
you used to work – the people had moved, but
she's caught up with them again – so you could
get a new position when the baby's born. And
there's some sort of letter that they found up in
your room – you might like to have it. It's from

331

your ma, I think.'

Fanny, who had been white-faced and shaken, broke down in sudden tears. 'So Miss Alicia's got it? Does she know what it says?'

'Something about your father being cruel to you. Says he could go in prison – Mr Lillywhite told her, and he ought to know.'

'Who ... who ... is ... Mr ... Lil ... lywhite...?' Fanny managed through her tears.

'Oh, he's the reason why I've come today. I meant to tell you, but I haven't got it out yet. Your aunt's left you some money, and I think there is a house. It's in Australia, but you can have it if you go. Mr Lillywhite will tell you. He's coming to the house.' She stopped, struck by a sudden thought. 'Didn't you say that you could have this baby somewhere comfortable? Well, if you've got money coming, couldn't you do that after all?'

Fanny looked at her, the tears still running down her face. 'You know, that might be possible. Especially if Miss Alicia knows the way things are, and won't think too harshly of me. Trouble is, no one will believe you, in a case like this. But if she's got the letter, she will know it all. My mother believed me, and she caught him out – she was going to come down here. And you know what happened. Wasn't his fault, mind. Well, not directly. It was a borrowed cart and my mother couldn't handle it – she was driving it herself and tried to go too fast. Funny thing, I think my father was really cut up by the loss – though it didn't stop him, did it?' She scrubbed her face with the corner of her sleeve.

back, barking and growling something terrible.

Edie shook her head. This was bewildering. 'I only hoped to have a word with him. It's about someone that I think might be his child. He came to our house once...'

'Well, if he got you in trouble, that's your lookout, not mine. I got my hands full looking after what I got,' the woman said. She turned in the doorway and called to someone in the house. 'Freddie! Get out the back and untie that stupid dog and let it loose. It'll see this girl off. Might as well earn its dinner for once in its damned life.'

There was a scuttling in the hall behind her, and what seemed to be a child ran in the direction of the back door and the yard. That was enough for Edie. 'It's all right, I'm leaving!' she said, hastily backing out on to the street. She thought of trying to shout and leave a message that she'd called, and that it was about Fanny – or rather Nellie Rouse – but the sight of a large and snarling dog dissuaded her from that. In any case, she thought, it might be better just to leave. Rouse was unlikely to tell her anything – perhaps she should have thought things out more carefully before she came.

She retreated, walking backwards, still keeping her eyes fixed firmly on the dog, which was now in the doorway straining at the leash, held by a smallish boy in ragged clothes who looked as if he might easily be tugged away with it.

'Here, look out, my 'andsome.' Something bumped her back. She turned. A bent old woman with a basket was peering up at her. 'Near as

256

'But that Miss Richie's come. Thinks you're going to Launceston. Shall I show her up?'

It was a longer walk to Trewendron than Edie had bargained for, and her boots had rubbed her stockings through and blistered both her heels. But she was exultant afterwards. She had learned such a lot.

Not, perversely, at the house itself, when she had finally worked out where it was – the corner of a little terrace, with a fenced yard at the back. She found it by the hand-painted notice on the gate, which read, 'Josiah Rouse: builder and carpenter. Roofing and thatching a speciality.' It saved her asking strangers and she went round to the front.

The door had been opened by a youngish girl – not a great deal older than Edith was herself – holding a squalling baby in her arms, and with an expression of suspicious resentment on her face. Her hair was almost as bedraggled as her skirts and pinafore and her face had the pinched look Fanny used to wear, though she was noticeably ample round the waist.

'Yes, this is Josiah Rouse's house. What is it to you?' She looked Edie up and down. 'Not another of his little indiscretions coming back to roost? Well, if it is, you'll get no help from me. You made your bed, you'll have to lie on it. And it's no good you performing. My 'usband isn't 'ome – and if he was he wouldn't talk to you. He's working on a building out at Altarnun. Now get off my premises before I set the dog on you.'

There was a dog, too. You could hear it at the

to offer any more, so in the end she prompted, 'What did happen to the wife? Didn't I hear something about a fire?'

They had turned down a narrow alley, where a jumble of small dwellings seemed jostling for room, and paused outside the smallest of them all. The woman turned to Edie. 'Lord love you, no! Road accident, it was. Cart turned over, and killed the lot of them – mother and three children. Only the little baby thrown clear and survived. They say the horse bolted – something must have startled it – in a narrow lane, and they were dragged to death. It was all in the papers – terrible affair. Proper nine days' wonder, it was, at the time. Still, why are we 'ere talking about such dreadful things?' She reached out and took the basket. 'This is where I live. Thank 'ee for the hand, my 'andsome. Care to come in and have a spot of tay? I believe I might even have a home-made split or two.'

Edie hesitated. It was tempting. She had eaten a good breakfast – that was all prepaid – but she had no money to buy anything else till dinner time. Yet Ma would say you shouldn't accept an invitation from someone you didn't know, because you never knew if they could really afford the extra cost. But the possibility of hearing more about the Rouses was too great, and she said, 'Thank you' and went inside the house.

It was a tiny little cottage – one room up and one room down. An open fireplace took up a whole wall, flanked by two small chairs with a table in between, and apart from a dresser –

258

nothing walked right into me and knocked me shopping clean out of me 'and.'

'I'm some sorry, missus,' Edie said at once. 'I was that worried by the dog, I wasn't looking where I went. Never hurt you, did I?'

The woman shook her head. 'Trod on me skirt, that's all. Though I am not surprised. Wretched dog's a menace – and that new wife's the same. Brought it with her – and that skinny kid. Spoil the place they do. Used to be a real nice neighbourhood round here.'

Edith said quickly, 'You knew the other wife?'

The woman nodded. 'Well, not to say knew her. Saw her in the street. I don't know of anyone who knew her properly. Kept herself apart, as you might say – not unfriendly, just didn't get out much, or have the neighbours in. Nice sort of woman though– not a bit like *her*!' She gestured to the end house, where the woman with the baby had slammed the door again. 'Terrible what 'appened to her in the end.' She hitched the basket up on to her hip. 'But I can't stand here gossiping, this 'ere basket weighs a ton.'

Edith said quickly, 'Can I carry it for you?' She took the shopping – it was heavy, too.

'Kind of you, my 'andsome. My old bones aren't what they used to be.' The woman bared her toothless gums in a delighted smile. 'I'll show you the way,' and she hustled off, suddenly more sprightly without her heavy load.

Edie hurried after her. She had been hoping for additional information about the former Mrs Rouse, but the old woman didn't seem inclined

257

'Perhaps I will come down and see Miss Killivant. Things can't be any worse. And they might be a good deal better, from what you're telling me. And I can always come back here, if there's any doubt. Though I shall be in trouble for giving the wrong name.'

'I put in word for you on that.'

Fanny smiled. 'You are a good friend, Edith, and I shan't forget. It will be nice to have my own name back again – and my own clothes as well, after these dreadful things they make you wear in here. Tell Miss Killivant that I will come tonight – though you had better warn her what a state I'm in. She might rather that I stayed up here.'

But Miss Killivant did nothing of the kind. In fact, when Edith got back from placing the order with the shops, and told her what had happened, she was quite furious – but not with Fanny.

'That poor girl,' she said. 'And that appalling man! Just wait till Mr Lillywhite hears this! Of course she must come here, and we'll do our best to help.'

She went to talk to Captain Halligan, who happened to be there, and he drove up to Madron later, in his own carriage, to fetch Fanny to the house.

Edwin Killivant could not believe his ears. 'You have decided *what*?' Whatever had come over Alicia today, he wondered. She was looking at him boldly, with her eyes alight, and there was a tremor of laughter in her voice.

'A dinner party, Edwin. You must have heard

333

of them?'

'With half a dozen people whom I've never met. This is preposterous. I demand an explanation. And who is to pay for it?'

'Why you are, Edwin, since you have taken the purse-strings of the household back. You will in fact be hosting the affair. And kindly remember these are Mother's guests, not mine – though it is true that I introduced them to the house. I'm sure I can trust you to be courtesy itself. This is after all her home, and she has been looking forward to tonight.'

Why did he feel as he had used to feel when Charles and Liss and Mary had all ganged up on him – helpless and furious and badly put upon? He knew that he sounded childish as he said, 'Well, I won't receive them, and there's an end of it. Who are they anyway? This jumped-up adventurer Halligan and his pair of friends, and some dreadful woman from the suffragists? Why should I allow them to dine at my expense?'

'Because your mother has invited them,' Alicia replied.

There was not a great deal that he could say to that, so he said nothing, merely fiddled with his drink. It was actually a very good brandy that she'd suddenly produced – no doubt kept for the benefit of the adventurer, he thought.

'Anyway,' Alicia went on, 'you're forgetting Mr Tulver. He'll be here as well. I thought you were anxious to have a word with him. He is certainly anxious to have a word with you.'

Edwin only snorted. 'I can see him at the bank.' Alicia was right, he realized with annoyance. He had forgotten Mr Tulver. And she seemed to think that she was right all round. There was something quite different about Alicia this time. She wasn't cross and argumentative, as she usually was, or sulky and snappish – but cool and logical. She seemed to be self-confident – and just a bit amused. And that was the damnedest thing of all to cope with.

She was sitting on the window-seat and smiling at him now; a curious little half-smile that made her look rather like a cat. Funny, he could sometimes see Caroline in her. 'I think he would prefer to talk to you in a social setting,' she said. 'He seems to feel he may have given you a false impression when he wrote. I think he'd rather that you heard the truth from other people first.'

He stood up abruptly and put down the brandy glass. 'The truth about what? That young jackanapes of yours? I've told you, Alicia, I will not meet the man. I have no doubt that he can be very charming when he tries – certainly he's managed to triumph with Mama – but it will not wash with me.' He looked into the mirror, seized his coat seams at the sides and pulled them sharply down over his hips. It seemed to him to underline the point. 'I decline to meet the man. A clergyman has a certain position to maintain. I cannot approve of your friendship with a casual nobody.'

She was still smiling, dammit! And now she was causing him to use improper language in his thoughts. He was about to say more but she was too quick for him.

335

'Then it will be difficult for you, Edwin. I intend to marry him.'

'Marry him!' He whirled around on her.

'Yes, I have been wanting to tell you, Edwin, dear. Captain Halligan did me the honour yesterday of asking me to be his wife. And I accepted him. I had no way of letting you know this before you arrived, but I hoped you would announce it to the company tonight.'

He sat down and drank the brandy without quite meaning to. 'And if I don't agree to this liaison?'

'Mother has already given her consent,' his sister said. She did not sound rebuffed. 'I don't believe that I need yours as well. Mr Lillywhite was telling me as much.'

'Mr Lillywhite!' he muttered angrily. 'The solicitor you think so much about? Has he been advising your Captain Halligan, as well? They are longtime friends, I believe you said? Advised him about your future prospects, possibly? So he can do you the honour of asking for your hand, knowing that he'll acquire your capital as well?'

'Not quite, Edwin. I understand that Philip – Captain Halligan – has money of his own. You rather underestimate his family, I think. He's the grandson of a major-general in Papa's old regiment. Hardly a nobody, Edwin, don't you agree? In fact I rather think Philip's grandfather commanded Father once.'

Edwin had been ready to stand up, but he sank back into his chair again. He reached for the brandy glass but he had drunk it all. 'Then why did you not say so when you wrote before? Of

336

course,' he ran a hand around his neck, inside his collar which was suddenly chafing him, 'this puts a different complexion on the thing.'

'But of course it does, Edwin.' She got up and rang the bell. 'But I couldn't tell you, because I didn't know myself. And nor, to do him justice, did Mr Tulver. Philip is too modest to boast of such a thing. I heard it last night from Mr Lillywhite, who used to know the family very well. He was a friend of Philip's father when he was alive. The family lived in Devon at that time, I understand. Quite a large estate.'

'Never heard of a Major-General Halligan!' He said it brusquely, but he was feeling enormously relieved. His wayward sister would be settled and accounted for and he would not have to worry about her any more. Though there was also a certain element of sadness in the thought. And there would still be Mother to contend with – though he supposed it would be possible to bring her up to London, somewhere close. It would mean she would be there cooing over Caroline a good deal of the time, but on the other hand he would be able to shut up Holvean House, or perhaps let it. It might work very well.

Alicia was talking. 'On his mother's side, of course.' She was wearing some sort of dark-blue shiny stuff tonight, and he had to admit that she looked magnificent. He had a damned fine-looking sister when she put her mind to it. 'That is why we did not recognize the name. But of course, I knew it the minute that I heard it.'

She mentioned a name of such distinction that it made him cough. 'Well, perhaps I was a little

337

over-hasty in my judgement there. And you must admit, Alicia, that you have often been...' He tailed off, searching for the appropriate way of putting it.

'Over-hasty in my judgements?' She was teasing him. 'Yes, I suppose I have. But if you're talking about Fanny, then I'm sure you will agree that my instincts in the matter have turned out to be right – though, as you have pointed out, I could not know they would.'

He had said so, several times, of course. He only nodded now. 'Quite a shocking business. It shook me, I confess. Poor child, she must have had a simply dreadful time. And as for her poor mother ... It defies belief.'

'Exactly, Edwin. I knew you'd feel that way. That's why I'm asking you for help. Mr Lillywhite is looking after the legal side of things – I gather there is money enough to pay for that, though I'm not convinced he's going to charge her very much – but there are other ways in which the girl needs help. She will have to find somewhere safe and clean to have this baby; somewhere people will not judge her for what she has done. And afterwards she will need someone to adopt it, so that she can be assured that it is looked after and loved. Isn't that just the sort of thing your mission's for?'

He was about to make some lofty answer about saving souls, but she was smiling at him – rather the way his daughter did. 'I suppose it could be managed,' he muttered grudgingly.

She came across and kissed him – actually kissed him – on the head. 'Edwin, we've had our

338

differences, but we are much alike. I knew, when it came to it, I could rely on you. You and your Christian works of charity. You're a good man at heart. Sometimes I think that I don't recognize how good, because I only see you in reference to myself.' She straightened abruptly and went and rang the bell. 'Now where has that maid got to? You're right again, you see. Servants in this house are lax at answering the bell.'

He found himself saying, 'Well, don't be hard on them. They've got a great deal on their plates tonight.' He found to his own astonishment that he had made a jest. 'Figuratively as well as literally, of course.'

It merited a smile.

'You rang, Miss Alicia?' Edith was standing at the door, trying to blink back the tears. She picked up her apron in her hands and half-buried her face in it. 'Oh, I'm some sorry, Miss Alicia. Just when you've got guests. But it's my pa, you see. They've had the doctor to him, but the news is very bad. They've gave him something, but they don't know if he'll pull through. And he's asking for me. My brother Abel's just come running all the way to fetch me home. And you with this dinner! What am I to do?' She stood there sobbing, with the apron to her mouth and the tears trickling into it.

She heard her mistress saying, in a peculiar tone of voice, 'Edwin is a clergyman and he's the host tonight. You had better ask him what he thinks.'

Edie looked up, too full of tears to speak. If Mr

Edwin was in charge of things there wasn't any hope. She'd have to give her notice and go in any case, she thought wildly. She gulped, about to speak, but he was already rising to his feet.

'She must go home, of course. I'll remember her father and her family in my prayers. Now don't you fret, my dear.' And to her amazement he came across the room, and actually patted her on the arm a little clumsily. It was more alarming than his usual snappishness.

She glanced at her mistress, who smiled at her and said, 'You heard him, Edith. You can run along. I'm sure that your friend Fanny will give us a hand.'

Edith boggled. Fanny? Serving at table, in her current state? Whatever was Mr Edwin going to say to that? But he didn't say anything except, 'Do you think she would?'

'I think that she'd be glad to, if you really mean it, sir,' she said in wonderment.

'I really mean it. Now go and get Fanny, and be off with you.'

'Yes, sir. And thank you – and, Miss Alicia, you too. I know how much this evening was going to mean to you.' But she was feeling happier as she scuttled up the stairs.

Fanny was astonished at being asked to serve, and looked a bit reluctant when Edie first told her, but when she knew the reason she agreed at once. ''Course you must go home at once and see your pa.'

Edie nodded. She was already tying on her shawl and bonnet. 'So I'll go down and tell them that you're on your way?'

Fanny smiled at her reflection in the mottled glass. 'Of course you can. Don't worry about me. I hope your pa's all right. He sounds a lovely man.' You're lucky to have him, was what she really meant.

Edith nodded, speechless. 'I'll come back when I can. Bless you, Fanny.' She ran back down the stairs.

At the door of the drawing-room she paused. Miss Alicia was speaking, and her voice was sad. 'Poor little Edie. What an awful shock. And just when everything was turning out so well.'

And Mr Edwin answered, in a gentle voice, 'There are no perfect endings. That's the way with life. But we do the best we can. And you've done your best for Edith. What more could she want?'

It was embarrassing to be listening to all this. Edie gave a gentle cough.

'Fanny's on her way, Miss.'

'Then you can be on yours. And ... Edie?'

'Yes, Miss?'

'Take Sammy with you for a bit of company. And tell your mother to have the doctor in. Tell her that this family will meet the bill for her.'

'Yes, Miss Alicia!' Edie spoke more joyfully this time. And suddenly the long, dark walk back home did not seem half so bad.

Epilogue

June 1914

The church was already packed to bursting point. There was Mrs Tulver – Elizabeth Richie as she used to be – looking as smart as sixpence in an enormous hat with a bunch of ostrich feathers on the side of it. Mr T, sitting beside her, turned round in his pew and noticed Edie looking. He gave her a quick bow, then faced the front again but he must have murmured something to his wife, because she turned and smiled.

'Look!' Edie muttered in an undertone, giving Sam a nudge. 'There's Mr Edwin's missus, coming in. And that dear child with her. Good as gold she is. You should see her, sometimes – likes to come downstairs, help Mrs Pritchard make a bit of cake. Not that she's much help, mind – more goes in her mouth and round her face than in the tin – but the child just loves it. Though I don't think her mother likes it very much.'

She didn't add what she was thinking to herself, that it wasn't the only thing the mother didn't like. Whiney sort of person, Claire Killivant could be – not an easy one to please. You

342

sometimes thought she didn't like being down this way at all, though they came quite often – once or twice a year – and old Mrs Killivant loved to see them and positively doted on little Caroline. And as for Mr Edwin!

He spoiled that child, that's what Sammy said. Not that Sammy was the one to talk. If anyone was spoiled, it was Edie Hern. Only had to say she'd like a drop of violet scent or a rattle for the baby, and he would bring it home next day. She smiled at her husband and he grinned back at her. There wasn't much she lacked, in a general way. Sammy was doing very nicely in his job, and the cottage was comfy – though perhaps a little cramped – and she'd been lucky that the Halligans had kept her on as well. Still found odd jobs for her, in spite of little Sam, and often gave her bits and pieces to take home to Ma.

Like today, for instance. They'd promised her some cake – a proper piece of it – to take home in a box. A tier of Miss Alicia's wedding cake it was – put aside on purpose for the first baby's christening. Didn't seem possible it was a whole two years since the mistress had walked down the aisle, but of course it was. And a few months after, Edie'd followed her, and even had the gloves – though she'd only worn a costume in a serviceable blue, and not a fancy wedding-gown like Miss Alicia, and there was no Miss Richie to hold up her train. But everyone had been there, even poor old Pa, though it was pretty much the last place that he ever went, and he'd looked as if he'd got up from his coffin to be there. Still, he'd seen her married, and he'd set his heart on that. And it was a mercy really, when he did slip away – those last two years had been a dreadful time and had taken their toll on Ma.

She wondered if Ma might have got here after all. She'd got a job scrubbing, now that Rosa was in school, but she might just have managed to get away in time. She squirmed around to see, but there was no sign of Ma. Only Meg, grinning in the backmost row, and Reuben beside her. That was no surprise. They were both working for the Halligans, these days. Started up at Holvean House, before the place was let, and then when the Captain's mother had moved back to Devon and old Mrs Killivant had moved in instead – those two had come with her, like Mrs Pritchard had.

And there was Mrs Pritchard, buttoned half to death, sitting in the corner looking proud as punch. 'Course, she was mostly the housekeeper these days; Captain Halligan employed two other staff to cook, and Mrs Pritchard was kept happy, finding fault with them. She caught sight of Edie fidgeting to look, and – though Edie was a married woman in her own right now – she shook her head at her.

Edie turned to Sammy. He was looking for the hymns. 'Hope they're ones I've heard of,' he whispered in her ear. 'I shan't follow else.'

It had been a revelation to her that Sam didn't read. It was not that he couldn't – he could make out the words, and was very good with labels and bills and things like that. It was just that he wasn't fast enough to get much joy of it. By the time he'd worked out what a sentence said, he'd forgotten half of what had gone before, so he couldn't read a story for the life of him.

So she always read the letters that they got from Nell, now that she was settled in Australia. He liked to hear about it: how hot it was out there, and how the house was nice – except there were spiders and snakes and things like that – and how Nellie'd found employment in the little town as a companion to the lady at the church (thanks to Mr Edwin, Edie rather thought), and how she'd met a fellow who had a bit of a farm, and how she was thinking of walking out with him.

Edith smiled faintly. Funny to think now, how she'd been such a fool – not spotting that Nellie was in the family way that time. She'd have seen it in an instant, if it happened now. Had done, in fact, with Mrs Halligan. Must have been last October. Baby Sam was very small at the time.

She shut her eyes, remembering. A warm day, it had been, and she had been in the cottage doing something there, when there was a sound of wheels at the gate. She had hurried out to open it and let the car come in. Lovely thing it was – great long bonnet and a folding roof. Mrs Halligan herself was driving it that day. She pushed down the windscreen and undid the muslin scarf that held her bonnet on.

'Hello, Edith. Here we are again. We had a lovely picnic, didn't we, my dear? And once the Captain got the car started, I drove it all the way, didn't I, Philip?'

The Captain smiled indulgently, the way he always did. 'You want to be careful, Lissie, don't go taking risks.'

His wife got out and smoothed her skirts down with a smile. And Edie knew at once.

'Here!' Sammy's voice was saying sharply in her ear. 'They're coming in the church! Pay attention!'

He was right, of course. Here was Mr Edwin, in his regalia, looking quite the part – they'd arranged for him to conduct the ceremony specially it seemed. And then the parents, looking proud as punch, and the baby in a gown that the mistress had made herself – all lovely gathers, quite a work of art – and old Mrs Killivant waddling in the rear with Mr Philip's sister, a pretty girl in green. Then the Lillywhites, who were to be the other godparents, came in and the service started.

The ancient words were very comforting, even in Mr Edwin's singsong kind of voice. It made you feel you were a part of things that had gone on for centuries and would go on the same for centuries to come. Sammy lost his place and couldn't sing the hymns, but baby Halligan was christened all the same.

And when it was over, and they were outside in the sun, Mrs Halligan let Edie hold the baby for a bit. Just for a moment, as though she were a friend, and not just a servant who lived on the estate.

'Mrs Hern is used to children,' she explained, to a stout man in uniform, who'd been holding forth about something called 'the Balkans' and how there was trouble there. She turned away and said to Edie, 'Where's your young

Sam today?'

'My sister Suzie's looking after him.' Edie looked down at the baby's crumpled little face. 'Hello, little one. Edwina Alicia Elizabeth Louise. What a big name for a little girl.' She gave the infant back to her mother. 'Called for her uncle, is she?'

'Of course. He's very pleased.' For a moment Alicia Halligan looked her in the eyes. 'I wanted names that had significance. So we settled on Edwina – such a pretty name. Or Edie, perhaps – for short?'

Edie was glowing as she took her piece of cake and walked back to the cottage with her husband, arm-in-arm. He looked back at the crowd.

'All that for a baby,' Sammy said. 'Nice little girl, of course, but she's not a patch on our little Sam.'